The Red-Handed League

HADLEY COLT

First published in the English language worldwide in 2016
by Betimes Books

www.betimesbooks.com

ISBN PRINT 978-0-9934331-2-2

The Red-Handed League is a work of fiction. Names, characters, places,
and incidents are either the product of the author's imagination or
are used fictitiously. Any resemblance to actual persons, living or dead,
events, or locales is entirely coincidental.

Cover design by JT Lindroos

Also by Hadley Colt:
Permanent Fatal Error

Women are naturally secretive, and they like to do their own secreting. Girls—that is to say, women in training—may be even more mysterious in that sense.

—*After Sir Arthur Conan Doyle*

TABLE OF CONTENTS

*Much of the following narrative
was excerpted from
the private Tumblr blog
of
Jona Ormond Watson*

MR. HOLMES

I am a brain, Watson.
The rest of me is a mere appendix.
—Sir Arthur Conan Doyle

1

I first met Mr. Holmes on the early morning of a late October day in the hallways of Cattulus High School.

Holmes was pale, slender and quite tall. On first glance, he conjured thoughts of a kind of a wan and whippet warlock. I already knew him to be twenty-five-years-old. His careless mop of unstudied, raven hair obscured a wide brow and ended in a punctuating, heavy comma curled over a perpetually arched right eyebrow. Those eyebrows of his—they were black and thick.

He was dressed in pleated black slacks and matching jacket just a shade too long to be in vogue, yet for him, it worked. The jacket was worn over a simple white cotton shirt buttoned all the way up but without a tie. Mr. Holmes was leaning against the jamb of the door outside his classroom, his legs crossed at the ankles and his hawkish nose poised over an iPad.

There was something at once insolent and compelling about his casually indifferent posture.

He was, in his way, rather good-looking. That fit the terrible template, of course.

As I looked him over, junior and senior girls—all of them cheerleaders—shot Mr. Holmes appraising looks of a far different sort as they pointedly flaunted their tight, ripe young bodies for his benefit.

Yet Mr. Holmes seemed utterly indifferent to the unsubtle displays of the gliding, flirty girls' budding sexuality. That definitely didn't fit the terrible template.

Moving through the hallway with my fellow students, bound for honors English and dressed just as provocatively as school codes would allow, on a gusty impulse, I started to distractedly move into Mr. Holmes' classroom. I smiled in feigned and confused embarrassment at him, pretending I'd mistakenly chosen the wrong room on this, the first day of classes at my new high school.

My posture and smile telegraphed this flirtatious overture: *Oh, God what a ditz I am. I really* am, *aren't I, sir? Go ahead, tell me so—but whatever you do, just please puh-lease* keep talking *to me, okay? Puh-lease?*

Of course I really just wanted to see what the man had on his tablet.

Holmes was one of eight suspect male teachers whom I'd been directed to keep the closest watch on. Something about Bill Holmes' decidedly sketch resume made him one of my new bosses' stipulated persons of greatest interest.

I saw that it was a Snapchat image on Mr. Holmes' iPad screen, a racy selfie of a hot young thing in a highly suggestive pose. She was probably fully nude from what I could see. Her already scant cheerleader's costume was cast aside in a crumpled heap of invitation—a tantalizing twist of fabric resting by bared and strategically posed arms, just obscuring the nipples of full and freckled breasts—a knowingly studied tableau calculated to kick a twenty-something man's libido into overdrive.

But for this strange glyph tattoo of a redheaded Medusa forever stamped upon her left shoulder, she'd be nearly as bare as the day she'd come into this wicked old world, screaming and bloody as we all do.

She was a buxom and pale-skinned cheerleader with an auburn mane. Prior research informed me was one Breeana Rourke. We'd be sitting in this very classroom together later today. Breeana had a pretty face and a killer little body. Even as I briefly studied her image on the screen, it faded from view.

That particular, wicked app: *So effing* vexing.

Yes, at two-o'clock sharp, we'd be sitting together in Mr. Holmes' room for our last class of the day. Now I knew something very unsavory about Breeana: Progress already, I congratulated myself. Seedy, but real progress.

Looking briefly my way, Mr. Bill Holmes pointedly turned his tablet's now innocent screen away from me and somehow put a little more imperious arch into his bushy right eyebrow.

I smiled awkwardly and tried to gloss it: "Sorry, but I thought this was my English room," I said. "First day here, ya know? Guess I'm all nerves." I flashed a copy of *Lolita* and said, "First book on my reading list. Can you believe this? Some old man perving on a young girl? *Really?*"

That stuff about the book being on the reading list was another lie, of course.

The Nabokov paperback was simply meant to be a potentially faster means to an investigative end. It really was not my idea, not at all, but I'd bought into the dubious gambit because I was fairly certain I didn't have a vote.

There was not a detectable flicker of interest on the part of Mr. Holmes in the charged paperback clutched in my sun-bronzed hand.

Backing out the door of his classroom, I made a point of fleetingly brushing his arm with my left breast to see how he'd react to that. "Still getting my schedule down," I said as he pointedly moved his arm away. I pressed a hand to my belly and said, "So much change. So many butterflies. It's like begging for ulcers, right?"

He didn't answer, instead giving me a long and appraising up-and-down look with his piercing gray eyes.

He didn't seem enticed by what he saw, not at all. He was in no way flirty as he addressed me. Something about that made me shiver. Maybe there was something wrong here after all, but maybe not quite the wicked-bad something I'd been dispatched to look for. Holmes seemed icily cold, even machine-like.

That Snapchat page, taken in tandem with the sexless way he'd appraised me (I'd been placed here, after all, very much for my youthful and appealing looks), spoke volumes in some way, didn't they?

Yes, didn't all that already add up to something very clearly wrong with the man?

I had already all but convinced myself they must. It was a visceral reaction, sure, but one also based on a solid enough foundation of on-the-fly deduction.

Yes, perhaps this Mr. Holmes is a dangerous and a bad man after all, I thought.

He shrugged and said without the trace of a smile, in the deepest and silkiest of voices that carried a mild British accent—positive catnip to young American girls raised on *Harry Potter*—"No worries, Ms. Sacker. Carry on."

He somehow already knew my alias. That gave me fresh shivers.

I said awkwardly, annoyed and even mildly angered to be knocked off stride so deftly by the handsome bastard, "I think you're my chemistry teacher later today. Actually, I'm sure you are that."

"I am indeed *that*," he said coolly. "So I'll see you again at two then, won't I?"

I smiled awkwardly and adjusted the strap of my backpack. "You will. Right. Definitely, yes." He was looking at my right hand, at the small white patch there. A chemistry class injury from a year ago.

Awkwardly, I walked away from him, convinced his eyes were still on me as I made my way down the hall, my skin crawling at the thought of which part of my body his gaze must surely be focused upon as I stiffly and self-consciously moved through the otherwise raucous hallway.

My walk *wasn't* the enticing thing my clandestine bosses would likely have hoped for, after all: I'd nearly severed my Achilles' tendon a few days back, still had a pronounced and vaguely painful limp that impeded any bid for a Lolitaesque and sexy sway. That injury had very nearly cost me my present assignment. Pain pills might have disguised the damage, but a congenital heart condition, longstanding and not to be played with, forbid their use.

Despite my limp, I could practically *feel* the man's gaze on me. Yet based on his previous behavior, Mr. Holmes' examination of my retreating silhouette would be something decidedly other than *sexual*, I figured.

Anyway, whatever the dark and wrong thing it was that fired the man, I had to concede round one to Mr. Holmes.

I promised myself I'd be better prepared—much more on my game—when our paths crossed again in the afternoon.

2

My journey to Holmes began just three days before that first day of classes at Cattulus.

I'd been unexpectedly called into my favorite *college* instructor's office. It was a gloomy, and ominously overcast autumn day. A tropical storm was working its way up the coast; days and days of heavy rains were forecast.

Cal Groves, my forensics teacher—something of a mentor and perhaps even a sometimes default father figure, as well—was seated close by a uniformed police officer.

I'd done nothing wrong, I knew that. This audience, and this pairing, therefore, merely intrigued me. I was certain that I was in no trouble.

The man's brass nameplate above his star indicated he was Police Chief Tony Briggs. I knew his name from the local newspapers' website articles. He had a solid enough reputation in the city of Portsmouth where he policed—one of the satellite bedroom communities, albeit a very expensive one, that orbited the Greater Metro area. The rich little town was roughly a forty-five minutes' drive from my college campus. If I hadn't recognized the name, the uniform would have gotten me there: it was quite ostentatious and had more than a hint of storm trooper lurking there, too.

Mr. Groves—fiftyish, sleight of build and graying—nudged his rolled-up shirt sleeves a bit higher on his forearms, then rested one hand over the other, obscuring his tight-fitting wedding ring. He had a habit of tugging and twisting at the band. He said, "Jona, this is rather unusual but I think it's a *real* opportunity that's coming your way. This is a chance for some very rare résumé building that might well kick-start your career after graduation."

I nodded, already excited by this mysterious *real opportunity.*

Yet something wasn't quite right about any of this.

I noticed that just like Chief Briggs, my instructor was looking at me in a new and particularly uncomfortable way. It was an unpleasant thing they were doing.

Briggs was a stranger, but Groves was a longtime association, so the new and nakedly appraising manner with which my instructor freshly eyed me was . . . unsettling. It was a very male way of looking at a pretty, much younger woman. My instructor—he was also my guidance counselor, more or less—had never, ever given me the sorts of *up and downs* he gave me now. Pure elevator eyes. It was all well beyond squirm inducing.

Then something in his manner changed, and he straightened up and abruptly lost the uncharacteristic predatory gaze. He said, maybe a bit red-faced to have noticed me noticing, "Please forgive me just now, Jona. For my own peace of mind, I had to try and see you through the lens of the vixen's role that's about to be offered you—I need you to accept that explanation. I simply had to convince myself you can plausibly pull off what will be asked of you. I feel very protective of you, I hope you know, and I won't see you put in a dangerous position. I never would do that."

Still blushing a bit, he cleared his throat and said, "Jona, I certainly know you see yourself more focused on the forensics side of policing after you leave here in a few months and begin building your law-enforcement career. That's certainly where some of your strongest gifts are to be found. I know you don't see yourself as a field agent at any point. Not a detective or the like in the use of your criminology degree. However, there's something to be said for having at least a little field experience to better inform your lab work and the dealings with all the others you'll encounter who are out there, moving in that world and working cases from the field." A hesitant smile: "They can be a breed apart, you see, Jona. We never really know anyone, I fear. Even the innocent can be a threat, pushed in a corner. Just a little field experience can be a boon in that sense—open your eyes to what really drives people . . . drives criminals."

He leaned forward a bit more and said, "You see, this is something of an undercover operation that Chief Briggs is here to offer you, Jona. I've talked to others at the school and they agree that we'll extend you work credits for the assignment if you take it on. These could perhaps even shorten the arc for you by waving some other remaining electives well outside your major so your graduation date won't be delayed. Frankly, if you do this, and if you bring it off, it will be a real feather in the cap of the university and perhaps even a game-changer for our budding little program here maybe opening the door to other field experiences for future upperclassmen who might one day follow in your path."

"*Wow*," I said uncertainly. "Okay, that does sound really interesting. I'm all ears."

A fleeting flicker of the elevator eyes returned in my instructor. I squirmed again and smiled uncomfortably. I assured myself, *He's just double-checking, just making sure.*

But what exactly was this all about? What *was* this undercover field assignment? And why single me out, a lab student as he'd explicitly pointed out? Why tag me for a "field assignment" of some sort?

And again, why these hungry eyes from these two much older men? Why were they looking at me in such a thinly veiled and undeniably carnal way? Precisely what was this clandestine assignment and where exactly was it going to take me?

Perhaps to a brothel? Possibly to some strip club? Was it in some way tied to a seamy, human-trafficking ring?

None of those prospects appealed to me, of course, not a bit.

A chill I couldn't hide seized me: Could there be something actually *worse* than any of those things?

The eyes of the men continued to minutely dissect me.

I tried to imagine what they saw and settled on a young coed, standing about five-ten, attractive and athletic. I ran several miles each morning and swam every night, or at least I did all that before screwing up my damned leg. Having been handed a kind of a death sentence while still a child, I'd early determined to throw myself into physical exertion—to harden my tender and damaged heart.

So far as the rest of my body goes—my outside, so to speak—apart from being fairly tall, I'm slender but busty. Pretty good from the back too (or so I'm told by a few aficionados of that portion of the female anatomy).

For now, I still had a between-semesters Miami tan that was pretty much an all-over affair courtesy of Haulover Beach.

That same Miami sun had bleached my usually sandy brown hair something closer in hue to ash blond.

But my left ankle was now just as noticeably bound in a traction bandage, the painful souvenir of some beach volley-ball gone awry after a night of too much drinking and too few warm up stretches before taking to the silken sand.

Mr. Groves looked briefly at some kind of dossier. I guessed it was my extant school file stuff full with all my records, and said, "You just turned twenty-three, yes?"

"That's right," I said, biting my lip. Giving them hard looks back. "Last month."

"Yes, on the twelfth," he said. "I'll tell you now that with the right clothes, a little less make up and just a little bit of coaching, I think you could still safely pass for seventeen or eighteen. That's really why you're here," he said, then rushed to add, "apart from your obvious skills and the fact you're more than something of a prodigy, one of the finest students I've ever had."

It was the strongest compliment my professor had ever paid me. I desperately hoped it wasn't driven by some cynical angling. I wanted, I *needed*, for my life's favorite teacher to *mean* it.

But no, it seemed genuine enough, as did his suddenly warm and familiar—even fatherly—smile back at me. He said, "This is entirely your choice, Jona. I can't lie and say that there might not be some small risk attached to this particular opportunity. Fieldwork is nothing if not unpredictable, even at the best of times. Are you still interested enough to talk more about this proposition?"

Another friendly smile: "And, yes for the record, it *does* pay something. It pays rather well, in fact."

"Of course, I'd like to know more," I said, "I really don't know anything about what you two are thinking right now."

The Portsmouth chief of police gave me a frosty smile and took a seat in the chair alongside me. He'd stopped with the elevator eyes, too. He said, "You may be aware we've had a number of pretty disturbing cases at a private school in my town, several cases in one high school, in fact, during the last school year. They all involved inappropriate interactions between educators and underage students. Everything from sexual conduct to inappropriate messaging. You know, *sexting*."

The corners of the policeman's mouth turned down liked he'd tasted something bitter as he gave voice to that last word.

The chief sighed and said dully, "Of course, one case with a single teacher would be plenty bad enough. But we've had four educators, teachers, coaches and a guidance counselor, implicated in separate cases in just over six months. All of them in one school. We have reason to believe there may be at least two or three more similar cases that might yet come to light involving current faculty. This stuff seemed almost organized to me, if you can believe it. At very least, it's something cultural within this particular school and among far too many of its staff members."

"I've read about those cases, of course," I said. "I was also shocked they were all happening at the same school. I do remember that some of it was very physical, as you said. Also that some of it involved exchange of texts and photos. But there's more?"

"Those latter, the messaging and the like, were probably headed somewhere physical too, if parents or friends hadn't tumbled to what was going on and blown the whistle," the chief said. "Here's the real thing, Ms. Watson: We think this is all already starting up again, and so very early in this school year."

As the old cop spoke, I candidly sized him up. He was in his mid-forties, I figured. Still had a decent build. He had black hair, graying at the temples, and a far-faster graying moustache. On surface, he seemed a solid and steady guy. Probably had a high school-age daughter and so all of this was perhaps ulcerating in a very personal way for this otherwise chill-seeming lawman.

Chief Briggs said, "Jona, I don't know what you know about Cattulus High School, but short-form, it's a private school and quite expensive to attend. Four years there results in a tuition bill that would make even a good state university blush with jealousy. We're talking about a private school that caters to the children of our most affluent citizens in Portsmouth. Let me just point out that the town's median income runs about ninety-thousand dollars. That's *median* income. And now patience in these very affluent parents' ranks is running very thin—that's something I fully grasp, of course."

That last sounded like a bit of political spin and a sop to a rich and badly burned constituency. Then I remembered the chief's appointed position was controlled by the Portsmouth mayor, who indeed had to stand for election in the fall.

And I at last now saw precisely where this was headed.

My looks, my deceptively youthful appearance? Yes, the nature of this undercover assignment was suddenly and all-too-cynically clear. These two fatherly men meant for me to embed in this tawdry high school as a student and then poke around from within. Probably they also meant for me to try to get myself seduced there while wearing a wire.

Mr. Groves all but confirmed it by saying, "Didn't you once mention to me you also did some cheerleading in high school?"

"All four years," I said unenthusiastically. "But I was mostly a football cheerleader. All that *Friday Night Lights*, stuff, yeah, and then some. And all of it done with no small and intensely private sense of irony. It was a status thing, I guess. It certainly wasn't hard to do. I can't say I loved or craved it as most of the other girls clearly did. It was more just a kind of private challenge to myself, to see if I could make the cut." A smile. "But you know that. I play to win."

"I do certainly know that," Mr. Groves said. "Indeed, you also swim competitively, you play volleyball here. You've maintained a remarkable level of athleticism in tandem with your academic studies. You live like there's no tomorrow—pushing yourself to the limit and beyond. So, doing a little cheerleading again probably wouldn't be such a terrible stretch, right? And, as a result of some concerned families pulling their daughters from Cattulus, there are now openings on the squad as it happens." A sly smile, "Irony, or no."

I smiled thinly. *God, cheerleading? Again? Dear Lord, gag me* now.

And yet, the idea of playing high school spy like this—and in the relative safety and controlled environment of a very exclusive private school, to boot? It was intoxicating. And anyway, what could possibly threaten me in such a silly, ritzy milieu?

"Shouldn't be so tough," I agreed aloud and perhaps too enthusiastically. To myself I thought, *No, not too tough at all, except for your fucked-up leg, genius.*

The chief then voiced that exact concern, of course.

Looking gloomily under my chair, Chief Briggs said, "I couldn't help but notice your limp when you walked in here, Ms. Watson. I see you're ankle is bandaged. How bad an injury is that? Judging by the way you move, I'm thinking cheerleading isn't in the cards anytime soon, and that's frankly a real concern."

He leaned in on one arm and said, "You see, the victims in all of these cases—well, nearly all—have been cheerleaders for this or that of the sports teams there. We thought ingratiating yourself with those types of students would be the quickest means of getting deeper and useful insights into the school and other possible problem faculty members. But now, looking at your leg...?" The chief of police gave a sad shake of his head. He sat back in his chair and raised his hands.

Mr. Groves nodded, frowning, and said, "Yes, I have to ask, Jona—it does seem to me you're still a good ways out from being able to push that leg much beyond slow walking. Exactly how bad is this injury? Has a doctor even looked at that ankle, or did you just wrap it yourself?"

It was the latter, of course. I felt the tremendous opportunity starting to slide through my fingers before it was even mine to lose. I couldn't bear to have it snatched from under me.

Pointedly using present tense, I said, "I assume you mean to drop me in this school as a transfer student. Seems simple to me: We just say I screwed up my leg cheering at my prior school. I can still talk the talk. I know too well what makes these sorts of silly girls run. I know what the little fools think they value and I can turn that on them to our own ends as needed. I know I can make this work. In a way, it's almost better."

The chief narrowed his eyes, freshly measuring me. "How is it better? Why don't you go ahead and explain it to me?"

I explained myself, trying to do so nonchalantly and confidently: "Injured, I'm not the kind of competition that will get their backs up," I said. "No threat to any of their individual squad positions, at least not from the jump. This could actually speed the process of ingratiation, precisely because I'm *so* much less threatening."

The two men looked hard at one another. Finally Mr. Groves said, "I'm with Jona on this, Chief. I'm confident she can pull this off, bum ankle or not. Like she said, it may even be an asset."

Briggs nodded and said, "Okay, then. I guess I'm game, too. Anyway, it's not like we're spoiled for options. We'll work out the less compelling details later. In the meantime, we have some files for you to study overnight, Jona. These will be personnel files of several male faculty members at the school who we think might bear closer watching. Seven are fairly well established faculty members. The eighth, a chemistry teacher, and a pretty strange young guy, I hear, came on board just under a month ago, on a temporary basis. You see his predecessor is on the tail-end of a maternity leave. I'd like you to closely study up on these men, to see if and *how* they interact with each other and with the female students. We'll also give you files on your would-be cheerleading peers."

The chief hesitated, then said, "As we dug into the cases we already know about, we found some unsettling connections. Confidentially, we caught wind—but sadly found no supporting proof—of some private parties that may have united several victims and perpetrators at a particular location on more than one occasion. These were kind of, well, frankly they were sex parties, we think. Maybe even sort of, well, student-teacher *orgies*. These would seem to go to what Mr. Groves characterized as a real fear that some of this abuse may have been organized or may even have become institutionalized, in some way. There's a suspicion that there may be a kind of festering culture of such abuse spreading through the high school. If there is such a conspiracy in place, we simply have no idea how far it reaches or how high up the ladder it runs."

Mr. Groves smiled and said, "Jona, it'll be your job to find all that out. If you will say yes to this opportunity."

"I do," I said, trying *so* hard not to seem over-eager. Of course, I was over the moon with exhilaration for the assignment. "I do say yes, I mean. You mentioned a salary. Will there be some kind of, you know, uniform allowance? I'll have to do some shopping to dress younger and—"

My instructor smiled thinly and said, "They have a quite literal uniform at the school," he said. "It's a kind of jumper." He shrugged and added apologetically. "Plaid, of course. Very tartan. Clan Lindsey, I think."

Oh, dear God.

"We also need to carefully consider rules of engagement and conduct," the chief said. "I can't have you entrapping anyone, of course—not that you ever would. But there is the challenge all undercover officers face—knowing how to edge up to certain lines without crossing them and compromising the case or becoming guilty of criminal conduct, yourself. We're sending you, a novice, into a kind of a minefield, I fear. Are you certain you're still up for this?"

"Dead certain," I said.

I immediately wished I'd phrased my exuberant answer differently. It was obviously very poor choice of words.

3

The cheerleading instructor was a pert and pixyish forty-something brunette named Honor Dasho. She was attractive and flirty with males and females alike—all zesty, beaming enthusiasm: plenty of buxom nervous energy packed into the lusty body of an aging, still-*kind of hot* ex-gymnast.

And that gravity defying, near motionless rack she fronted—I was sure it had been paid for. There was also her suspiciously smooth forehead that, to me at least, quietly seemed to confide between discreetly cupped hands *b-o-t-o-x*.

Regardless, "Coach," as she insisted we call her, was an impressive piece of work in the eyes of most men, and maybe even some attractive young ones.

On that latter note, I wondered if she had ever tried to work her MILF charms on Mr. William Holmes, assuming that she even found him attractive. Given the object of budding carnal interest he seemed to be for the younger set around the school, I figured it must certainly be so as well for at least some of the older crowd. He was fit, handsome and he had real presence.

And just like Holmes, Honor Dasho had a naked left ring finger, so they seemed likely to be mutually available.

But then, on further reflection, there was also that age gulf. Maybe Holmes wasn't into hot cougars and liked them exclusively young.

Maybe Mrs. Dasho wasn't into being a hot cougar. (That prospect seemed quite dubious, to my mind: After all, what attractive older woman wouldn't want to consider herself sexually enticing to younger men?)

Either way, at lunch, Honor made a point of finding me in the cafeteria line and then ushering me limping and tray in hand to the cheerleader's table where she made a point of introducing me to still-surviving (that is to say, still-enrolled) squad members—the rag-tag but plucky survivors from the previous school year's sex scandals.

If my college instructor and the Portsmouth police chief made me feel like a piece of meat with their fleeting examinations a few days before, the way these girls sized me up was every bit as acidly appraising and perhaps even more brazen.

It was actually *worse* to endure the girls' gawking, because I knew they were going to places in their heads that those older men's lustful minds wouldn't think of traveling to.

Body image stuff, for instance. Looking for early-onset cellulite or the intimation of a double chin or . . . ? Really, just all kinds of wicked stuff like that. The stuff of fingers poked down throats and juice purges. I'd seen it. Here and there, I'd lived it.

After all-around introductions, Coach Dasho signaled they should make room at the table and she pulled up another chair for me. I put down my tray and slid in.

Titan-haired Breeana—her racy and buxom selfie's milk-skinned image was positively burned into my brain—smiled and said, "That ankle looks like it hurts, *a lot*. Bad dismount?"

I wrinkled my nose. "Nah. A scorpion gone *way* wrong," I said. "Base collapsed. And then an epic fail just down below. Domino principle. At least I landed on my feet."

Breeana, who was fairly petite relative to me, said, "Figured you'd be base, tall as you are and with your shoulders, not a flyer."

A compliment or a dig? It could be either, or both. Maybe *neither*. So I simply decided to just let it go.

Another of the girls, much closer to my height and build (but with a little less up top, chest-wise)—olive-skinned and with the blackest hair and eyes (her name was Maria)—smiled and said, "*Ouch*. Yeah, good thing it was your feet you landed on, like you said. On your head, you'd be, you know, dead, or moving your wheel chair with puffs through a straw. How long 'til you're good to take the floor again?" She made a sad face and said quieter to the other girls, "We're like, what, three down, now?"

Mrs. Dasho corrected, "Four." Then the coach excused herself, presumably so I could bond with the squad without the awkwardness or inhibition posed by her lingering presence.

Do I have to actually say the next forty-five minutes were intensely torturous?

I spent the time trying to look interested and engaged and *so* thrilled to bask in the squad's thinly tolerant presence that I could feel my jaws starting to ache from the long, forced smile I'd painted on, trying to blend in with the little bitches.

By the same token, it was proving time well spent in terms of assimilating all the silly things I needed to re-enforce my cover as a high school student. Always a kind of a sponge, I almost immediately found myself talking more with my hands, employing these big and sweeping teenage girl gestures that were melodramatic and over-broad manifestations of life lived to the top and very much *always in the moment*.

I soon enough began carpet-bombing my sentences with "likes" and "you knows" and a flurry of unnecessary punctuating and affirmation-seeking "*rights*"?

I found myself ending the most unambiguous of my observations and assertions on similarly ascending intonations that made them all sound like questions or intimations of nagging doubt.

Of course, high school wasn't really that long ago for me.

But had I really been this vapid four or five years ago? Had I ever really been *so* out of touch with the ground and cut off from reality as these little rich witches manifestly were proving themselves to be with each and every silly utterance?

I tried to console myself it probably wasn't so, that these shallow, callow girls had certain advantages in distancing themselves from every-day reality that I had not enjoyed. They had the advantages of family wealth, most pointedly. Money let anyone, young or old, evade some significant proportion of reality. And money also often buys an effective enough escape hatch from so many of life's consequences that the un-wealthy or outright poor must face down or find themselves utterly destroyed by.

About a half-an-hour in, talk turned, as it inevitably does among teenage girls in any numbers, to *them* and to *that*.

That is to say, to *guys* and to *sex*.

This talk didn't just center on boys their own age, not completely. Some of the dudes the girls gushed over were faculty members.

The girls polled me for my opinions of some men and boys in the school, but I deflected nearly all of them, pointing out quite reasonably—and factually—that I was only four hours into my first day of school, and so hadn't encountered most of the boys or the men that I was being pressed to assess.

Then Breeana specifically brought up Mr. Holmes.

The other girls exchanged these funny, slightly off-kilter smiles I couldn't quite figure out. I was on thin ice here, I knew, particularly since Breeana was very much guilty of sending Mr. Holmes naked photos of herself on Snapchat. She saw him as a *get*.

Weighing my words, I said, "He's kinda of interesting in an intellectual, geeky way. I mean, I only saw him for like, a *minute*. Got confused and walked into his class this morning, thinking it was English." I looked around, then lowered my voice. "Honestly? He was kind of, you know, *remote*."

A honey blonde named Jess shot a pointed look at Breeana and said, *"Right?"*

Breeana said to me, searching my face, "But you *do* think he's hot? And that accent? That's to die for." She exchanged glances with the other girls, awaiting my final verdict. *Her* "Right?" was implied.

Again, a round of funny little smiles erupted.

"Sure," I said, looking straight at Breeana. "Don't you think he's hot?"

"Maybe," Breeana said neutrally, sizing me up, but in a different way, now.

This time I really couldn't read what was going on behind her pretty mask.

One of the girls then asked Breeana if she was up for a movie. She just sighed and shook her head. "Huh-uh. Have to go to Unc's tonight. He's tutoring me in math and chemistry. Old bastard is pretty much the only thing getting me through. Lucky me, huh? I mean, having this mathematical genius uncle to keep me in the game?"

4

I checked my phone: Just ten minutes remaining until chemistry class. I realized my palms were slightly damp. My pulse was significantly elevated. What was it about this dude Holmes that was doing this to me?

My schedule had been arranged as best it could to secure daily classes with four of the seven men on Chief Brigg's so-called "watch list."

None of those other three men had seemed particularly compelling or off-putting to me in the course of my earlier-in-the day sessions in their classes. There had been nothing to raise eyebrows, at least not so far, in any of their behavior or conversation.

What was it about this particular remaining man that prompted such a deep and visceral reaction from me? This young teacher—this near-peer of mine—named "William Scott Sherlock Holmes," had already gotten well and truly under my skin.

And my simple reaction to the man, my abiding uneasiness about him, served only to ratchet up my grudging suspicions.

In their manifest attraction to the ascetic but undeniably attractive chemistry teacher, even the silly-ass cheerleaders still had enough brains to know something was at least a little off about their "kinda hot in a nerdy, hipster-way" chemistry instructor.

I closed my locker, nervously twisting the lock and then hugging my chemistry books closer to my chest, completely undermining my strategically chosen, bust-emphasizing ensemble.

Catching myself in this silly moment of throwback to my own wrenching high school years' shyness and self-consciousness about my early-budding breasts, I shifted my books to my side, straightened my back and braced for the leg and lower back pain as I tried to enter Mr. Holmes' classroom with at least the specter of my sexiest, pre-injury strut.

Mr. Holmes nodded at me and pointed to a vacant chair. "Your seat is right there, Ms. Sacker," he said.

Damn: It was literally *front and center.*

So much for quietly blending in.

Showtime for Mr. Holmes.

How to describe Bill Holmes' teaching demeanor?

Seductive? Calculated to entice hot young things?

Decidedly *not.*

Was it condescending? Was it simultaneously patronizing and impatient?

Absolutely.

Yes, it was certainly marked by all of these lamentable and acidic aspects.

It was also peppered with fast-racing and under-the-breath muttered asides: these jibes you just couldn't quite make out, try as you might, and so you couldn't quite get really put out by any of them, even if you knew and knew down deep, that his barely perceptible digs were directed squarely at *you*.

And yet Mr. Holmes clearly knew his stuff. It was just that he also just as clearly had no facility—or perhaps more accurately, he simply had no patience, none whatever—to effectively transfer his percolating and vast knowledge to the unworthy. He seemingly had no sense of obligation to convey what he knew in any meaningful or engaging way to just anyone.

Ten minutes in, I knew the imperious and somewhat tightly wound and attractive-in-an-aquiline way Mr. Holmes knew infinitely more about chemistry than just about anyone else I'd known.

My God, Holmes would even have easily run rings around Cal Groves; he'd have done that five or six times over, never breaking a sweat, I thought somewhat bitterly.

Foregoing the digital Smartboard, Mr. Holmes instead favored the ancient chalkboard hanging behind it.

He assaulted its scarred black surface with flurries and volleys of fast-written equations unleashed in tandem with barely comprehensible explosions of explanation.

All of these "lessons" were delivered with his back to us as he jabbed at the board with squeaking and frequently snapping sticks of yellow chalk.

Holmes' dizzying, fast-moving presentation was a kind of eerie and mesmerizing performance art unto itself.

It was clear to me the man should not be teaching as a day-job, yet this hour in his classroom was in a perverse way fast-becoming the highlight of my day.

Versed in the subject as I was, I began to see that I might be the only one in the room who really understood anything the man was conveying, and, still more perversely, I was the only one who might actually leave the room richer for the experience.

Despite lingering misgivings about him placed in my head by others, I found myself drawn in by Holmes' presentation, assured in the heady knowledge I was the only student in the room who came close to getting it.

As he scrawled more equations across the board, now and again some epiphany would seize him, and he'd suddenly go darting down a rabbit hole of abstract chemical theory I knew was begetting students' notes that would be utterly incomprehensible to them later and perhaps even destructive to their eventual grade point averages.

And yet, here and there, I could just about keep up with his whiplash tangents and the intense, slender man's dizzying flights of improvisational and hypothetical reasoning.

I even dared to pose a few questions about some of those assertions that didn't result in Holmes veering off into yet another muttered paroxysm of thinly veiled insults flung my direction in a fit of barely concealed contempt and exasperation.

After my third or fourth such question, Holmes paused and looked at me with something like fresh eyes. This focused interest on Mr. Holmes' part in a student—male or female— was something unprecedented in my admittedly limited experience in his classroom.

Something electric and eerily quiet in the atmosphere of his room made it just as clear to me that such interest on our instructor's part was quite unprecedented in the experience of all of my classmates, as well.

A smile teased the corner of his lips. His gaze flickered briefly toward the ceiling and he said, "Good God, have you sent me an actual student, at last?"

Shifting his gaze to me, Mr. Holmes said, "Kudos to you, Miss Sacker, for grasping Ariadne's delicate thread and for nearly finding your way out of the labyrinth I've constructed behind me." He vaguely gestured at the scrawled-over chalkboard.

That rather thinly tempered compliment made me ridiculously proud.

It also drew scowls and some potentially damaging suspicion from clearly still-at-sea cheerleaders, including the almost equally bosomy Breeana who had this very day sent this brainy and strangely compelling man near-naked and swiftly vanishing photos of herself and her impressive chest laid so nearly bare.

The last bell rang: there would surely be a few crackling last announcements, then dismissal for the day.

I'd been issued a loaner, brushed-silver, new-model Ford Mustang that intimated its raw horsepower in smoothly contoured metal lines evoking mature and oiled muscle. The sporty Ford was calculated to further the illusion of me as some moneybags daddy's too-pampered princess.

I was looking forward to pushing the car through its paces on some of the winding, hilly roads outside Portsmouth. I'd been looking forward to that all weekend, but Mr. Holmes's strangely spiky compliment had instantly invested me with still more nervous energy that needed to find outward expression, and very soon.

A fast tear through the surrounding hills' hairpin turns making my way back home to the city just might fit that bill.

As the principal droned on about this-and-that humdrum nonsense, I noticed Mr. Holmes was suddenly back behind his desk, his elbows on its scarred and battered tabletop, his long, slender fingers tented under his chin. He was watching me *so* closely. There was something in his look that evoked that of a sleek cobra.

Feeling challenged, the mongoose in me looked back at him and didn't break off its unblinking, returned gaze.

I sensed other female eyes were watching us watching one another—Mr. Holmes and I brazenly sizing up the other. I'd struck some primal nerve in this strange and brilliant man, exactly that much was clear to me. But what larger reaction would that struck-nerve produce?

Would he follow me home? Would he maybe just send me a Facebook friend request?

Or perhaps he'd just start following me on Twitter to facilitate some steamy, direct messaging. If not any of that, would I be getting solicitations this evening for some fleeting but intimate Shapchat photos? (As students, we'd all had to provide email addresses on our registration forms—presumably, full faculty had access to same.)

What exactly would come next?

Something, surely: Of that much I was certain.

The principal finished his monotone monologue with a flip of some distant, off-switch that triggered a blasting cascade of shrill and piercing squelches that made us all wince.

All but our teacher flinched at the din; the instructor still only had eyes for me. Holmes remained motionless, staring at me with hooded eyes. It gave me these mixed sorts of shivers—at once fearful and yet, frankly, well, yes, *enticed.*

His velvety baritone drawl fast followed the din from the overhead speaker. Holmes' voice was almost a hypnotic balm after all that messy noise. He said, honey-toned, "Miss Sacker, could you possibly stay behind for a few moments?"

Another, much smaller shiver: Other eyes were on me again—all the girls in class, but particularly those of the cheerleaders. The latter shot me slack-jawed stares.

"Sure," I said with a smile at Mr. Holmes that some might call suggestive. "I can do that. No problem."

A dangerous spark of competitive spirit strewn amongst some of my would-be cheerleading peers was instantly struck. It was unprofessional of me as an undercover "operative," I knew that of course, but a maverick part of me driven to impulsive gambits simply didn't care about any of that.

My classmates filed out, eager to flee the school grounds.

Breeana was of course last to leave. She threw me a death stare on her way out the door. I smiled back and shrugged.

This intriguing man's simple request to linger behind for a time had just made me a terrible enemy among the cheerleading class.

There is more than one way to solve any puzzle, I tried to convince myself. *You don't need these silly and horny girls to learn the truth of whatever is going on in this tony hellhole.*

When they were all gone, when it was just the two of us alone together, I smiled at Mr. Holmes, braced for anything he might throw my way. Deep down, I was thrilling at the chess game I sensed loomed. I was determined to be up to this match.

Some part of me, the worrisome sliver of my soul that likes pushing other people's muscle cars fast on unfamiliar roads and laying alone, basking stark naked and glisteningly enticing on distant nude beaches—the never-to-be-denied adrenaline junkie in me who for so many reasons positively embraced the live-today-for-tomorrow-we-die ethos—yearned to go toe-to-toe with this perhaps dangerous, yet oddly brilliant and queerly beautiful mind.

If Mr. Holmes was indeed the monster the Portsmouth police chief suspected him of being, I was surely going to be at least a little troubled for a very long time for having helped to bring him down. He might be evil, or even a fiend, but he was just as clearly a genius in his own right—that I'd come to see and very swiftly after a single hour sitting in the man's class.

Meeting his intense gaze, I said huskily, "Should I close the door, sir?"

"Absolutely not," he said suspiciously loudly. He remained at his desk. His fingers were still tented as his burning, gimlet gray eyes worked at me.

I could hardly help myself: I said, "Why should the door stay open, sir?"

"Because closing it with us alone together in here would be untoward," he said. "You're a student and I'm your teacher. In the wake of certain bad and actually criminal recent events, the school has implemented a new if lamentably belated policy. No one-on-one, private communications between teachers and students are to be tolerated."

Holmes rose suddenly, uncoiling all at once, languidly but deliberately. For all his stillness and his apparently slender build, I sensed hidden reservoirs of strength and endurance. During his own high school years, I guessed, he was probably a long-distance runner. He had just that kind of turned-in on itself, focused personality.

An old soul.

He came close—stepping very much into my personal space—and sleekly leaned in *so* near to me his lips lightly brushed my thrice-pierced ear.

The intimate contact thrilled me. I feared I was poised to blow my undercover assignment on Day One, for I suddenly knew that I was vulnerable to wanting to seduce this man, but entirely for my own pleasure.

He said softly in his silky British baritone, "You know as well as I do the sex crimes that have happened in this high school, my friend. And, oh yes, it's quite clear to me that those are why you're here, Miss Jona *Watson*."

The use of my real last name cut like a cracking whip's lash. Now I was starkly terrified. I tasted blood and realized I'd bitten through my lip.

Holmes quickly whispered, "Now please be very careful what you say next, my dear, because I think we can safely assume that earthy Breeana who sends select teachers naked photos of herself is likely still lingering just outside that open door, eavesdropping on us."

Feeling his breath on my ear and at my throat's pulse, my heart began to race harder. Had someone in the police force confided something about me and about my true role in this school to Mr. Holmes for some reason? It didn't seem possible, and in no way logical. Holmes was possibly a prime suspect of theirs, after all.

Then a much worse thought came to me: Had I that badly played the role of student in just these few first hours to so utterly and catastrophically blown my cover nearly from the start?

How did this man know my real last name, for the love of God?

Holmes whispered in my ear, "That you are some kind of undercover investigator is a certainty. Exactly who you're working for is the only thing that presently eludes me, although I'll confess to certain strongly-held suspicions. The local police force is the first and the most logical choice among those that present themselves."

There was a sour tone in his voice as he uttered the words *local police force*.

Seeing something in my expression he evidently accepted as confirmation of my employers' identity, he looked somehow more disappointed but said in what I gathered he thought to be a consoling tone, "In our rarified field, we must of course find the blessed work and opportunities where we can, yes? From your expression I'm now convinced I'm right about your overseers." The hint of a frown: "Sincere condolences on your employers."

He checked the door and said, "These walls may have ears other than those of that silly girl, you know. And, anyway, there's much to clean up in here as a result of today's earlier, decidedly less than OCD underclassmen. Will you help me scrub up some beakers and test tubes by the sink where we can talk more discretely under the white noise of the water tap? Are you agreeable to that prospect, Jona? I presume you don't have a bus to catch as you arrived before the first of those things pulled in this morning." He pulled back and his icy gray eyes searched mine. "You will *so* disappoint me if you say you're not available to me."

I narrowed my eyes. "Of course I'm agreeable," I whispered. "Of course I'll help you clean up, Mr. Holmes. I positively relish the prospect of talking more deeply with you. And, clearly you're some kind of an investigator, too. I'm serving you notice now that I mean to ferret out your bosses as they obviously can't be the local police. Perhaps the school board?"

His face was impassive. On instinct I said, "Or more likely some rich girl's parents? Maybe a school benefactor who's arranged this gig for you as teacher in exchange for their building a new wing or something?"

Holmes gave out an exultant "Hah!" It struck me as confirmation of my last guess.

Then he said softly, "Excellent, Miss Watson. Your arrival in these dismal halls is actually quite fortuitous and exquisitely timed. Having found a potential colleague in you is in fact welcomed by me, as I'll explain to you directly."

Standing up and shooting his sleeves, speaking loudly for any who might still be listening—most probably Breeana, of course—he said, "Now let's clean up this mess those ridiculous and grubby sophomore swine left behind."

5

With the gush of water from the sink to cover our hushed discussion, Holmes, his shoulder occasionally brushing mine and so making me wonder if it was deliberate, said softly, "This is frankly still no place for a real talk, Ms. Watson. I think we should set a proper rendezvous this afternoon."

Leaning in closer, his lip almost touching my ear again, he said softly, "For safety's sake, and protection of our mutual covers, it should be miles away, I should think. Perhaps at least an hour's drive from here."

I nodded, passing him a beaker to dry. "Sure," I said. "How about the city, but at the east end? It's where I actually live." I was speaking of my campus dorm.

I set to scrubbing the last in a line of scorched-bottomed, Pyrex-manufactured beakers. "Where do you live presently?"

"Oh, the city too, of course," Holmes said. The ghost of a smile: "A teacher's salary, even in this absurd school, and certainly on an independent consulting criminal investigator's uncertain fees, can't cover costs in this ridiculous town. There's simply no affording this farcical place on anything less than a CEO's salary."

Holmes made a sour face. "So it's a temporary place I'm in for now. A residence hotel just this side of seedy, some would probably say. I have my eye on a fine apartment in the city, but it's a bit out of my reach, currently." He shook his head. "So I'm reluctantly looking for a roommate. So far, quite unsuccessfully. You know–someone to split costs."

The city's rush hour traffic didn't sufficiently scratch my itch to push my still-untested loaner Mustang on the hilly county two-lanes far from the city's sprawl, confusion and its infuriating gridlock.

Holmes had chosen a Starbucks situated squarely downtown for our "rendezvous"—a place very much in the city's center, but a good ways from Portsmouth, from its jailbait cheerleaders and the town's too snappily dressed police force.

I stood outside the coffee shop under an umbrella, checking my watch again. I'd been loitering for a long fifteen minutes in a thrashing, late-afternoon rainstorm. It was a steady downpour and I thought it would likely continue well into the night.

A taxi suddenly slid curbside, just missing splashing water on me by a scant three inches. Holmes settled his fare and slid out, deftly ducking under my umbrella. As he opened the coffee shop's door for himself—pointedly not for me, as he slid through first—I said, "I suppose your car's in the shop?"

"Oh, I don't have a car," he said. "Never got a license to drive this side. Not officially. But we have your car—the one I watched you leave in and that's now parked there." A hand wave in its general direction. "Let's get our drinks, then you drive. We'll talk on the move. Probably not a good idea for us to be seen in public like this, as a fair number of the school's students' parents work here in the city, after all."

"Sounds about right," I agreed.

Holmes again gave me a head to heel sweep of his gray eyes—still nothing sexual there at all. "On that note, do you have a coat or something you could put on over that uniform? Even away from the school, the two of us together with you looking like fresh-scrubbed underage sex appeal and sporting that silly schoolgirl jumper telegraphs a decidedly unsavory message. The most innocent of the possible explanations being that you're engaged in some flavor of erotic cosplay, which is, of course, not so very innocent at all."

While Holmes remained safely dry under my umbrella, I ran in the rain to my car to fetch my black duster that nearly reached my ankles.

I ordered a venti coffee, black: Somehow, I figured Holmes would probably echo that order. But I badly undershot in my prediction for Holmes' jones for über caffeine. How could I possibly anticipate his truly monstrous capacity for the stuff? When it came his turn, he said, "Just a venti espresso, thank you."

The barista, tattooed, twenty-something and instantly rendered slack-jawed by Holmes' order said, blinking, "I beg your pardon?"

"A venti espresso," Holmes said again, this time curtly. Her relented and gave her the ghost of a smile. "Here, I'll save you the math—it's essentially equivalent to roughly twenty standard espressos," he said. "I'll pay accordingly, of course."

"That's a killer drink." The barista bit her generous lower lip. "Honestly, mister, I work here to pay for classes for my real next day job—that's to be a doctor one day. I'm pretty sure what you're trying to order really can kill you, and pretty fast."

Holmes waved a hand. "Absurd. Been doing it twice-a-day, for five years at least, and here I stand. Anyway, haven't you heard the saying the customer is always right?"

A wry but cautious smile. She said, "Okay, your funeral, good sir. But this may take several minutes."

It of course actually took *many* several minutes for her to prepare Holmes' "killer" drink. Other patrons gave him death stares to rival Breeana's glare at me after Holmes had asked me to hang around alone with him after the close of class.

But Holmes seemed oblivious to our fellow customers' resentment. In fact, he seemed very much out of touch with any public scene, more inwardly directed and ignoring all that passed around and before him. Or so it seemed to me in that strange moment. I'd be proven desperately wrong about how keyed-in he was at any given time, and quite soon.

She at last handed him his drink and said, "I think I'm going to have to say this is on the house 'cause I just don't know how to price the sucker." She hesitated and then confessed, "I'm pretty sure making that drink's going to cost me my job, mister."

Holmes scowled and said, "I've done this before, as I said, and occasionally in this very Starbucks. In fact, I'm known to your manager." He handed her thirty dollars. "Five of that is for you—" he checked her nametag and said, *"Krista."*

Krista the barista and possibly doctor-in-waiting just shook her head and said, "If you really drink all that, I think you'll be shaking—actually vibrating so much that you'll be able to pass through solid walls, mister."

I was with her in that assessment, and then some.

Holmes just gave her another little smile and raised his travel cup in tribute to her. He took a sip and said, "Remember exactly how you achieved this for the next time, because it is perfect, Krista. You could be barista to the Gods."

Ignoring the angry stares of the other patrons, Holmes took my umbrella from me and led the way to the front door and back out into the needle-spray rain.

I slid my coffee cup in the caddy between our seats and got the Mustang in gear. I flipped on the wipers and set a course for the hilly sticks I'd been so aching to drive, fast.

Holmes said, "You're brimming with questions, of course."

I figured Holmes had already drunk maybe half of his insane, jumbo-sized espresso, yet he still seemed damnably calm and steady. His slender musicians' hands weren't even shaking from all the caffeine that had to be hammering his heart, and so very hard at that. God, the head rushes the man should be experiencing from just a few sips of that crazy brew should surely be overwhelming.

He sampled more of his bizarre drink and said, "You're wondering how I identified you this morning, but even more, you're wondering how I know your real name."

"For starters, yes," I admitted. "Sure, I wonder at all that. At that, and a ton of other things."

He nodded. "Your alias was no particular feat beyond simple memory," Holmes said, looking out his window. "Every student has a student ID photo taken. They're made available to all staff members. I prefer assigned seating because the seats match the corresponding chart with all of your mug shots that I keep on my desk. It's insulting, after all, not to know one's students' names." A beat and he added, "Even those of the dullards, which is to say, nearly all of you, or, rather, nearly all of them."

"You truly don't do it simply because you're just passing through here fleetingly and so don't have time to learn the names as a regular teacher would?"

"No," he said bluntly, "It's because I truly don't care about any of them as individuals. Not one bit. I simply can't afford the storage space in my brain to retain the names of silly teens who ultimately mean nothing to me and who spark less than no interest in me intellectually or otherwise."

"Well that does explain that," I said evenly. "And it also explains why you pointed me to that specific chair when I entered the room. You'd already selected it for me to match your seating chart. A minor mystery is now revealed. And it was really no mystery at all, was it?"

A deep sigh. He said acidly, "My dear, everything becomes commonplace and diluted once explained. And we're just starting that tedious process." He shook out a cigarette and cracked the window. "I do hope you're not going to forbid me smoking in your loaner car. Its real owner is obviously a prodigious fellow smoker, after all."

Loaner? Mr. Groves smoked?

How had Holmes figured any of *that* out?

The ashtray was immaculate. I'd detected no scent of cigarette smoke in the Mustang.

Well, I'd let those tangential mysteries linger for now. I said, "It's not my car, as you've somehow figured out. So go for it, only not in my direction, please. I don't smoke."

Holmes nodded his thanks and said, "Of course deducing you were no simple high school student wasn't any great stretch either." He smiled thinly and said, "But no worries about others repeating my discovery. As you've no doubt already decided of me, I'm a singularity in those hallowed halls back in Portsmouth. Rest assured you're right about all of that."

The corners of his mouth turned down. "Such as it is, your mask is well and firmly in place for all of the lemmings who roam the halls of Cattulus. I'm sure of precisely that much, Jona: You're pulling it off for all of the rest back there, I'm confident of that."

Precisely that much.

It is one of my favorite and frequently used words, yet so rarely, so fleetingly, does it prove apt as used by others.

I said, "But just how *precisely* did you find me out, Mr. Holmes?" With just a little insinuation injected into the loaded phrase I said, "Precisely how'd you *make* me, sir?"

"Simple observation and some eavesdropping at lunch," he said. "I'm fairly certain you don't know I was seated just behind you in the cafeteria today." He sighed and expelled twin streams of smoke from his flaring nostrils. "My God, the conversations those girls have. They hardly rise to the criteria that the word 'conversation' connotes."

Mr. Holmes, sitting behind me?

So that's why the other girls were exchanging those knowing, crooked smiles when Breeana pointedly asked me about Mr. Holmes and his possible attractiveness—when they'd plumbed for my assessment of Holmes as boyfriend material.

She'd deliberately asked me with the man himself sitting in earshot.

I was left seething at the slutty little bitch's destructive angling.

We'd at last reached the sticks; I dropped the hammer. The Mustang's engine roared and the Ford surged forward, pushing us both back in our seats. Yet Holmes seemed unperturbed by our increasing speed. He instead said, "You gave me enough in shared admissions to your fellow students for me to check against, and to confirm certain things I'd already observed that had triggered their own cascade of further questions and deductions, all of them informed by half-remembered memories and some jiffy computer-assisted researches. In other words, some admitted Googling."

Once again, he said that last like it was a dirty word. "The Web's a cheat of course, but undeniably, a timesaver. And, anyway, one must know what to look for in the first place in order to find answers online. Junk in, junk out, otherwise, yes?"

"Yes, but explain more about how you found me out, precisely," I said. That *P*-word again. "And be very explicit, please. I need to know exactly where I screwed up so I don't repeat those mistakes."

Holmes laughed softly. "I'm not sure that phrase applies— *screwed up*. It's exclusively me after all who found you out, Jona. It wasn't anything you necessarily did. It's more a matter of who you are, who and how I am, and how bloody anyone else but me behaves, anytime. As always, it's about what they do, how they move and how they choose to dress. It's about the life decisions they make that produce something very much like fingerprints that are easily detectable to the trained eye. It's really more about what I alone in this tepid world make of behavior or signs related to individuals and what I conclude from those things than about anything you did or didn't do."

"You've frankly lost me." I shot him a look as we lofted a hill that briefly seemed to raise my stomach to my throat. Holmes still seemed utterly unruffled by my aggressive, edgy driving.

He said, "When we first officially met this morning, certain things were simply observed, of course, just as I've said. In a sense, it's exactly that simple. Where others see, I, perhaps quite uniquely, truly observe. The distinction, while obvious enough on face, is still something precious few put into conscious practice. This world is ripe with obvious facts and waiting revelations that virtually nobody remotely perceives. People look but they refuse to *see*. They hear but they never listen. My method is largely founded on the keenest observation of things the rest of you—or most of you at any rate, for I'll give you the benefit of the doubt for the moment—never detect or absorb."

He sipped more of his venti espresso and said, "For the point of illustration, let's consider the matter of *Ms.* Jona *Sacker* and her impulsive detour into my classroom this morning, shall we?"

I gripped the steering wheel harder, bracing for it. I hate justified criticism. I hate to fail. "Yes, why don't we do that? What did she do to betray herself?"

Staying with the tactic of speaking of me in third person to my face, Holmes said off-handedly, "Of course her limp was the first thing I noticed. It's the first thing even a dullard would notice. That, and her rather fresh suntan, which, through her somewhat strategically and cynically chosen wardrobe—her loose fitting top that reveals so much of her breasts when she hunches over her notes—made clear her recently acquired tan likely runs something in the vicinity of crown to toe. That tan of hers also emphasized the chemical burn I see even now showing so extra whitely on her right hand, just at the intersection of thumb and forefinger."

He held up his far paler right hand that bore its own scar, nearly the twin of mine. The fact we had something so rare in common left me prickling inside. Yes, I was a perhaps already a goner for this strange man.

Fool, I chided myself.

Holmes continued, "Clearly, you're a fellow chemist or more correctly a *student* of chemistry—a somewhat clumsy one I would have to guess, much like myself, or clumsy at least *once*." He smiled ruefully. "I owe my accident, and several sequels, to a penchant for pesky and sometimes painful distraction." A shrug. "The mind does race . . . "

He smiled conspiratorially and pressed on. "Anyway, it was undeniable that Jona and I are clearly marked with the same chemical burns, so I can only deduce that given the particular chemical in question, Jona got her mark in the same way and from the same source that I received my own laboratory war wound. The chemical is rare enough in common practice in more routine chemistry classrooms. It's an acid, of course, but one used for only one purpose—one within which what can best be described as a very narrow niche of employment. Forensically speaking, that is. So I concluded this morning that Jona and I are birds of a very particular chemical feather, so to speak."

So there was that. It was all soundly deduced, and all devastatingly accurate.

I said, "You mentioned sitting behind me in the cafeteria today."

Holmes nodded. He switched from talking about me as someone else to speaking to me directly again. "Yes. At lunch, you told those addle-brained girls you injured yourself executing some silly cheerleading pyramid dismount, or the like. For reasons I'll explain later, I already doubted your alleged age and so therefore equally doubted any recent forays into high school or even college cheerleading.

"But I also noticed you are right-handed, Jona," he raced on, picking up speed. "You see, my dear, nearly all runners and athletes who are right-handed are also right-footed. It's a different statistical equation for left-handers, for obscure genetic reasons that don't at all interest me but whose statistical dependability is solid and so therefore indispensable in the commission of my craft. In this case, as in so many others, I bless the knowledge and curse the lesson. So, at first I considered the possibility you more likely injured your right ankle in a starter's block, perhaps as a result of running and not stretching out first. Or perhaps in some *other*, similar sports pursuit. Before settling on running as the cause, I looked at the rest of your body. For my part, I'll confess that this morning I'd nearly all but settled on volleyball being the cause of your ankle injury."

Eerie. I shivered and said, "Why volleyball, of all sports?"

"Because of the quality and texture of the flesh on your tanned forearms. Spiking the ball has calloused your arms, exactly midway between wrist and elbow. In light of your all-over tan, I'm thinking beach volleyball caused this particular injury. As there aren't beaches around here, and because of that exotic tan, I take it to be a between-semesters injury probably spent in Florida and probably in Miami, you see. That also again points to you being a college student. Returning to the clue of your injury, it was *probably* fueled by uncharacteristically heavy drinking and resultant dehydration, thus sharply raising the risk of a muscle tear. You're decidedly fit otherwise, so I don't see you as a habitual drinker and you certainly show no signs of smoking, despite the clues and the lingering evidence this car presents as belonging to a cigarette fiend. On balance, you're careful with your health and body at least in terms of diet and exercise. No, it's clear to me, with that injury, as well as your physique and your exotic tan, that your ankle's present condition is a byproduct of a rare interval of debauchery. Again, that marks you a college student. Virtually all roads, deductively speaking, lead to that salient fact regarding your current station in life—that being that you're still in school."

"That's all very accurate and very logical so far, I guess," I said slowly. "I mean, again . . . now that you have explained it to me."

Clearly frustrated, Holmes said softly, *"Omne ignotum pro magnifico.* All things unknown seem grand. Explanation makes the world so much smaller."

He smiled neutrally and emptied his cup. He cracked the window further and then simply flung the empty container out the window into the wind to go bouncing off behind us.

Cigarettes, coffee cups and other people's egos: The world was Holmes ashtray.

He suddenly arched both eyebrows. "So I *am* right about the volleyball? Your swimmer's back, broad shoulders and rump are unmistakable manifestations of intense and consistent swimming. Different sports foster different body types. But the implied underlying scar tissue of infinite volleyball impacts to your forearms are something quite apart from anything to do with water sports—beyond water volleyball of course, if I've indeed called it correctly. I believe I have because water volleyball would result in buoyancy to your body in motion that would inhibit the possibility of the sort of ankle injury you've suffered."

"You are right, as I've already told you," I said softly back. "I went for a return early in a match on a Miami vacation. It was beach volleyball, as you first guessed, and I nearly severed my Achilles' tendon. No stretching out first, just as you said."

A rueful smile and I allowed, "And I *might* have been slightly hung-over. Long Islands sneak up on you, sometimes."

"Hah!" He laughed and then bowed his head in thanks for my confirmation. Then, apparently remembering one word that ulcerated for him, he said, "And it was no guess. It was all deduction based on observation, Jona. Guessing is a shocking habit and it's destructive to the logical faculties. When you guess, or when you fantasize, you inevitably find yourself twisting facts to suit theories. No, the correct sequence of deduction is to gather data first, then twist your theory to encompass and fit the data you've amassed."

It struck me then this strange young man could build mansions on next-to-nothing with his so-called *observations*.

I said, "So you deduced I'm a forensics or criminology student and not a high-schooler. You know I'm a *plant*, just as you seem to be. But you know *my* real name, too. Explain that, please? What gave *that* away?"

"Just building on what I've already shared with you. For everyone else at Cattulus, I'm sure, you pass as a high school student, and I again congratulate you on that, Jona. It's no mean feat to be so convincingly insipid and vapid for hours on end, yet you manage it quite well." He smiled wryly and said, "And there's also that wrist of yours."

"My wrist?"

"Despite the wristwatch you use to try and hide the tattoo on your left wrist, it's still visible enough when the band slips up or down your arm. The tattoo 'round your wrist is a very particular and highly stylized iteration of a Celtic chain. It's very unusual and nearly always favored by young women of a certain age—specifically the mid-twenties—who became obsessed with that dreadful film starring What's-His-Name a few years ago."

I could feel the fan-girl blush in my cheeks. He'd called it.

"There was female character in said dreadful film whom had just such a tattoo on her left wrist," he continued. "That particular illustration in eternal ink enjoyed a thankfully fleeting vogue among women of a particular age-range and temperamental disposition. This is where I confess no facility for retaining names or details attached to popular culture beyond the ones that might directly exert themselves upon my needs for executing my trade. So I can't tell you the name of the film, the names of the actor or actresses, let alone the silly characters' names. I *can* tell you the year in which the film was made, the interval at which it exerted its mystifying weight and influence on men and women of a certain age and I can, therefore, fairly accurately tell you how old someone is within a year, either direction—encompassing the interval between cinema and digital, home-use release—who sports that particular tattoo. Suffice it to say, no authentic contemporary *high school* student bears that particular brand of tat."

He threw the stub of his latest cigarette out the window and immediately got another going. "For the life of me, I can't fathom why anyone mutilates themselves with ink, but tattoos' proliferation is germane to my investigations more often than one might think. So I've made quite a study of them. I even wrote a little eBook on the subject."

He made a face and confessed somewhat contritely, "It would be available in paperback, too, but I lost patience trying to figure out the pagination process. And anyway, hardly anyone seems to read physical books anymore." Holmes scowled suddenly and said, "By the way, that paperback copy of *Lolita* you were flaunting throughout the day was more than a shade heavy-handed, Ms. Watson. Far too on the nose, so to speak. I do sincerely hope that was not your idea."

"My employer's," I said, commiserating with Holmes. "I argued strongly against it, of course, but was overruled. If they'd thought of it, they'd probably have had me blasting The Police and *Don't Stand So Close to Me* on my iPod all day, too."

That was a pop culture musical reference that clearly got by Holmes. He just nodded distractedly and said vaguely, "No doubt you're right about that."

Yes, it was clear to me he wasn't *sure* at all about this particular aside of mine regarding The Police and that song title. Holmes had no context whatever regarding what I was talking about, it was painfully, awkwardly obvious. It was the first of many similar voids I'd experience in terms of Holmes' staggering disconnection from current culture and politics; from really anything that didn't potentially inform his "trade" or what I'd eventually come to hear him describe with unabashed reverence as "the art of deduction."

I thought about all he'd deduced about me and gave into the reality:

Score yet another round to Mr. Holmes, the *so* unsettling logician.

I said, "Do you have any tattoos you want to tell me about, Mr. Holmes?"

He was taken aback. "Absolutely not," he said. "Christ, no. It's disfigurement, as I've said. And a waste of money. And most importantly, it's a too easy clue to any enemy or potential antagonist with half a brain, as I've demonstrated to you, particularly when one is playing a role—something I'm doing now, and do often. Your impulsive tattoo—probably chosen on a drunken whim while on some other hedonistic holiday between college semesters—utterly undermined your cover the moment I saw your arm. Fortunately for you, not everyone is me."

"Okay," I said chastened, palming the wheel on another mounting, curving hill that again put butterflies in my stomach. Certainly it must have done the same for Holmes, but he still showed no signs of any such an effect. He still showed no fear of the speed I was managing to maintain on the wet and snaky roads. Hell, he wasn't even wearing a seatbelt.

I said, "So you suspected me to be a college student and one majoring in forensics and probably criminology since I was likely planted here by local police in your mind. But how *did* you learn my real name? You never answered that question."

Holmes looked disgusted with himself. "Google again," he said with a hint of dejection. He looked almost as if I'd struck him across the face for pushing him to that dreaded admission.

He said dully, "It's a cheat in a sense, of course. But as I pointed out earlier, one must input the proper search terms to hit pay dirt, you have to allow me that. Let's start with the first name, 'Jona'. Fairly unusual, of course. It's not an obvious or natural choice for an alias. It's the kind of name that struts and bounces, which is quite at variance with the goal of fitting in and not drawing attention to oneself when one is trying to operate clandestinely.

"But given your youth and college status, it's a safe deduction this is a first assignment for you," he continued. "You're green, and some kind of special recruit since I've determined for myself you do not yet possess your college degree. That being so, it stands to reason every contingency would be taken to ease your path on this first operation by the probable dullards who are your controllers. I therefore decided from the outset that 'Jona' is your real first name. I had your approximate age courtesy of your dated tattoo. I had the knowledge of your scar and thus your chemistry background. I had already let myself settle on volleyball and swimming as athletic pursuits of choice.

"With 'Jona' and those three search terms tossed into Google—chemistry, volleyball, swimming—a cascade of honor roll listings, sports reports and scholarship announcements pointed me to one Ms. Jona Ormond Watson. A newspaper website's photo of you in a damp and clingy swimsuit, smiling, matched up nicely against my seating chart mugshot of you and personal observations of your anatomy. Parenthetically, your visible tan lines were different in that photo from the ones you sport now up top, again leading me to believe you've recently spent time on a clothing optional beach."

Again, it was all so absurdly simple when explained.

Thank God I resisted the impulse to say so again. I suspect Holmes would have again taken my head off for diminishing his deductive accomplishments.

"You know so much about me, but I still know comparatively little about you," I said. "Are you hungry, by the way? I'm starving. I'll buy dinner this time and you can tell me more about yourself, Mr. Holmes. Interested?"

He smiled. "I'm not at all interested in talking about me, but in talking more about our respective missions? Very much so. In eating? Again, not so much at all. When I'm on a case, nearly all appetite abandons me. But I'll watch you eat and I could certainly do with more caffeine. That and nicotine are really all the fuel I need to sustain operations most days when on the hunt. In tandem, they focus the faculties."

"So dinner for one it is," I said.

"Yes," he said dryly, looking out his window again. I realized finally he was concentrating on the passenger side rearview mirror. He said, "But first we have a another decision to make."

"What's that?"

Holmes had nearly smoked down another cigarette. He said, "Despite your lead-footing in the rain, we're being followed, Watson. The question is, do we confront our tail, or do we simply try to lose him?"

6

"**I**'m pretty sure I can shake him," I said.

It was a white car back there—that's all I could be certain of given the distance and the winding road that made me focus my attention fully forward rather than on the rearview mirror.

"I'm pretty sure you could do that too," Holmes said. "You drive like a wheelman for the Mafia. I'm convinced you'd lose him or maybe kill us in the trying. He's stayed this close, this long, and you've been pushing this borrowed car aggressively in the rain. I'm therefore leaning toward confrontation as the better course."

I bit my lip, at last finding some circumspection. "What if they have guns?"

Holmes shrugged and said, "What if *I* have a gun?"

That gave me butterflies without the push of another fast-taken rise in the road. "Do you have a gun?" I waited a beat and added, "Do you have one on you?"

"Rest assured, I'm always armed, often variously," he said. "This time it does happen to be a gun." He pulled his suit jacket's flap back to reveal some sort of revolver hanging there in a chamois leather shoulder holster. *Well, well.*

"So what's the plan?"

Holmes slid his gun out of his holster and rested it on his thigh, pointed well away from me, thank God. "Slow down—slow a lot, or even park. There's enough shoulder for that. Let's see what he does when you bring us to a full stop." Holmes was decided. "Yes, stop. Do that now, please, Watson."

Inchoately trusting in Holmes, I gave the Mustang some brake and drifted onto the gravel shoulder.

I kept one hand on the wheel and the other on the gear-shift in case we needed to get moving again, *fast*. My toe twitched on the brake as I stared into the rearview mirror at the far-less-distant white car: It barreled on toward us after only a moment's hesitation.

I said desperately, "Should I give it some gas? Should I get us moving again, Holmes? Tell me *now* because we don't any time at all."

"Just stay put," Holmes said firmly. "I think he means to pass us by and fast. That's telling. There's no good place to turn around so he has to stop and confront us, or he has to blow by us."

I said, "But if he has a gun and takes a shot as he passes?"

"At this speed, driving with one hand, shooting with the other and through one glass window—maybe two if he can't get his own window down before he gets here?" Holmes smiled meanly and shook his head. "Hitting one of us with such a shot would require an act of God if there was even such a being, which of course there isn't."

The car was coming *so* fast now—half-a-mile; a quarter mile and now it was almost upon us.

I thought of ducking, but then something about the car struck me as mildly familiar. I had to see it through and try to get a look at the driver. I refused to cower below window level as the thing whipped by us—any risk from guns or no.

I also remembered a class guest speaker—a cop—who sneered at the notion of all those TV police and detectives who took shelter behind cruiser doors when exchanging gunfire with armed opponents.

Our speaker made it clear that test firing of firearms of even mediocre stopping power resulted in bullets frequently passing through *both* doors—and test dummies seated between them—of myriad police cruisers.

When our pale shadow did pass us by—owing to its extreme speed and the narrowness of the road—it actually buffeted my sitting-still loaner Mustang, setting it rocking side-to-side. Urgently, I said to Holmes, "Should I try to follow now?"

"No, turn around and let's go back. But first explain to me why you're blushing so furiously."

Dammit. Found out.

I said softly, "Because I *know* who that person was. *Is*. Whatever."

Holmes just looked at me and said, "Then you must tell, Watson."

"It was my chemistry professor," I said thickly. "I think he's just playing guardian angel. Probably even has some GPS tracer in this car to facilitate keeping tabs on me. That's his second car that just whipped by." I gripped the steering wheel tighter.

"And this, presumably, is his first car." Holmes exploded in laughter. "A middle-aged man's sports car . . . And he's playing chaperone for the tyro undercover agent! *Excellent.* Now I *have* truly seen it all, I think!"

For that moment, I truly hated Holmes.

Then he made actually made it *worse*: "He has some sort of crush on you, I take it. Based on the glimpse I got, he's at least sixty. My God, are there no teachers in this world who aren't trying to bed their much younger students? Good Lord, this bloody sorry world is indeed a sordid one."

"*No*," I said, feeling my pulse in my ears. "It's not like that! Not at all! He's more of a father figure. He's just very protective of me."

Mr. Holmes, who I had already decided was mostly lacking in simple empathy, seemed to sense he'd struck a particularly sensitive nerve. He quickly relented: "Then he's a good man and wise enough man in some respects for you're indeed in greater danger than you grasp. What's his name?"

Still angry, I said, "Professor Calvin Groves."

Holmes startled me: "I've read several of his published works. He's quite worthy and you're indeed fortunate to have him as your instructor. I'll confess I'm more of an autodidact than effectively properly schooled in some subjects. His first book on forensics was my little Bible starting out. You really must introduce us when all of this is over and we can be ourselves. But for now . . . ?"

He reached down between my legs and flipped a lever. Then he got out and popped the hood on the Mustang. "Just because I don't have an operator's license over here doesn't mean I don't know cars," he called to me. He fiddled a bit, then slammed shut the hood. He tossed me a little black box with a couple of severed wires dangling out one end. "There you are," he said. "Now you're invisible . . . in a sense. At least he won't be able to track you through this car."

Holmes then took a deep breath and let it out slowly. He reached for yet another cigarette. "And, anyway, Mr. Groves is quite right to worry about you, Jona. These are far darker matters than just tawdry student-teacher shenanigans rippling through that snooty private school back there. We're both treading far deeper and bloodier waters than that. You just don't know it yet. But don't worry about that—I doubt your police masters grasp it, either, and they're so-called professionals."

"Once again, you have to explain all that, Homes," I said as I tried to turn the Mustang around on the narrow road.

"I'll do just that thing, but over that dinner you earlier suggested," he said. "I now find myself a little hungry. And it will be my treat this time."

I said, "So, what will it be? Pizza? Italian? Chinese? Mexican?"

"It's all the same to me, as I told you. I'd be happy with a deli sandwich and a beer, frankly. You choose."

I thought about options, watching the mirror to see if Mr. Groves would take up the pursuit again. There was someone else back there, but likely on a motorcycle: there was the lonely blaze of a single headlight behind, quite distantly. Its lane position convinced me it was a bike, not a car with a blown headlight.

But after the embarrassment of our last undetected shadow, I held my tongue this time, just assuming Holmes was equally aware of this possibly new vehicle shadowing us and, like me, holding his tongue for the time, keeping his own council.

Petty of me? Probably.

Would my silence prove a mistake?

Maybe. And yet I held my tongue, at least for the moment.

7

I introduced Holmes to my favorite Chinese restaurant, Wo Hop. Business was light: three other solitary diners— two female and one male—and then us, the only apparent "couple."

Taking our seats, I said, "I'm afraid I can't make it too late tonight, you know."

Holmes scowled and picked up his menu. He said, "And why is that? You struck me as a night owl. Heaven knows I am."

I made an equally glowering face and said, "Homework. Apart from you, nobody else in that school knows I'm a plant. For the sake of the other teachers and my cover, I have to do the coursework, like all the other students. God, high school homework again...shoot me now."

Holmes brushed the comma of dark hair back from his forehead and said, "Well, at least you can skip your chemistry homework. You've already passed the course and with honors, so far as I'm concerned. Straight A's, all the way. You're the only one in the room who grasps a scintilla of what I'm saying, the only one with the merest wisp of understanding."

Looking over the menu—I always scanned my options, but I also invariably ordered the same "Happy Family" entrée—I said, "On that note, as we've established you are more than just the world's surliest substitute chemistry teacher, what exactly is it that you *truly* are? So, you're like, a private investigator?"

I could practically hear Holmes' eyes roll as I gave that one voice. "Emphatically, no, Ms. Watson. I'm very decidedly not that sorry thing. God! Now you're insulting me, Jona." He looked truly appalled.

Smoothing his hand over the white linen tablecloth, he took a breath and then said icily, "No, Ms. Watson, I'm not a *private investigator*. If one were to chart the investigatory evolutionary chain, you'd have police as some organism slithering out of the swampy muck and into the mud. Below even those dullards would be private investigators for the latter define the bottom rung of the evolutionary ladder. They are usually little better than voyeurs with cameras who mostly dabble in tawdry marital strife—cases that nearly always crescendo in a sleazy little sting operation hinging on some bosomy female operative who entraps the straying male in some squalid bar. She cadges some drinks, then suggests some hourly-rates, hot-sheets motel for some compromising photos to leverage a robust divorce settlement. Dullards hear the term 'private investigator' and think of Marlowe, or Sam Spade—maybe that dreadful obsessive-compulsive TV idiot Monk. No, Ms. Watson, fictional PI's are all absurdist drivel, actually more execrable than the real articles, if that's at all imaginable."

"God, so sorry," I said. "I hear you and I understand your taking offense. A thousand apologies, Holmes." I poured myself some hot tea from the silver pot sitting between us and asked, "So then what are you, exactly?"

Holmes seemed to think about it, then said, "I suppose over here you'd call it being an 'independent contractor.'" He browsed the menu for a time then said, "I more or less invented my calling. If I must be called anything, I prefer independent consulting detective."

Okay.

It seemed like splitting hairs to me, but it clearly mattered very much to Holmes so I embraced the job title he'd coined for himself. "So you're a problem solver, but for a price?"

"Or perhaps a problem eradicator for price. A man has to live. And money honestly earned ensures I stay flush enough to continue to help other people with their little problems."

I nodded and smiled as our waiter came to take our order. When he left I said, "And so who's keeping you flush now?"

"Some girl's concerned parents, as I assume you logically earlier deduced." Holmes was reaching for his cigarettes again, then caught himself and sighed. "I'd helped the father's employer in solving some intellectual property theft of a deliciously diabolical nature—diabolical in its conception and execution. Anyway, for this man, I was a known quantity as a successful agent for problem solving."

"And are you known to anyone in the school—that is to say, known to be what you really are by anyone else in the school beyond your employer?"

"Only the school principal has an inkling. He had to make the rather hasty hiring decision regarding my employment, after all."

Our waiter arrived again to take our order. I decided since we had the place mostly to ourselves—not to mention being a regular and so known to the staff—I doffed my overcoat. I intended something spicy and didn't want to sit sweltering in a coat with some Szechuan sweat on.

Holmes ordered comparatively little: just some green tea and a bowl of hot and sour soup. He argued after how hunger sharpened one's mental faculties.

I volunteered my medically informed opinion that hunger—and ensuing blood sugar crashes—actually weakened concentration, generating confusion and dulled memory.

Holmes just shrugged and said, "But it's not like that for me. Quite the opposite, actually."

I checked my phone for the time. "I think I can give this another half-an-hour, then I've got to hit the books," I said. "Got that cover to maintain, you know."

Holmes checked his wristwatch. "So let's put the remaining time to good use and get down to cases. That cover of yours—it has implications for mine, too, you know. That river runs in both directions, as you'll have no doubt gathered by the deliberate attention I paid you today in class. By the rumors that attention will no doubt have started among your peers and, perhaps, some key faculty, as well." A smile. "We can only hope . . . "

"Yes . . . "

But, no, that was a stall: I really wasn't yet certain where Holmes was headed with all of this.

I hadn't *gathered*, not at all.

He continued, "In our respective roles, certain behaviors are expected—perhaps even required of us. Those are particularly expected by our nemesis, you'll agree."

"Of course, sure . . . " I was still completely flummoxed. Who in God's name was this *nemesis?* Did any real person living a real life have such a thing as a "nemesis"?

"But embodying those expectations could compromise our positions as investigators, not to mention the possible court cases we're working to give foundation," he dashed on. "We simply can't commit crimes in order to solve or prevent other crimes."

I was still at sea. I said, "Of course we can't. So, go on . . . ?"

"The obvious fact is, I can't sleep with underage girls to protect underage girls," Holmes rued. "And you can't be seducing and entrapping male teachers to build cases against them for sleeping with their students. Still, we have to make a convincing case for ourselves as libertines and *players* if we're to penetrate to the very core of this carnal cabal, for lack of a better term."

A "beard"—that's what I began to grasp Holmes saw in me. Pouring myself more tea, I said, "You're suggesting we let the world think we've hooked up."

He scowled. "Forgive me: *Hooked up?*"

"You know that we're, well, lovers. An item."

He smiled and pointed. "Exactly! That's *exactly* it, Ms. Watson." He seemed palpably relieved to have had me be the one to give it voice. "If it's assumed that you and I are *that*, well *then* . . . ?" He snapped his fingers. "It obviously solves a serious problem for both of us. It saves you the coarse attentions of these poisonous teachers and it cools the fires for a certain Breeana Rourke and some other underage girls who have me in their underage sights."

Leaning in on crossed arms, I said, "Yes, about Breeana and that photo. When you talk about blurring lines and jeopardizing prosecutions, you must surely see that friending these horny girls on Facebook or Instagram and trading photos on Snapchat is itself a criminal act, regardless of your intentions or quasi-official status. They're indeed underage, and Breeana sent you naked photos that are therefore illegal for you to possess or for really anyone to have. She may have a woman's body, but she's still a kid in the eyes of the law. Those pictures are child porn, legally. And if you've reciprocated . . . ?"

He was clearly taken aback. "I haven't taken any Selfies in this lifetime," Holmes said archly, "nor will I ever. As to soliciting photos, no I haven't done that, either. Two days ago, I strategically left my iPad unguarded and unlocked on my desk when I ran down the hall for an announced ten minute absence. Three girls—Breeana being the first to make use of the resulting opportunity—used my iPad to friend themselves on several social networks. I'm walking a tightrope with no net, I know that, Watson. But there's still a veil to pierce and the stakes are much higher than tawdry student-teacher relationships, as I've intimated. These are worthwhile risks I take in the cause of a righting a far greater wrong."

I checked my watch again.

He smiled and said, "You really are concerned about this silly homework, aren't you? Really, you need only be mediocre as a student, you must know. You're not staying long enough to complete a school year, one hopes. So what if you flunk out?"

"It's not my nature to just get by," I said. "I'm competitive and results-driven. It's just the way I'm wired. I can't play the idiot."

Holmes smiled. "I'd frankly probably be the same in your position. If it will take some pressure off and buy us back a little more cooperative time in the days ahead, give me your math homework going forward. It'll be relaxing in a way, kind of like five-finger exercises between grading papers. My God, those papers . . . " A forlorn shake of the head. He said, "Anyway, I get in very early, so just give me your locker combination and I'll leave the completed homework in there each morning before you students arrive."

I smiled. "Thank you. That does help. Don't suppose you'd take on history, too?"

"Not if you truly value your grades," he said. "Not history, or English—these subjects are not in my so-called wheelhouse.

Now back to our investigation: There's a party Saturday night. I need you to be, you know, kind of like my, well, my date for that. You'll do it of course?"

If I could see his feet, I had a sense he might be twisting his toe. His sudden awkwardness was strangely endearing.

I said, "What party? What kind of party would ever possibly allow us, student and teacher, to be there as, well, you know, as a detectable couple?"

Holmes' gray eyes glistened. "By hazy account—and some admitted deduction—a very unusual and exclusive party," he said. "I've been invited twice and made excuses fearing I'd be forced to cross those lines we've spoken of and their resulting challenge to us in maintaining convincing cover. I doubt refusal of this third invitation would earn a fourth invite. So again, your arrival here is quite timely indeed, Jona. You'll at last afford me access to these steamy soirees."

Holmes lightly punched air, beaming. It was an unexpected, boyishly appealing and wholly spontaneous gesture. It was clear that an ulcerating point of frustration had just evaporated for Holmes. I was pleased to have made that possible simply by showing up, as it were. Well, that was all that had been required *so far*. I started thinking about this party and what it might really be like.

Chief Brigg's description of these fabled parties suddenly came back to me, giving me butterflies: "Orgies" was the word he'd used for them, wasn't it?

"Invited," I said, thinking aloud. "Invited by whom, for God's sake? Who would risk crawling out on that crazy limb? Seems like a hell of a gamble, doesn't it? If they read you wrong and you then ran to the police . . . ?"

Holmes shook his head. "No, there's no possibility of that. I've shamelessly talked the talk to a couple of fellow male faculty members in the privacy of the teacher's lounge to help secure those twice-declined invitations. These are, parenthetically, male faculty members whose very real and unsavory interactions with students remain still undetected by your police friends, or so I gather."

Drumming restless fingers on the tabletop, Holmes said, "I'll confess now that this morning I was toying with forwarding on a copy of Breeana's naked photo to my perverse peers to further my cover. A rather desperate and yes, illegal activity, but one being committed by a man on the side of the angels, as you know. Anyway, happily, you made the scene and now we have this much better angle of attack, working as partners in a variety of senses, yes?"

Yes . . . Yet that phrase "partners in a variety of senses" tantalized me.

And, my God, I was coming to see that Holmes might pay lip service to the letter of the law, but he actually lived and operated in a far grayer space. I sensed he was well capable of breaking the law in his efforts to enforce it.

I said, "Anyway, you couldn't have shared her picture—the whole point of Snapchat is the image disappears—" now I snapped my fingers "—just like that."

Holmes just smiled and shook his head. "I took a screenshot. You have to be quick of course, and it sends a notification to the other person that you've made a permanent copy of their fleeting photo—although there are ways even around that if one takes the trouble. But in this case, I think we can agree the silly twit will probably take my effort at achieving permanency of her racy photo as a sign of my interest in her."

"That's probably too sadly true," I said. I warmed my hands on my teacup. "So, I just point out a last time you have essentially child porn sitting on your iPad right now, *partner.*

She's a minor in the eyes of the law and naked in pretty much anyone's eyes. If you turn it over to someone now it's still evidence. If you hold onto it much longer—"

"It's a criminal act," he said sourly. "Here's my thought—I'll send you a copy. I suppose it serves my cause to have your employers on the page regarding my relative innocence as I potentially find myself pushing the envelope going forward. I trust they will keep the confidence?"

"I'll try to make sure that they do," I said.

"That would actually be an improvement in my quality of life in some ways," he said. "Frankly, their rather ham-handed suspicious inquiries after me these past few weeks have been both inhibiting and irksome. If I was given to further alliteration I might add *inept* too in there. Possibly *incompetent* would be a candidate."

I held up a hand. "Enough of that, Holmes. These men are my bosses after all, and anyway, you have me at a disadvantage in that sense. For all I know, your illustrious client could be—"

"A monster in his own right," Holmes finished for me. "It's quite possible, of course. Men of power and earned influence tend toward ruthlessness and narcissism. One simply must sometimes take the rough with the smooth, yes?"

"This party Saturday night," I said, "Tell me more about—"

"There isn't time for that now," Holmes said curtly. I sensed he really didn't want me to know what I'd agreed to, fearing I might balk with any clearer understanding of this "party."

A smile and a dodge: "We have our homework, after all. And I have my summary raft of C's to hand-down to your lackluster chemistry classmates—with the noted exception of Miss Jona Sacker, who is singularly not hopelessly at sea in my class."

Holmes paid the check and passed me a fortune cookie. "Dinner again tomorrow night?" He asked it as I unwrapped my cookie, then broke it in two, extracting the strip of paper within. I read my fortune aloud: "Silence is golden; duct tape is silver."

Holmes snorted softly, then shared his: "Stand clear, or be trodden under foot."

I wondered aloud, "What does *that* mean? They usually aren't this, er, *oblique*. Certainly not this menacing. They must have changed vendors between your cookie and mine."

Holmes just tossed his un-sampled cookie aside and said with a curled lip, "Fortunes in a cookie? It's even sillier than astrology."

"Given the hour and the distance," I said, "why don't I save you a taxi fare tonight and drop you at home?" I was curious to see at least the outside of this rather sketchy place where he'd settled while he sought a roommate.

Holmes said, "Yes, thank you. That's very kind. I'd just about decided to ask you to do that very thing. It's only fifteen minutes' drive or so."

A single headlight blazed behind us. I finally mentioned it to Holmes. After all, I didn't want to lead someone straight to his home—assuming, that was, they didn't already know where he lived.

Holmes said, "Yes, I think he was following your teacher who was following us. When the former panicked and then fled, our friend back there lost his cover."

"Then should I drop you somewhere other than home? Should I try to outrun him? I suspect I maybe could with this car."

Holmes was firm: "No, I have some suspicions about who he might be, or, rather, who he *serves*. Consistent with what we discussed earlier this evening, it was our *friend* back there who decided me on asking you for a ride home before you beat me to the punch."

"Okay . . . But why?"

He wet his lips, hesitating. He said finally, "Because we simply *have* to fulfill certain base expectations going forward from here. We have to do that starting right now, I fear."

"That doesn't help me at all, of course." Annoyed, I said, "You want me to pull up right out front?"

"Yes, right out front. Front and center," Holmes said. "The assumption being—no, that's not right; not assumption but rather, the deduction—that they already know just where I live."

I palmed curbside. The neighborhood wasn't the greatest, not at all. Holmes' building was a dingy old brownstone— tagged and tagged over again with gang signs and random graffiti. "You really need a better place," I said. "This looks like a crime scene waiting to happen."

"Yes," Holmes said, suddenly distracted. "As I confided earlier, I found a good place across town, I think, but—" He hesitated, then veered: "You live in a dorm now, I take it?"

"That's right, in my real life, that's to say. Right now, in my fake life, I live in a house with a sham family. An illustrious guardian who works for a prominent Portsmouth employer. About that dorm arrangement, though: I candidly abhor my roommate."

"There are roommates, and there are roommates," Holmes said. "Are you graduating soon?"

"Yes, quite soon. This little gig is worth some pretty significant credits, I'm promised. They say it might even shave off some time."

"Good for you," Holmes said. "Then we should talk further about living quarters."

Well, of course *that* got my attention. But before I could possibly react to that loaded and leading statement, Holmes said quickly, decisively, "I need you to go with what's coming next, Jona. But it's necessary, so please forgive me."

My stomach kicked. God, what exactly was *this* mysterious thing that was coming?

Holmes turned around in his seat to face me. He draped his left arm around the back of my seat. Searching my eyes, he used his right hand to stroke my hair behind my ear.

His arm touched my neck, curled around there, then exerted pressure, urging me toward him.

My God, was this really happening? My heart kicked into overdrive.

Holmes held my gaze until the last possible second before our lips made contact.

I went with it, even slid my tongue in his mouth as I found myself so much loving it. The kiss was hard and lingering and intensely passionate. Then I was half aware of a flash of light going off, like that of a camera. For a moment, I thought it was all in my head.

Holmes broke it off soon after that flash of light. "Please forgive me," he said. "We simply *had* to fulfill the Professor's expectations, Jona. That image that was just taken of us kissing will fill the bill quite nicely, I should think."

Dizzied, slightly panting, I said, "What professor? What bill?"

Holmes seemed wholly collected; intensely focused on everything but me. I sensed dully our kiss had maybe meant same as nothing to him.

"Yes. Consider it a teaser. No spoilers, not yet. I'll explain about the *Professor*—and yes, that's very much with a capital 'P', tomorrow."

Dazedly, still a little passion-drunk from our kiss, I said, "That motorcyclist—he'll follow me home now. Shouldn't I be concerned?"

"No," Holmes said. "Not afraid. He's followed me several nights and never touched me." He hesitated and said, "But it wouldn't do for him to know you live in the city, too. When you drop me, you need to lose him if you mean to go to your dorm. Do that in the direction of Portsmouth, of course. If you're going back to your fake family, then just go back to your fake family."

"Of course." I smiled cunningly, hoping to entice him into another kiss, maybe. "You just trust me to lose him if I choose that route?"

Holmes smiled back. He leaned in, seemingly impulsively, and kissed me once more. "Emphatically. After all, I've seen how you can drive, Jona."

I drove home to my false family in a daze, remembering the sensation of Holmes' lips against mine and half-focused on that motorcyclist behind me. Those kisses: I still tasted his mouth—the wine, coffee and, yes, all those cigarettes.

And I still feared our kiss had been nothing more to Holmes than a ruse.

For my part? *Well . . .* It had been the mother of all kisses to that point in my life.

But that single headlight was still back there in my rearview mirror, stubbornly dragging my otherwise giddy thoughts in unhappy and sinister directions.

Might the man on the bike be this mysterious Professor with a capital 'P'?

This much was certain: I couldn't lead him back to my dorm room, just as Holmes had said. I'd already started the longish journey back to my place in Portsmouth. Still, I didn't really want him knowing too much about my so-called *life* there, either.

I toyed with calling Holmes. Maybe I'd explain I just wasn't having luck shaking my tail and so needed to hit a convenience store like it was always planned, and then return to Holmes and his hovel. I might beg the right to sleep on his sofa, maybe.

But from the outside the place really did look like a dive and so Holmes probably wouldn't want me to see inside. He had his pride in some places—that was manifest.

There was another thing, too: If I called now and begged sanctuary with him Holmes might correctly fear his calculated, strategic kiss was already going sideways on him, that it had triggered some too-real loving notions in me.

No, it was better to make the drive back to Portsmouth after all, but lose my tail on the commute—get home to *family* and burn the midnight oil completing my homework.

Still, just for fun, in the end the man on the motorcycle proved ridiculously easy to lose.

I got him on the straight away to Portsmouth, then I dropped the hammer. I tore off around an exit ramp, passed five minutes in a dark parking lot behind a rambling old warehouse, before getting back on the interstate.

When I got home, I dug out my hand-me-down antique revolver. At some point, the line ran out of sufficient numbers of sons and so I inherited one of the family's ancient weapons after my parents' fatal car crash. My elder brother had inherited my Colt's twin. I had a concealed carry permit, but could hardly carry the gun to either of my schools.

But *home* at last, I shoved the gun—loaded and with the safety off—under my full-size bed's guest pillow, then showered.

After, wrapped in a big, warm terry-cloth robe, I cracked the books, and worked at my assignments until one a.m.

When I finally turned off the lights and pulled up the covers, my dreams were quite troubled with wicked, sultry imaginings about Mr. Holmes.

8

I was fifteen minutes from leaving home in the morning when my cell phone rang: It was Professor Groves.

Sheepishly, he said, "Jona, about last evening—"

"Your heart was in the right place, but you could have seriously compromised me," I said as forcefully as I could manage. "I'm fine. Anyway, Holmes is an undercover investigator, too. He's another secret embed. So we are, for now, more or less allied."

Cal Groves was clearly sent reeling by that revelation. "Jona, this man is regarded by police as—"

A suspect, I know. Idiots. I yearned to give that estimation voice.

"Please," I said too quickly, yet firm in doing so. "The police are so desperate that they've asked someone like me to help them crack their case. So, please understand they're clearly flailing on all fronts. Holmes is on the side of the angels." That last line had sounded far more convincing coming from its silver-tongued source.

"Jona, you've spent only a few hours in this man's company. Holmes is—"

"A genius, in his way, yes, that's true. Both as a chemist, and as an investigator. He's already aware of the parties the chief alluded to. In fact I'm invited to one with him on Saturday night. He's already identified two other teachers the police don't even know about as being involved with students."

The tone of his voice indicated my professor was clearly torn on the issue of Holmes: "You're certain this man is to be trusted? And you're not actually going to one of these parties *with* him? His behavior in the classroom by all accounts—"

"Is that of a genius," I said. "I've *seen*. He's off-the-charts brilliant in chemistry, forensics and the art of observational deduction. Admittedly, in other far less important areas, he's a hot mess. It's possible he has a mild form of Asperger's Syndrome. Just *possibly*." I gave it a beat and said, "You should know now that he knows and admires your work."

That gave him at least a little pause. "Really? Is that truly so?"

"Truly," I said, smiling so he'd hear it in my voice. "Really."

"What else do you know about him, Jona? What else has this Holmes told you?" There was suddenly static on the line. Cell coverage—at least for my provider—was not particularly good in the smaller, ritzy city—so called NIMBYism—"not in my backyard" sentiments thwarted construction of critical cell towers in vital, pretty neighborhoods.

"I'm driving and the weather is less than great," I said. "I really need to focus on the road."

"Of course," Prof. Groves reluctantly said. "When can I expect to hear from you again?"

"When I know more, I'll call you. Please don't ever follow me again. I can handle this, really. And now I have an ally. A formidable one, at that. I'm sure it's so."

"These two other teachers your *ally* has identified—?"

"More on that soon," I said. "Traffic is picking up. I really need to keep both hands on the wheel now."

"But your promise we *will* talk soon?"

I said, "I'll call you—or the chief (for he was the one paying me, after all)—as soon as I really know anything worth sharing."

There was a motorcycle waiting in the parking lot of a Starbucks adjacent to the school which was pretty much the same as road's end. It was *the* motorcyclist, the same one that followed us the previous evening. He was waiting for me, clearly intent upon following me again. Well, good luck to him.

High school and college: Different enough, in a sense.

I was beginning to see from my older perspective that high school was really mostly just a kind of performance art practiced for the benefit of fellow inmates.

College was a blessed reboot: In college, in many respects, you were a cipher. A college student, at least in the fairly early going, was at sea and an unknown quantity to her peers. Education really was the focus there, overall.

High school, every sorry minute of it, was just undeclared drama school: I could at last see that now, hard and clear.

There were dark circles under my eyes and bed hair I didn't have quite enough time to rectify in order to mitigate others' low opinions of me on this, my second day at school.

Yes, on day two of high school, I was already drawing askance looks from The Squad. They were probably already making me for a hard-partier. No un-ringing that bell.

Holmes was standing in the door of his classroom just as he had been the day before, peering at his iPad. I sensed he saw me, but he didn't allow me a flicker of acknowledgement. That was just as well, I thought, particularly as The Squad and Breeana were very much with me, for the moment.

I stopped by my locker and the other girls drifted on without me, but clearly talking about me as they moved through the hallways like a plaid-skirted escadrille.

Good to his word, Holmes had left my math homework there in my locker. Smiling stupidly, I closed the door and spun the dial.

Breeana was suddenly beside me again. She said, "What was it—wine? Margaritas?" With a hint of disappointment she said, "Was it beer, Jona? Tell me at least it was *craft* beer."

"It was simply homework," I said.

Dubious doesn't begin to adequately describe her expression. She said, "Really?"

"Swear," I said. "My last school was kind of not remotely academic like this one. I never got slammed with homework like this before. This fucking sucks."

A sly smile and darting gaze, left and then right. Quietly she said, "I've got something that will wake you up. Helps with the weight, too. You want?"

"No, I'm good," I said coolly. "Why God invented Coke—as in cola—and Starbucks."

"Your funeral," Breeana said doubtfully.

Thunder rumbled, low and close, overhead. There had been some weather warnings on the radio of the potential for severe thunderstorms, possibly even for tornados. Another crack of thunder that startled us both. Thinking of tornadoes, I said, "Does this place have a basement?"

"Has," Breeana said. "But it's closed off ever since the custodian caught Tisha Wagner—the ex-Squad captain—down there blowing Mr. Coyle. He *was* the band director, by the way, and not very physically fit, I have to say." A crooked smile. She added, "Tisha played flute. Draw your own conclusions and make your own dirty jokes."

My second lunch at the cheerleaders' table. *The Roundtable* as the girls called it: How staggeringly and inappropriately Arthurian for this catty gathering. Still, at least it was evidence someone must have actually read at least one book in AP English, I thought.

Eating a yogurt in *super* slow motion—really just teasing the content with a plastic spoon—Breeana said, "You leave his tubes—his *test* tubes—all squeaky clean?"

I gave her a withering stare to rival the one she'd shot at me leaving chemistry class the day before. "I was *asked* to stay by Mr. Holmes. You know that. You saw."

She shrugged, tracing the liner of her yogurt cup with her spoon for the last of it. "And now what?"

I leaned into the table, crossing my arms. "What's it matter? You asked me if I thought he was hot." A little shrug. "I do. I think he's very fucking hot." I snorted softly and said, "But all we did was wash up some beakers and those test tubes you mentioned. That's all. Boring doing the dishes stuff. That was it. "

"Not how I hear it," Breeana said. "That's not how I hear it at all."

I sipped my orange juice and said, "Just how did you hear it, then? And who *said* it, because, since they were so wrong, they're obviously an idiot and so someone needs to set 'em straight. Who said it?"

Breeana lowered her head. Speaking toward the tabletop, she said, "You'll be coming Saturday night, I hear." Her gaze shifted: meaningful glances around at the other girls.

I bit my lip, letting the silence hang in the air between us for a long awkward time. When the tension was crazy thick, I at last said, "Pretty sure I have no clue what's you're talking about. No clue at all."

A mild sneer, "Sure, Jona . . . "

At last, chemistry class—and another mine field of a school day winding down.

My ankle was better now: I figured sometime next week I might even be able to start training with the girls. Then things were going to get *really* incendiary and treacherous amongst them. I'd instantly move from novelty to threat, at least for some of the less athletic.

Today—probably uncharacteristically based on the slack-jawed expressions of my duller classmates—Holmes had dialed it down several intellectual notches. Some of the students actually looked like they were almost grasping some of what was being taught them.

For my part, I laid very low: I wasn't the cascade of questions I had been yesterday.

Holmes' dark rings under his piercing gray eyes echoed my own. I was pretty sure that congruity wasn't lost on Breeana, at least. Also, she'd evidently decided to adopt my inquisitive posture from the day before: It had worked for me, after all—at least it was so from her perspective.

But it *so* wasn't working for her.

After her fifth obtuse question, Holmes, looking very hung-over, twisted knuckles in his eye sockets, squeezed the bridge of his hawkish nose and said in a gravelly voice, "Ms. Rourke, let's try to master the bunny hill before we try to take the ski jump dive into the far loftier concepts, yes? You need to learn to ride the bike without training wheels first."

Now *Holmes* was treated to the cheerleader's death stare, but one coupled with a furious blush of embarrassment.

He'd gone too far: She'd probably tattle to her parents who would rush to the principal, demanding Holmes' head.

He sighed and checked his watch. Fifteen minutes until final announcements and dismissal. I thought I heard Holmes mutter in lament, "*Cursed ennui . . .*"

The bell at last rang. Another crackling string of half-listened-to announcements ensued. I waited to see if Holmes would ask me to stay behind again. As students packed up to clear out, it was clear Breeana and I were in a race to be the last to leave his classroom.

It got so pointless and strange—Holmes just staring at both of us then ordering me out with a darting gaze to the door and back again—I stood and lightly limped out the door.

Making my way to my loaner Mustang, I saw my friend the mysterious motorcyclist, again. I bit my lip and thought about it: I could probably outrun him or lose him again. But I wanted to sleep in the city tonight, back on campus at least, and that was in the wrong direction from the current *family home*.

There was an old, still-working payphone in the entryway to the school. I rolled up alongside, dropped some coins, then called up Chief Briggs and told him I was about to call in a complaint about a suspicious man on a motorcycle. I told him my planned path so they could intercept him. The chief agreed and said I should call later in the evening and he'd fill me in.

I made my way back down the steps. The bad weather was gathering force again: the sky was freshly darkening and there were more low rumbles of thunder that rattled window glass. It was just starting to sprinkle as I swung into the Ford and got her in gear.

This time, I didn't even try to lose my tail. I just drove along my pre-planned route toward my faux home and waited for the Portsmouth cop's party lights to force the biker curbside for some pointed questions.

Halfway to the city, my phone rang. It was Holmes:

"Where are you, Watson?"

"Halfway home. I mean to my real home. My dorm. Staying there tonight. Are we still thinking dinner? Because you still owe me a lot of explanations about this party, and about this Professor with a capital *P*, you know. Where are *you*, Holmes?"

"In a cab, somewhere far behind you, no doubt, given your lead-footed tendencies."

"You might be surprised. You might actually be in front of me this one time. I had a complication." I told him about what I'd done with the motorcyclist.

Holmes thought about it, then said, "Probably for the best. I have some thoughts about who he probably is and certainly for whom he works. Anyway, he served his purpose taking that photo last night—establishing us as being properly improper together." His tone shifted. "As to dinner, yes, that's still the plan if you're game."

"Oh, I'm very much game," I said. Fortunately, homework was light tonight—just some math that it was on Holmes to complete. He said, "There's a seafood place I'm partial to." He said he'd text me the name and address. He added, "It goes without saying, don't be followed there, Jona."

I said, "You're in a damn taxi. I assume you'll take steps to avoid a tail, too?"

"That's right," he said. "I'm being dropped elsewhere. I'll go the rest of the way to the restaurant on foot. See you at five-thirty."

My gaze flicked to the rearview mirror: All clear.

9

I found Holmes in a back corner booth, waiting with a
bottle of Rombauer Chardonnay on ice. He'd also ordered
an appetizer—a plate of calamari. It looked like he'd already
sampled some of the latter.

A menu sat waiting in front of my empty seat. I slid off my
damp raincoat and folded it and put it on the seat, then slid in.

Holmes presumed to pour me some wine. We tapped
glasses. I said, "We drink to?"

"To the game, of course," Holmes said simply. "So, do you
now know who the man on the motorcycle is?"

After checking my watch I said, "In two hours or so I
will." I helped myself to some of the calamari between us and
then sipped the wine. Scooping up a menu I said, "This is
your haunt, you said. So what's good, Holmes?"

After ordering a salmon salad and a cup of seafood bisque
for myself (Holmes hewing to his earlier insistence he didn't
eat much at all when on a case) an email tone alarm caught my
attention. It was the Portsmouth Chief of Police—I'd rather

whimsically set a ring tone for him that sampled the *Law and Order* "*DUN-DUN*" riff.

Holmes arched an eyebrow when my phone went off. "Your boss, I take it?"

"That's right," I said, tapping in the password the chief and I had agreed upon to ensure it was indeed us at either end of any email exchange. I hit "send."

"Suspect I'm getting the 411 on my motorcyclist shadow a bit earlier than previously announced," I said.

Holmes nodded. "Then while we wait, I'll venture what I think I know about this man. I believe him to be a man named John Clay, age twenty-six. He's a computer hacker of no small skill. He did two years of a suspended six-year sentence for hacking into one of this city's major bank's databases and redirecting three-quarters of a million dollars into a private account. He was released from prison this past April."

Wondering if Holmes would somehow again be miraculously proven right, I stared at my phone, awaiting its verdict. Five long minutes passed.

DUN-DUN. The ring tone startled me when it came.

I scanned the email. I tapped back, "OK" and dimmed its screen.

The ghost of a smile on Holmes' pale and handsome face. "So what's the verdict, Watson?"

"Just as you said. It's Clay." I drummed my fingertips on the table, then sipped some more chilled white wine. I said, "You somehow deduced this? How?"

"Nothing like that," he said. "I got a decent look at the man when he was following me before he shifted his focus to you. I checked him against my personal collection of mug shots."

His fingertips brushed his smart phone. "Dwelling in the cloud, you know. It's a staggering amount of data. The letter

'M', just by itself is massive, the primary reason for which I'll soon enough explain, just as promised."

Holmes raised his goblet to his lips. I suddenly found myself remembering the taste of his mouth, our tongues darting, tangling. He said, "Now that we know for certain what we know about our shadow, we'll need to be extremely careful with all of our electronic communications. You and your police friends, too. *Especially* you and them. I suspect there's very little to which Mr. Clay can't lay claim in the digital realm when he sets his mind and hand to the task."

I put my phone and away and said, "That was my first police contact on my cell. Perhaps I'll make it the last. Maybe we should go back to the old ways . . . exclusively landlines, which I've been using some since taking on this job and for that reason—who knows how to tap one of those old phones anymore? Maybe we should do the same—not that we've had any electronic exchanges so far other than straight up phone calls."

"Maybe we should indeed think about stepping back from smart phones and email," Holmes agreed. "I know a simple but effective code using stick figures we might try. Maybe we could use the chalkboard in the old lecture hall they're renovating to trade messages as needed."

He frowned suddenly. "You know, it suddenly occurs to me that our lack of electronic exchanges may be its own problem in the other direction."

I frowned, propping my chin on my palm. "Explain, Holmes."

His eyes darted left and right, not really seeing me. As much to himself as to me, I suspected, he said, "If Clay's already hacked in to one or both of our phones, he would rightly expect a certain level—to be more precise, a certain *kind*—of communication to be occurring between you and I."

Despite sensing where Holmes was headed, I still wanted him to say it for various reasons. "Elaborate, Holmes."

The corners of his mouth turned down. "Oh, you know well enough. Sexual messages. Perhaps even pictures."

Now it was my turn to arch my eyebrows. "Are you seriously suggesting we start sexting one another? To even exchange photos of our bodies?"

Some dark part of me actually hoped he was making that pitch. Not that I'd ever do that—but just the idea of doing that was undeniably exciting.

Holmes shrugged indifferently. "It's something to seriously consider at the least, I think. You, at least, *ala* Breeana, should probably be sending me such photos."

"We'll think more on that," I said neutrally. "In the meantime, who is John Clay beyond being a gifted hacker? How is he tied to all of this stuff with the teachers and students and their tawdry little affairs? Are you saying he'd directing these hook-ups, or even making them happen in some way? If so, how? And to what end?"

Now Holmes leaned in closer, crossing his arms on the table. Softly, so only I could hear, he said, "No, I don't say he's directing things. He's a tool in his own right. His master, the grand architect of these sordid trifles with the sleazy educators and their underage lovers, is someone far above even Mr. Clay's not-inconsiderable and formidable intellectual talents. Clay answers to a much higher, still more devious master. Of that much I am certain."

Our waiter came to clear our decimated plate of calamari.

When he'd left, Holmes stared intently at me. "Have you," he said quietly, yet rather fiercely, "ever heard of a Professor Moriarty?"

10

Looking back on it now, it's far more ominous—*far more of a moment*—than it seemed that rainy night in that rather shabby seafood restaurant favored by Holmes just off the plaza.

I think I remember blinking—looking back rather densely I'm sure Holmes thought—then saying blankly, "Moriarty?"

"*Professor* Moriarty," Holmes said softly. "Yes."

"No," I said dully. "I don't believe so. I'm pretty certain not. Is he someone in, you know, the field of chemistry?"

Holmes shook his head, frowning. "Mathematics is more his forte. Possibly astronomy, too." He sat back, spreading his arms out on the back of the black Naugehyde booth, once again shaking his head wonderingly.

"And so there it is," he said with a hint of exasperation. "There's the confirmation of his genius and his remarkable subtlety," Holmes said. His eyes grew intense and fixed on me. "The professor is the dark architect of this sordid series of tawdry sexual liaisons that have drawn you and I together, and yet his name and his very existence are unknown to your police overlords, just as they remain unknown to nearly everyone in this world but me."

An old tune was playing on the sound system: Queen and David Bowie dueting on *Under Pressure*.

I shrugged off a vague chill. Holmes' expression was utterly ineffable.

"How to put this in context for you?" He bit his lip and said somberly, "Moriarty is the Steve Jobs or the Bill Gates of crime I suppose."

"But I've never heard of him," I said, quite reasonably, or so I thought at the time.

"And that's the terrible wonder of it all," Holmes lamented, raising his arms, then dropping them again in dejection across the back of his booth. "Watson, I know you hardly know me, but you must surely grasp even by now that I'm a man firmly rooted in reality. I'm not given to hypothetical indulgences or flights of fancy. I tell you without exaggeration that this man—this professor—is the source of myriad far-reaching and infinitely malignant criminal schemes of often incomprehensible scale."

My hand was drifting toward my phone. Of course, I meant to Google the name "Moriarty."

Holmes practically swatted my hand in its reach for my smart phone. "No!" It came as a vehement hiss from my companion. "Remember Clay! If he's already hacked into your mobile and is mirroring your actions on his own devices he can't know that I even know of Moriarty's existence. That's the one critical advantage I currently enjoy over the Professor."

Holmes eyes urgently searched mine. "I tell you, Watson, without a trace of exaggeration, the professor is the closest thing to evil incarnate I've encountered in my investigative career—one which encompasses sociopaths and psychopaths of the first order. This man's schemes here in this city and back in Portsmouth are vast and nearly unfathomable."

I narrowed my eyes. "But not unfathomable to you," I said. Despite myself, a hint of accusation entered my voice. "You've been keeping secrets from me."

"No, not unfathomable to me," Holmes said. "Eyes wide open, *seeing* where no other does, I grasped a delicate thread and I traced it through countless twists and blinds back to the Professor." A frosty smile. "As to keeping secrets, I'm telling you now. You're the only person on earth I've confided this to, or ever would confide to at this point. You see, I do trust you and deeply value your partnership in this investigation, Jona."

I simply didn't know what to say to any of it. In just a few moments, Holmes had punted our sleazy little high school sex case into the stratosphere. Now the culprit behind it all was being painted by Holmes as some mysterious mastermind.

My loss for words hardly seemed to matter, for Holmes raced on:

"This isn't a series of student-teacher affairs, Watson. It's so far more than that."

Rubbing my arms with my hands I said, "What exactly is it, then?"

Holmes gave me a chilling smile. "We find ourselves, we two, in the midst of a monstrous and devastating criminal conspiracy. A scheme whose full scope and final ends I can't say with confidence I yet firmly and fully grasp."

I said softly, "Holmes, I find that admission . . . terrifying."

He just knitted his bushy brows and said distractedly, "Really? Because I find it quite exhilarating. How seldom does one find oneself surprised or even truly threatened in this shabby, dreary world, after all?"

"And that truly excites you?"

"It would excite anyone, wouldn't it? What other feeling should it inspire?"

"Fear maybe? Terror? The need to hide?"

Holmes shrugged. "Not in me."

I nodded and sipped my wine, wishing it was red and far more robust. "So tell me more about this Professor," I said, hearing the wine starting to work its way into my voice, slowing my tongue.

A wicked smile. Holmes said, "Yes, more about the Professor is indeed in order."

THE RED-HANDED
LEAGUE

*The emotional qualities
are antagonistic
to clear reasoning.*
—Sir Arthur Conan Doyle

11

Professor Moriarty," I repeated aloud again. "Where exactly does he teach?"

Holmes shook his head. "Perpetual teaching isn't a prerequisite for retaining the rather ambiguous title of *professor*, of course. That said, at some point, really not so terribly long ago at all, he was mathematics professor at one of your ivy league universities. The Professor was a hair's breadth from attaining tenure."

On a hunch—one without any foundation other than a kind of wispy intuition, and so something Holmes would abhor—I said, "You cost him that position, didn't you? You screwed up his shot at that tenure?"

Holmes searched my face. "A guess, Watson?"

"Call it intuition," I baldly admitted.

"Smacks of sexism of course, but then again I have seen it proven out too many times not to allow that the impression of a woman may now and again be more valuable than the conclusion of even the most potent of analytical reasoners," Holmes said.

Smiling, leaning in on crossed arms and so mirroring his posture, I said, "What did you do to this man, Mr. Holmes?"

He couldn't keep a trace of pride from his voice. Holmes said, "It was more of a Pyrrhic victory in the end. I derailed one of the professor's early schemes. I damaged his reputation and cost him his post at the university, yes. Fortunately, I don't think I left fingerprints that time, so I remain, for the moment, a mystery to him. But he evaded the bigger, more enduring net, back then. Escaped arrest, let alone prosecution."

"But you did hurt him," I said. "You drew blood."

"Anonymously," Holmes said. "Or so I hope. My anonymity is key to fighting him even now, as I earlier told you. Even if I don't yet grasp his scheme in all its totality, I know enough to confidently say the Professor's previous crimes pale in comparison to this plot's scope."

Now he had me firmly hooked.

"What exactly is this man's bigger, newer scheme? At least tell me what you're confident enough to share, Holmes, won't you?"

He said, "Well, so far as I can discern, it's like this—"

Holmes was cut off mid-sentence as two uniformed men stepped up to our table, hands on their service weapons. Behind them, Chief Tony Briggs stood with his own weapon drawn. A city police officer in a tamer uniform—a liaison or "host" law enforcement authority, so to speak, stood with the older cop who was my boss.

The chief leveled a finger at Holmes. He said, "Mr. William Sherlock Holmes, I'm placing you under arrest upon suspicion of exchanging illicit photographic materials with a minor. Lace your fingers behind your neck and slide out of the booth! Do it now!"

I realized my mouth was open. I found my voice and said firmly, "No! This is wrong. Holmes is—"

Both the chief and Holmes warned me with their eyes. I realized then others who might have a darker interest in how this was playing out might also be watching. Some might even be this mysterious Professor's spies. I stopped cold.

The cops cuffed Holmes' hands behind his back and read him his rights.

Chief Briggs said gruffly, "We'll take you with us, missy. Your folks—who I'm guessing are going to be quite pissed and rightly disappointed in you—can pick you up at headquarters after we've talked about this man and what he may have done with you or tried to get you to do with or to *him*."

I was told I would be allowed to drive my loaner car back to Portsmouth . . . with a police escort at my side.

Professor Groves was out front and he was the one assigned to ride with me. *Damn it.* I frowned, dreading the next thirty or so minutes of conversation as we made our way back to that dirty little rich town.

At least the Professor consented to let me drive his car, allowing me the option to now and again feign road distraction or safety concerns as reasons not to answer every question he might put to me during our commute.

A cruiser transporting Holmes and the chief was just ahead of us as we headed back to the too-rich village. Seething, I said to my instructor, "I sincerely hope you weren't behind this arrest in some way. Because if you were, I swear to you—"

"Not the kind of sentence you should ever finish, Jona," he said curtly, cutting me off. He seemed to think he held the higher ground.

Gripping the steering wheel of the man's sporty Ford tighter I said, "Holmes is innocent. He's completely on the right side of things, as I've said. He's a colleague of ours, how can't you see?"

"He's perhaps that," Professor Groves said. "He's perhaps many things. But it seems to me that *innocent* is hardly the proper word to describe this man. The more I know about him, the more I must regard him as a malignant narcissist. Perhaps even a sociopath. The thought of you two alone together appalls and terrifies me, Jona."

On a dime, I found my attitudes toward my mentor further turning, souring still more. "You're just wrong," I said bitterly.

The sharpness of my tone set him back—I had him blinking and momentarily at a loss for words. He finally said, "I only wish this was what you think it is, kiddo."

I think he knew he'd burned some bridge between us coming here to witness Holmes' arrest, perhaps even having set it in motion. I suspected then that was indeed so—he had actually somehow prompted Holmes' arrest. In the moment, I loathed him.

We rode in silence the rest of the way back to the city, a long and painful interval of noiselessness broken only by the text alarm on my phone.

They signaled a few incoming words from Holmes:

"Hold your tongue, for God's sake, J. Things aren't what they appear to be. SH"

They desperately tried to keep me from Holmes.

Professor Groves bit nervously at his fingernails all the while: For the first time I noticed they were indeed stained yellow and I also saw the small vertical wrinkles at his lips that hinted at years of pursing his mouth to inhale smoke. Even as he fidgeted, he tried to pull more information from me again after our awkward and mostly silent ride over together.

I dug in my heels: "You need to get me in that room with Holmes, *now*. He's my partner and he's our lifeline to finding out what's really going on here. He's way ahead of you—of *us*, I mean—I really believe that."

"You don't hear the hint of pride in your voice that I hear as you say that," the older man said. It struck me as a haughty tone. "That's another sign you've already lost your compass points," he said. "Yes, I'm afraid we put you in over your head, Jona. It's my fault really, not yours."

Something in my expression must have unsettled the professor. Certainly I was feeling naked hatred for him in the moment. I also felt betrayed—and deeply so. It all must have shown on my face.

He said quietly, holding up his hands, "We simply need to know more about this Holmes before we put you two back together. The chief and I really believe that." I wondered if the chief really felt that—or was he maybe just an unwitting tool of this lusting old man's misdirected interest in me.

"I can't tell you more," I said firmly. "Partly because I don't know all that much more, and partly because he can't tell me, either. You see, Holmes has his own client. Some client with wealth and power. And even stripped of the client's status, there's a privilege factor at work here. You know—the privacy of investigator-client privilege."

"I'm not even sure there is such a thing outside of television police procedurals," Grove said.

"Either way, Holmes is now my colleague, not a perp."

"Jona—"

"No. Don't speak to me in such a patronizing tone. This is, I think, a bigger thing than just teachers and students fooling around, there's a far greater threat looming."

"What exactly is this greater threat, Jona? You have to explain that."

I held fast: "Get me in that room with Holmes and we'll be able to do some of that together. I'll try to draw him out and get more on the record for you two about what's really in back of these sleazy sex cases."

Giving my professor a hard look in the eyes, I said, "There's far more here than just the sad fact of older men lusting after their too-young students, professor."

Holmes and I were at last reunited in the chief's office.

Professor Groves, red-faced, stood quietly, glowering in the corner, one elbow resting on a battered filing cabinet. Message received: His interest in me—and my awareness and dismissal of that interest—was now manifest.

Chief Briggs said, I thought mostly for my benefit, "First, Mr. Holmes, my apologies for this so-called arrest. I think you'll agree that bringing you here under any other circumstances might have destroyed your cover."

Holmes' gaze flickered briefly my way. He was seated behind a battered table, his hands now cuffed in front so he could drink from the not steaming cup of coffee sitting in front of his manacled hands.

Jailhouse java: It was clearly tepid judging by its color. It also smelled slightly burned. Holmes, the venti espresso fiend, must surely find the stuff nauseating, I thought. Certainly from the beverage's present level, it was also all but untouched.

I wouldn't have sunk to quaffing the stuff, so how could a caf-feine fiend of Holmes' elevations be expected to lower himself so very far?

And Holmes—he had a black eye and a fat lip. The same two cops from the restaurant who were standing behind him now sported their own facial wounds. Holmes had appar-ently given a good deal worse than he'd gotten. He said to me, "Watson, it's good to see you again."

"Holmes . . . Likewise. I see our friends here are flirting with a personal injury suit once we get you out of here."

Chief Briggs gave me an angry look. "So you two are quite well-acquainted now, I take it?"

Holmes looked meaningfully to me. He was letting me state cases, being chivalrous, in his peculiar way.

"Acquainted," I said. "Yes, we are that. You might even say allied, up to a point."

The chief snorted softly. "Terrific." He nodded in Holmes' direction. "I've granted your request, Mr. Holmes. She's here, now. Now you both owe me some answers, but let's start with you, Bill.

"I prefer Sherlock."

"Okay, *Sherlock*, who are you working for?"

"Strictly privileged information," Holmes said. "I'm a licensed investigator, after all. Shall I quote state law—cite a case history?"

"You're a foreigner who is here on a work visa," Briggs said. "Those can be revoked, often quite easily. Just one phone call to Homeland Security and I figure I can send you pack-ing, Sherlock."

Holmes held up his cuffed hands, somehow cowing the chief to abrupt silence. He said, "My work visa is hardly of a common nature. My family—my brother, specifically—could be said to be the British government in some respects, you see. You can clear my credentials through MI-6. I'm here, you could also say, and very fairly and accurately, at the good graces of your allied intelligence services and with the full support and knowledge of your Homeland Security, for whom I've also worked, from time to time."

Holmes smiled and said, "I think it no exaggeration to say a call from me to that latter agency would produce infinitely more grief and fallout for you than the reverse. The simple fact is that you're chasing after whipping leaves in the eye of a lethal hurricane. The target we seek is well above your present aim." Sherlock shot a glance at Professor Groves. "It's certainly well above *you,* with all due respect, and, as a private citizen with no official police sanction, why *are* you here, *Mr.* Groves?"

Holmes looked to the chief of police and said, "When I invoke my right to counsel, this man's presence will be a primary feature of my eventual claims lodged against you and your department, *Chief.* This man has no place here, and anyway, in certain primary respects, he's little better than those teachers at Portsmouth who so concern you. An old man with a wandering eye after his young charges."

The chief's face freshly reddened. "You could say Groves and I are allied. And there's nothing you're going to gain by insulting us," he said. "We've established you're not a suspect, and you're not even under arrest, really. This is . . . " The chief lost his way.

Holmes said, "Very well. Taking you at your word that I'm not under arrest or a suspect, let's then stop posturing. Take off these handcuffs and then I will cheerfully tell you what I can in the spirit of civilized cooperation."

The chief and Groves exchanged long and pained looks. Then they turned to me.

I shrugged and said, "I trust and respect this man, implicitly. He's owed the respect you'd demand for yourself as peers."

Holmes again raised his hands and said, "The keys?"

12

Holmes, at last un-cuffed and resolutely unflappable, had his long pale fingers gripped around a large Starbuck's travel cup of espresso—a police paid-for confection that had Chief Briggs stealing disbelieving glances at the receipt next to his cup of jailhouse brew.

Sherlock was closely contemplating the chief and my professor. Lord only knew what Holmes' caffeine stoked computer of a brain was further deducing about the two men and their private lives in these quiet, charged moments: they'd given him so long to worry those bones . . .

The chief finally broke the silence. He said, "I'm told precious little by my embed beyond the fact that you seem to believe there's something far more significant going on here than just age inappropriate sexual conduct and interactions."

Holmes rolled his gray eyes and laughed. He said, "Sex itself is nearly always about more than mere sex, even in non-criminal contexts," he said. "Haven't you found that to be nearly always so in your experiences, professional or otherwise?"

Groves said coldly, "You're *certain* there is more here this time?"

Holmes put down his coffee cup and tented his fingers under his chin. "Girls and teachers misbehaving—is that really all you see here? Is that truly the extent of it for both of you?" He looked from the professor to the police chief. "Is that as far as your collective vision extends?"

Holding my tongue, I watched these three men joust. I also found myself waiting for the name *Moriarty* to crop up. But that last was not to be.

Instead, recalling some of his Socratic classroom approach, Holmes pushed forward as if he was trying to guide some dawdling young chemistry students to a first meager epiphany.

He drank more of his killer drink, then said, more than a shade patronizingly, I thought, "Finish this sentence, gentlemen: 'Every young woman is . . . '"

After several seconds of awkward silence, it seemingly dawned on my increasingly disappointing mentor and constable boss that they were indeed being asked to answer a question, or at very least, to supply some words to finish Holmes' sentence— at very least, to venture an opinion.

Every young woman is . . .

"A student," the chief said first.

Holmes, the ersatz and eternally disappointed substitute teacher, sneeringly said, "You might find yourself surprised on that point. And, anyway, wrong! Try again."

Every young woman is . . .

"An object of desire," Professor Groves said.

That one left Holmes looking nakedly askance at *my* teacher. I was left squirming; my teacher still more so.

"'There is that, for a sorry few," Holmes said. There was that vague hint of insinuation in Sherlock's voice. "But no, that's not the right answer, either."

Now Holmes was staring at me. There was something hopeful in his look—some sense of him imploring me to properly finish his sentence for him after the two older men had failed in their attempts.

Holmes raced ahead, confirming my suspicion: "Watson, your colleague and admirer turns his hopeful eyes to you for some illumination for the benefit of our associates." Holmes voice dripped sarcasm upon those last two words.

Goddamn, I thought.

Every young woman is . . .

Damn . . .

Every young woman is . . .

Racing for an answer, I reached for the clearly obvious one, instantly hating myself for it. I said softly, "Every young woman is somebody's daughter."

Holmes leveled a long pale index finger. He said, looking directly into my eyes, "Thank you, Ms. Watson. Thank you for seeing. For perceiving *precisely*."

Holmes turned to face the cop and the college instructor. "All girls are daughters . . . of people. Simple science, yes. Tawdry sex affairs hold mild interest for me only so far as they relate to criminality, but they are hardly the stuff of life and death and certainly hold no intellectual challenge for the *pure* investigator. When I was approached by my present client—and that person will remain nameless throughout this shared experience of ours, there'll be no further debate or compromise on that point—I of course wanted to know more about him. That compulsion spurred me on to research the parents of your other high school students who've become involved with their instructors. Even my cursory research to that end was revelatory."

My mind raced, flinging myself down the path Holmes had just revealed to us.

Portsmouth: A rich village full of obscenely well-paid people.

It's most noted and largest employer was The Partington Port Authority, a military industrial complex whose primary clients were various branches of the United States military, top secret and cutting edge defense technology and spy tech contractors.

I said that all aloud, unthinkingly.

Holmes pointed at me, beaming. "You see, you fellows chose quite well indeed in your embed, gentlemen. This young woman is a prodigy." He smiled at me and said, "That's really excellent, Watson. At least twice you've surprised me. That might even be a kind of record. Every girl is somebody's daughter, but these victims of yours aren't just *anybody's* daughters. And that's by *somebody's* dark design, of course."

Somewhat amazingly—certainly stubbornly—Holmes had little to add after prodding me to lead my bosses to the revelation of what might really be driving the sexual improprieties bedeviling the Portsmouth private school.

For the moment, the chief and my professor seemed oblivious to Holmes shutting off the tap: No, they were far too busy Googling victims names and trying to replicate Holmes' claims.

For our part, Holmes and I sat sipping our Starbucks: Holmes looked infinitely bored. I just wanted this terrible and awkward confrontation to end.

The name "Moriarty" had still not been given voice.

If Holmes didn't seem impelled to put it out there, I certainly had no intention of doing so: It didn't seem mine to reveal.

The two older men continued to banter back and forth between their efforts working the phones and tapping away at a shared laptop. Holmes eventually sighed and checked his watch.

The chief suddenly remembered us then. He frowned at my partner and said, "I'm sorry, are we boring you, Mr. Holmes?"

Holmes gray gimlet eyes were hooded. "Candidly, yes, and painfully so. I told you how things are, sometime ago. Watching you and your academic friend replicate what I did many, many days ago is patently tedious for me and for my friend and colleague." He nodded in my direction. "How could you imagine it to be otherwise? It's also quite insulting to both of us."

More red faces. To his credit, Groves asked the central question, redeeming himself ever so slightly:

"So I gather you think these girls are being targeted in order to place leverage on their fathers and mothers employed at the port authority. Presumably to blackmail them with threats of revealing the girls' roles as victims and trashing their reputations in order to gain access to military intelligence or technology?"

"The scales at last fall from his eyes," Holmes said, looking to the ceiling. "What else? Yes, that is the goal, I believe."

Moriarty. The name reverberated for me, yet it still hadn't been invoked by Holmes. *He must have his reasons*, I thought. He'd said his apparent unawareness about Moriarty was an edge in fighting him. I supposed that must still explain his silence, even to the authorities.

Chief Briggs said, "So there's this party tomorrow night . . . "

Another chill: I had a strong sense the chief was pushing this about Saturday night at the behest of my instructor. That really made me squirm. Once again, it seemed to me, Groves' attempts to me keep from the party clearly weren't just a manifestation of surrogate fatherly concern, but instead of his very real jealousy, indicative of a sense of ownership. I felt freshly queasy. I glanced over and saw Holmes studying me. The look he gave me was a mixture of fascination and pity.

I looked again at my professor: Jesus Christ but how I despised him now, and for all time, I admitted to myself. All was laid waste between us. Now he was just another horny old man unleashing the dogs of lust in an impossible-to-realize bid for the affections of a much younger and wholly uninterested woman. Yes, I quite despised him.

Holmes continued to give me this searching look; something in his expression was increasingly compassionate. I'll confess here that I loved him for that: despite evidence and even self-made claims to the contrary, it was clear to me Holmes was indeed capable of great sympathy, or, at least, of real empathy.

My true partner said, "There is indeed a party Saturday night, one I fully intend to attend with Ms. Watson as my companion. For the purpose of securing and maintaining our respective covers, it's plainly obvious we must both attend. It is therefore fortuitous indeed that Jona and I find ourselves in the happy position of being able to cover for one another in the context of this party and within the walls of that school. Attending in concert, we two investigators can outwardly live down to expectations—to play act the randy instructor and the comely young cheerleader that our peers and their conspirators demand of us. Jona and I can save one another from having to, well—to really go there. Surely you must both see that."

Professor Groves wasn't having it, not even a little. In fact, he seemed almost apoplectic. He had to be pushed back in his chair by Chief Briggs as he exploded, "It's an orgy you're taking this child to!"

Holmes scowled, unflappable in the face of my professor's fury. "Absurd. And you're being insulting. She's a woman and emancipated and one studying to be a criminologist. She's no child. And anyway, risk is a facet of our trade and it's insulting you attempt to marginalize Jona by dismissing her as some waif to be protected from the job." I thought he'd leave it there, but Holmes, didn't of course:

"You both chose Jona for this undercover operation. You two dropped her into this cesspool to fix something nobody else could. So let her do the task you quite rightly chose her to complete."

"An orgy," Professor Groves said again.

Like some manner of mocking or snarky Boy Scout, Holmes raised his hand in sign of pledge and said, "I promise you both I'll be acting entirely *appropriately* tomorrow night. I expect Jona will do nothing other than the same. The only way for either of us to advance the case is to move into the inner circle of these conspirators. As it happens, the man you selected to play guardian for Jona in her secret role is by delicious happenstance a man of some real importance at the Portsmouth Port Authority. He will therefore be a person of profound interest to our puppet master. So you see, gentlemen, the stars are aligning in our favor. By attending the party together, by providing the illusion of walking the walk and talking the talk expected of us, Jona and I will have advanced the ball many, many yards by this time Sunday. Surely you will now release me to go home and prepare for tomorrow night and this event of such critical importance to us all."

13

We rolled the dice and decided to ride back into the city together to further discuss things.

Holmes asked I make certain I wasn't being tailed and then to pick him up six blocks from the police headquarters in an unlit, back alley running behind the town center's easternmost row of commercial buildings.

It was nearly one in the morning as Holmes slid into the Mustang and I made a run for the state route back to the city. A gathering drizzle was following us. I nudged the wipers on their slowest intermittent setting and said, "You never mentioned Moriarty."

He squeezed the bridge of his nose and ran his fingers back through his black hair. "Neither did you," he said. "I thank you for your judicious restraint. They aren't prepared for that revelation yet. I don't have enough ammo to put him out there as the grand architect of all this that I know him to be."

"Tell me the truth: Even if you had the evidence, would you ever truly hint of Moriarty's existence to them?"

Holmes rubbed his jaw. "It's a fair question. The answer is, I rather doubt that I would, at least as things stand now.

Moriarty is simply too far outside their realm to fathom. He's the Leviathan and they are minnows. Those two men, honorable as they may be in some humble ways, are Lilliputians by comparison. You must see it's so."

I sighed. "What you said back there, is it really true? Is Moriarty after military secrets of some kind?"

"It's really more along the lines of leveraging military intelligence and infrastructure to his own ends, I think."

I at last pulled curbside in front of Holmes' building. I was exhausted almost dizzy with my crashing blood pressure. I'd entertained visions of Holmes being kept in jail for some period of hours or even days. But he was free and my bundled nerves unraveling.

Holmes turned a bit in his seat. "You look absolutely wrung out. Not safe to drive any distance. He reached out and stroked my hair behind my ear. His fingers trailed down my throat and grasped the back of my neck, urging my face toward his. I didn't resist, of course. Pulse quickening, wetting my lips I said, softly, "For the benefit of more watching spies?"

"There are none I'm aware of right now, actually," Holmes said. I could feel his breath on my lips. "This could be rehearsal for tomorrow night. We must seem very practiced at this, after all."

Then his tongue was again in my mouth, his hands on my breasts for the first time. I responded eagerly of course, my own hand straying. After a time he pulled away and said, "As I said, you're exhausted. Come on up and stay the night, why don't you?"

Panting, hardly believing he'd offered, I said, "To further our cover, or to practice some more like this?" I burned for him; I yearned for more *practice*.

"No, just to sleep and to spare you becoming a traffic casualty," he said.

I kissed him again, the aggressor this time. It was delicious. I said, "We should continue this upstairs a while longer, shouldn't we? As you said, we have to be convincing."

"Something tells me we'll manage that," Holmes said dryly. "Anyway, I'm not leaving you the luxury of decision. I fear for your safety, tired as you are. You're coming up, no arguments. For the sake of chivalry—that tired conceit—I'll even offer you the bed and I'll take the couch."

"But . . . " my hand was still there on him. His body was responding, if his heart and mind apparently weren't. *That isn't nothing*, I told myself. He gently pushed my hand away. I saw now that he was panting lightly, too.

Angry, frustrated with longing, I never the less locked up the sporty Ford and followed Holmes up the sooty stone stairs to the spray-painted front door.

14

Saturday morning. I awakened to the smell and sounds of breakfast being prepared—Holmes had whipped up an omelet and toast. It was more than competently prepared; quite delicious, in fact.

Holmes, not surprisingly, also brewed an excellent—if crazy strong—cup of coffee.

No homework, no school: I already had my school uniform on me that was my stipulated ensemble for the night's dirty party, of course. But it was twelve hours until that event started. We had time and no commitments. I was wondering where the intervening hours might lead us; how those hours would end up being spent.

Sipping my scalding, pitch black coffee, I surveyed Holmes' present home. It was under-furnished to the point of being Spartan. Just two rather battered but comfortably inviting chairs arrayed next to what appeared to be a non-working fireplace.

Along one far wall was a scarred and stained white pine table littered with beakers and stands and racks of chemicals and bottled powders. Two bookcases between windows facing the street were burdened with volumes on chemistry, forensics and various studies in criminal psychology. On a stand by one of the tables was a MacBook and a police band radio.

The fourth wall of the apartment was lined with boxes overflowing with magazine and newspaper clippings; with file folders and scrapbooks. These were what hadn't yet found their way into Holmes little corner of The Cloud, I guessed.

In one lonely corner I spied a music stand, a stool and a violin case.

I said cheerfully, "Homey."

Holmes gave that a frosty smile it deserved over the rim of his coffee cup. "Please, Watson, it's anything but that. It's also decidedly not an intimation of how my next dwelling place will appear. This is a weigh station, that's all. For now, I subscribe to the axiom that a home is an engine in which one can best live."

He got his first cigarette of the morning going and opened his laptop, scanning the website of the daily paper and some select crime reporters' personal blogs. "Looks like it was a quiet night overall," he said in a kind of disappointed indictment of the criminal classes.

"And your arrest didn't make the papers?"

"As there were no charges filed, and no formal arrest, no, of course not," Holmes said. He considered me through the haze of his steam coming off his coffee. "Let's veer back a bit. I told you I thought I found a rather wonderful place. It's on Baker Street."

I met his gaze. "So you did."

"Portsmouth is not the future for either of us, I think you'll agree there, Watson."

"Emphatically," I said. "I'll never afford that place and wouldn't want to be there even if I could manage it. It's like hometown by Disney, or something."

"Here in the city, I'll never lack for cases, nor will you. What do you say I show you this place I've found? In a couple of months or less, you'll be graduated, out of the dorms, and so in the market for a home. I can go solo that long in terms of rent. Take a look with me?"

I really didn't think about it nearly long enough, of course. After a few passionate kisses and the hungry groping of one another's bodies, what might moving in together actually portend?

And, if it didn't foreshadow some form of at least physical relationship—friends with benefits—when I brought someone home some night or for a weekend of trysting, or if Holmes did that, though I couldn't imagine him with anyone but myself for some reason, what then?

But impulsively, I said, "Sure. Let's take a look. Why not?"

Holmes gave me a once over. "But we can hardly do it with you looking like *that*." He wrinkled his nose at my school uniform.

"No, I agree. And I really don't want to spend the day and the night dressed like this, believe me." I reached in my purse and plucked out a debit card. "I have something of an expense account and I've barely touched it. Pretty sure it can stand the hit of a pair of jeans, a couple of cheap tops and some down-market tennis shoes."

Holmes stubbed out his nearly spent cigarette, then reached for another. "There's an Old Navy and a Payless four blocks north. We'll walk it."

Seven in the morning and he was already on his second smoke of the day: Not good.

Still, there was something oddly appealing about his morning personality. He was subdued, almost mellow. His shower damp hair still showed comb tracks. He was wearing

a long gray lounging robe and had been intermittently brows-
ing over a book on binomial theories. I at last saw the byline
on the volume's spine and nearly spit out some of my coffee.
"It's by Moriarty."

"Yep."

I held out my cup for a refill and said, "The book, it's
readable?"

"Barely."

"Comprehensible?"

"Utterly, but not wholly engaging. It sold better in Europe,
I'm told, where it's had some small influence."

"Aha," I said. "I don't suppose there's an author photo?"

Holmes finished filling my cup. "Unhappily, not. His
appearance, I fear, remains a mystery, although I've heard
some second-hand descriptions. Tallish, but hunched. A high
and wide forehead. Sunken eyes. He may or may not have
some form of palsy for they say he has a strange side-to-side
head movement now and again. I've heard it compared to the
way a Cobra moves when raising its head before a strike."

"Charming." I put down my mug. "When do you want
to go shopping? I really want to stop feeling like school girl
fantasy night at the bordello, particularly as that's the life I'll
actually be living tonight, God help me."

Holmes said, "Then why don't we go shopping this
morning?"

I bought a pair of jeans, two tops and some sensible flats.
These all came cheaply enough —no reason for the overly
financially endowed Portsmouth police to get anything in a
bunch about my spending.

Walking through the park, Holmes said, "I much prefer you looking this way—like a real person."

Holmes slid his arm through mine. I leaned in closer. "Is this for show, or—"

"We're being followed, if that's the *real* point of your question."

I gripped his arm with my other hand. "You have your gun?"

"Naturally."

"So we'll confront him?"

"Of course not."

"You said I look more my age, Holmes—enough to threaten my cover?"

"Don't be silly. You can't dress in plaid all the time. You look like you're in off-school mode, that's all. She'll take it that way, I'm sure."

"She'll?"

"Yes, our shadow *du jour* is female," he said. "In fact, she checked out just ahead of us. She bought a perfectly perfunctory sweater and some sort of hat."

"The redhead with the funny eye?"

"Some sort of infection, I think. Pink eye maybe, so more's the reason to keep a distance." As if an afterthought, Holmes threw in, "and, as you'll probably have noticed yourself, she's left-handed, asthmatic, has mild astigmatism. She has a pet Angora cat and her mother is in the advanced stages of Alzeheimer's."

"You're going to have explain how you got to some of that, you know?"

"Later, perhaps."

"She's Moriarty's agent, though?"

"Much too competent for police, so I'd say yes."

Grating—his latest dig at the police. Yet I hooked my thumb in the rear pocket of his black jeans, playing the happy girlfriend. I said, "This party tonight—you said we'll behave *appropriately?*"

"Yes," he said distractedly. "Quite so. We will indeed behave appropriately."

Hm.

We stopped at Parm for lunch. I ordered spaghetti; Holmes again ate very light—just a bowl of soup and a chunk of bread along with a shared bottle of Chianti.

I ran my fingers down my thigh, stroking the soft denim. "This damned party—having to wear that plaid uniform and play the naughty school girl, it crawls my skin, you know?"

"I know," Holmes said. "Most of your peers, by all accounts, don't keep the ensemble—or a single other stitch—on for long."

I might venture onto a nude beach in the company of strangers or with a lover to provide familiar company, but to go to a party and show my body to teachers and fellow students and in such a sexually charged context? Not a chance that was going to happen.

I said, "You're not actually expecting me—"

"Hardly," he said. "Don't worry. Do nothing you're not comfortable with tonight. Believe me, this isn't my scene either, but we won't get another shot like this and so..."

And so.

After our meal, drifting through another cold rain, we wandered along Baker Street under a shared umbrella, headed to look at this apartment Holmes kept going on about. In any other context, it would have been a lovely day—good breakfast, great lunch and a mild wine buzz. Walking in the rain with an object of desire to look over a possible new shared love nest. It was potentially the start of a great romantic adventure together.

The building to which Holmes guided me was constructed of white stone with arched entryways at street level. Where the second story commenced, the building transformed into red brick and spans of black wrought iron.

An elderly, gray-haired little woman with a soft Scottish burr greeted us at the door. "This is Mrs. Martha Hudson, this wonderful place's primary manager, Watson," Holmes said.

The little woman smiled and shook my hand. "The fiancée at last, and, *Watson*, what an unusual first name, my dear," she said to me.

Smiling and squeezing her hand I said, "It's our little joke. That's my maiden name. I'm Jona."

Fiancée! I was strangely delighted Holmes had trapped himself like that.

It was imminently logical in its way—logical to a mind like Holmes', that is to say. Yes, I could see how the reasoning machine got there: A lease agreement for a not-romantically attached male and female would pose a risk-inherent proposition: the probability of flight or a breaking off the living arrangement would loom freshly, over and over at each of the living-together partners respective, succeeding romantic entanglements. A single jealous boyfriend or girlfriend in the mix could spell disaster for the alliance and thus for the landlady.

So Holmes had cannily pitched us as newlyweds waiting to happen. So be it.

But Holmes, being Holmes, hadn't thought through the logical extensions of that ruse. He hadn't let his imposing mind run down all the alleys of implications and expectations shacking up newlyweds could and inevitably would demand of the players.

Again, so be it.

I kissed "my man" playfully and chucked under his chin with a softly swung fist. Holmes looked like he wanted to smash me. Beaming at Mrs. Hudson, I said, "Bill here's gone on and on about this place. Can't wait to see it!"

Holmes managed a smile and said, "And here we are at last, darling. Lead on, Mrs. Hudson!"

Walking up the stairs behind the little Scotswoman, Holmes leaned in close and said, "I hate the name, William, and Bill even more so. If you have to use anything but Holmes, go for the middle name."

"Scott?"

"No, the longer one. Sherlock. Just as I told your friends last night."

Over her shoulder the woman said, "It's just one floor up, so no great bother. Only seventeen steps, aye? It's number 221, suite B."

It seemed a nice enough space: A largish sitting room with a *working* fireplace blending into a kitchen. Two bedrooms and bathroom with a Jacuzzi tub.

Mrs. Watson excused herself briefly to allow us a few moments to experience the space "alone, which is to say, as a couple."

Once we were *alone*, Holmes stepped away from me. With a neutral voice, I said, "Your cover story about a looming marriage will continue to demand ongoing effort on our part, you know that."

"I see it now," Holmes said, looking slightly pained. "Oh, well, spilt milk. Can't erase what the moving finger has writ in this instance. A necessary evil. As you probably deduced, an unattached man and woman—"

"Would elicit a rejection from that bustling little Scot," I said. "I quite like her already, by the way. She seems . . . formidable."

"Your intuition, again?"

"What else?"

"I could go on," Holmes said.

"Sure. But later, perhaps. I think I want to discover this woman in all her facets for myself. *If* we go through with this." I smiled and shook my head. "I haven't known you a week and we're toying with moving in together. This is crazy, Holmes."

I looked around again. "And a lot of square footage for the city. Can we really afford this?"

"Cheaper than you might think," Holmes said, "so, pooling our resources, I think yes, it's well within our grasp."

"I still don't see how that can be. This much space in this city is not going to come cheaply."

Holmes considered me for a moment, then crossed the room. He placed his boot toe against the edge of a heavy, long throw rug. "It's been on the market for a while. There's a reason . . . people get jittery about certain kinds of places. They get silly superstitious feelings about them."

"Holmes, you've lost me. What happened here?"

Holmes kicked back the rug. I stared at the stained hardwood floor. It would take a sander and a lot of effort and refinishing to take out that big stain. I said, "Is that what I think?"

"Yes. Domestic issue. Lover one had an extensive collection of edged weapons. Lover two experienced a severed femoral artery. There were other—and quite energetically headline engendering—complications. *Wounds.* You know the old realty saying, 'location, location, location'? Nearly everyone knows this location, in the worst way. So it's a buyers market." He smiled and squeezed my arm. "Lucky for us, eh?"

I certainly wasn't squeamish, or superstitious.

It was a *crazy* amount of space in the city for such a price. I said, "But I don't have a stable paycheck yet."

"You will—you're a whiz kid. I've seen your GPAs and read a few of your papers that have found their way online. You'll be snapped up by the city police or the county sheriff, no question of that." He smiled and said, "Particularly in the face of the notoriety you'll inevitably enjoy when we crack our present case."

Holmes stood by the window, looking down on Baker Street. I could imagine him there always, morning and night, standing hawkish sentinel over the darkened city, a violin under his chin and a fire going in the winter . . .

His back to me, he said, "You like it? Is this a go, Watson?"

I thought more about it, watching Holmes watching out the window. Fortunately, I liked Chinese, Italian and Indian cuisine, which were the most abundant of this neighborhood's dining opportunities.

"It's pretty wonderful," I said.

Holmes clasped his hands behind his back. "You're amenable then? I'm prepared to write a check for our deposit right now."

I hardly knew what to say. It was true—we hardly knew each other in any real sense of the word . . . just days acquainted. And yet . . . And yet.

Sharing this space with Holmes, the notion of living with him here: I found it an act of imagination that came surprisingly easy. I had no current boyfriend of course—it's own terrible story—but I was a free agent so nobody could get jealous. I had no parents in a position to judge.

"I am," I said, clear voiced and determined. "Let's do this thing."

"Excellent," Holmes called out. He let out one of his triumphant "Hahs!"

Behind us, Mrs. Hudson clapped her hands. I had no idea how long she'd been there; how much she might have heard. She just smiled and said, "Now let me just fetch those papers." She hesitated and then said carefully, "You're not thinking children here, are you?"

"Good God, no!" Holmes exploded.

A frosty smile from Mrs. Hudson. "Aye, good then. For there's a no bairns policy . . . " An apologetic smile cast my direction. She said, sadly, "Mr. Hudson, ya ken . . . he loathes children."

15

More cold rain, coming down much harder now. We were huddled close against one another under the umbrella again, drawing warmth from each other's bodies. I said, "She's still back there?"

"Of course."

"What do you think our shadow will make of our real estate excursion? It won't pose issues for our investigations?"

"Possibly just spark mild confusion," he said. "It'll probably result in the amateur's leap in logic: You know, a slightly older man trying to bind a young and pretty female to him with empty promises of a real and enduring commitment. The ploy of putting starry-eyed notions of marriage and a dream loft together in the Big City in the mind of the hot-blooded little high-schooler. How couldn't *that* Jona be enticed by such a prospect?"

Indeed: how couldn't she be?

Holmes had many enviable qualities—so many startling insights into human behavior and an uncanny grasp for seizing on human weaknesses.

But a sense of irony? I think that was quite beyond him.

Metaphor? That was equally outside his comprehension, and perhaps more accurately, quite past his simple caring.

I stopped us there for a moment, our stalker be damned. She had no umbrella so let her stand there and get further soaked as she was stranded between sheltering shop canopies. I stood on tiptoe and kissed Holmes passionately again. Holmes played along, but when I at last ended the kiss he said softly, tellingly, "I think we're sufficiently practiced, don't you, Watson?"

"It's not that," I said innocently. "We're past practicing, Holmes. It's just me, playing the role, right? What you said just now reminded me that I'm a starry-eyed high-schooler who just went apartment shopping with my sexy older teacher-lover. Certain actions are expected of me now. I could be forgiven for jumping your bones right here, on the street and in full view. I have to live down to stormy hormonal expectations. I ask myself, 'What would Breanna do?' In that context, hell, I should be pulling you into an alley right now and getting down—"

His fingers pressed to my lips. "I get the point. It's all very well-argued." He kissed me back, like he *meant* it. It was wonderful. I stroked his face. I said softly, "The next time we kiss, and it should be soon and at your initiation, you should cup my hips in your hands, pull us together hard so we're pressed tightly to one another, *down there* . . . Probably you should even insinuate a thigh between my legs. Do you know what I mean?"

"Yes," Holmes said, "I do. More solid strategy, Watson."

I smiled to myself: I thought so too.

Prepping and primping for the party: Of course I'd never been to an *orgy*—this was blue skies territory for me, and for Holmes too, I figured.

(Honestly? I wasn't quite convinced he maybe wasn't perhaps still a virgin.)

I asked him what he'd be wearing. He said it would be pretty much his usual rig—black jeans, boots and a black jacket over a white shirt—"but open collar for this evening of debauchery, of course."

Of course: What else? And Holmes really only had one "look" as I'd been learning. I'd stolen a glance in his closet—a row of white shirts, black jeans, three identical longish-cut black jackets, four identical sets of black shoes and two long black overcoats.

Of course for my part, I was relegated to my perv-stoking plaid school jumper. It might have been marginally better if these twisted older men had insisted we go "cheerleader" tonight. But not really that much better of course.

Yes, tonight Holmes and I were going to see sex crimes committed—adults consorting with legally-underage girl, whatever those girls' bust sizes, level of experience in bed or their own desires.

An orgy . . .

That reminded me. I opened the container and took the day's stipulated pill from its slot, washed it down with the dregs of a can of Canada Dry sparkling water. Only five left. I hadn't yet called for a refill. It was Brad who'd got me started on them as our relationship went to "the next level", as he'd put it.

That *next level* had imploded a week before meeting Holmes.

After so many months with Brad, and then still seeing no end in sight, birth control pills seemed to make sense. Now they were almost a habit. And, maybe if only for tonight with *Sherlock*, a crazy, fantasy-filled just-in-case.

Brad: I became angry at just the thought of the name. The bastard. After his betrayal, I'd endeavored to burn out his memory with a hedonistic sortie through sultry Miami, but that only made it all worse.

Then along came Holmes. A rebound romance? If so, what a remarkable and sideways potential rebound he posed.

I closed the case with my birth control pills and brushed my teeth. I checked my look in the mirror: I now hated the tattoo at my wrist. Holmes led me to that epiphany, too. I'd have to save up money to have it erased. But even that would leave a kind of scar, of course.

But then what in this world didn't result in those in one way or another, pretty much all over, and nearly all of the time?

I turned down off my get-ready music: A moody mix of songs, presently Lynda Kay's *Dream My Darling*.

As we were leaving, I moved to take my iPhone off its charger.

Holmes said, "Don't bother with that, Jona. Best to actually leave it."

I said, "But I might be able to take some surreptitious photos . . . for evidence."

"That exactly why all mobile phones are confiscated at the door. I was cautioned on that. They also have a signal suppressor in case one somehow gets through screening. It's a smart phone and camera-free zone for obvious reasons."

Damnable, irrefutable logic, as always.

I said, "I could leave it in the car."

"I suspect those get searched for these very things and more while guests are distracted living it up," Holmes said. "No, I think we can agree that we don't want to give Mr. Clay ready access to phones, laptops . . . to anything. For that reason,

I similarly suggest we strip the glove compartment of your loaner of most of its contents. I doubt Groves or Chief Briggs had the forethought to remove titles, pink slips . . . maybe not even spare or back up packages of Merits." The ghost of a smile on Holmes' lips. "His brand, that is to say." The corners of his mouth turned down. "Appalling choice. Rubbish."

16

S oft and steady windshield wiper slap that almost calmed; the soothing sound of tires on wet pavement, even if moving at speed. I was again allowed to control the tunes, so I was delving deeper into my moody mix, the sultry trill of Julee Cruise's old *Questions in a World of Blue*:

When did the day/with all its light/turn into night?

The windows were cracked not just to let in the scent of the autumn rain but to draw out the smell of Holmes' cigarettes. His *unfiltered* cigarettes, I'd noted for the first time after his cutting remark about Groves' cigarette brand preferences.

Holmes was too right: I needed to sharpen my sense of observation and I'd begun to do that, to observe and draw more conclusions.

To wit:

Holmes was an extremist in all things: smoking, coffee drinking and his career—he was the consummate workaholic.

If we actually had sex together tonight, I let myself wonder, would it be the same? That is to say, would it be extreme in some fashion? Holmes did nothing in half-measures, after all. Why would it be different when it came to bed?

Sherlock's steady, deep voice, posing questions from the darkness at my side: "You seem suddenly sullen, Watson, somber."

"I was thinking about a lot of things. My instructor, for one."

"Groves?" Holmes shook his head. "I'm sorry. That taints everything of course. And it's a terrible reminder of the very case in which he's complicit in tangling you up."

"There is all that." Which was my way of saying, there were other things on my mind. If he caught it, he didn't rise to the bait. Holmes sighed and said, "It's terrible to lose respect for a trusted authority figure, I expect."

"Ever happen to you Holmes?"

His left fist, already closed, the only one clearly visible to me in the low light, clinched harder. His knuckles went whiter. "No, but I can well imagine."

"You've not been there yourself?"

"Never. I don't believe in heroes."

"I wouldn't go that far," I said.

"And I can't grasp why that would be," he said.

"You can't grasp it because you're negative by nature. A hardened cynic."

Holmes softly snorted. "History, particularly criminal history, is on the side of the cynics, I should think you have to agree. And do you actively and truly regard yourself as an optimist, particularly after these wretched past few months you've endured?"

I flicked the speed of the wiper's up a notch as the rain began falling harder. "What do you mean by that?"

"There's more troubling you," Holmes said. "Tell me, are you getting over Mr. Brad Hawkins, even a little, yet?"

I shot him a look; I couldn't keep the flare of anger from my eyes or the indictment from my voice, which now descended into a kind of husky snarl: "How do you know that name?"

Holmes knew he was suddenly on very thin ice with me—it was there in his stricken gray eyes. He stared out the passenger window and said in the direction of the falling rain, "When I met you, when you became known to me, I researched you, as I would anyone. I scoured your Twitter and Facebook accounts, your Instagram and publicly available Tumblr accounts and all the rest. They're a social media library—no, a romance's archæological repository, if you will—one of trysts and week-end trips together. Photos of entrees split and movies seen . . . All the detritus of a fleeting love affair in bloom, then slipping into comfortable stasis, then at last spinning down into decay. This man betrayed you. Worse, he *hurt* you. That makes him a cretin and a fool."

"Why precisely is he a fool, Holmes?"

He didn't answer, maybe pretending not to hear me. He just kept staring off into the rain. He said quietly, quite earnestly, "You have only to ask of course, and I'll hurt him back . . . all of it quite legal and nonviolent, but administered in a manner consistent with my nature and talents. I promise you I'll do that if you'd like. This man should be taught a les-son so he doesn't ever do the same to another."

We rode the rest of the way in mounting silence.

The party house had once been a tony old country club, recently restored to something like past glory but now a pri-vate party venue located amidst rolling hills and wooded acreage halfway between the city and Portsmouth—a kind of policing no-man's land owing to certain current budget challenges facing the sheriff's office.

"So it's same as completely private in its current incarnation," I said.

"Very much so, about the same as a private residence would be," Holmes said. "For all the squalor of the city, it's remote and isolated places like this one—far from anywhere, anything and anyone—that most fill me with dread. It's place like this where the most evil can act with a kind of arrogant impunity. In the bustle of the city, there's always a potential witness, an eavesdropper or a possible Good Samaritan. Out here in solitude, it's all lawlessness and the hushed maw of the bloody void."

Holmes grew rueful: "People think cities are wicked and dangerous places, but I'd place them well below country houses and lonely farm holdings for real menace. It's the remote places where people can live and act out with impunity that I regard as harrowing. Give me Times Square on any given night over a remote country house, three miles from any neighbor and far further from a police station."

Holmes edgily eyed the stony edifice of the three-story mansion as we rolled toward the parking space. I forewent valet parking and palmed into an empty space.

"Who owns this place now?" I wondered aloud. "Perhaps Moriarty?"

"Perhaps. Almost certainly it's so. It's buried under a thicket of DBAs—that's a tax designation for "Doing Business As" shell companies. I'm still trying to run down the definitive owner. In the end, that fact isn't paramount to the larger investigation and so not a priority for a one-man band as I've been to this point."

I turned off the engine. My palms were wet; my stomach all butterflies. "This is crazy, you know that?" My voice was thin and tight to my own ears.

Holmes, now seemingly very attuned to me and my moods rested a big, firm hand on my shoulder. "I do. And it is. But we have one another to lean on, Watson. We'll come through this just fine together. You must trust in me." His hand drifted, brushing up the side of my throat and cupping my chin. He urged me to him—a deep kiss; darting tongues. His hand drifted under my skirt; I spread my legs and pressed against him, lightly shaking but thrilling to his touch there.

I broke away, panting, lusting for so much more from him. "I do."

Holmes was very still then. He was still looking at me, but almost seeing through me, it seemed. He said in a kind of incantatory voice, "Watson, from the moment we step out of this car until we return here, we must live in the moment and improvise as appropriate. That said, my understanding is that *all* girls are regarded as imminently available to *all* members until it is made explicitly and unambiguously clear that it is otherwise. Monogamy isn't much of a factor for these people, as you might well imagine."

For the first time since accepting my assignment, I found myself wanting to stand down—to bag this "investigation" and go back to my old school and student ways . . . *If* only I could do so and yet somehow keep Holmes in my life.

Holmes took my hand and raised it to his mouth. His lips brushed its back. "We're first-timers, so it's reasonable to expect and even demand that there be some latitude granted us by the initiates. We have that on our side. To further protect ourselves, I suggest that we stay very much together and overtly coupled to the explicit exclusion of any other.

"Meaningful eye contact, public displays of affection. We need to seem as if we can't keep our hands off one another. Do you think you can manage that for two or three hours, Watson?"

Oh, I could manage. That, I could relish.

I said, "No problem there, Holmes. No trouble at all."

"Good." Holmes squeezed my knee. "Here we go then. The game is afoot, Watson!"

With shaking legs, I slid out of the Mustang and once again joined Holmes under his big old umbrella. Possibly I held too strongly to him. If he thought so, Holmes didn't remark.

We weaved our way around expanding puddles and through a sea of Humvees, Escalades and Jaguars, then up a meandering run of stone steps to the grand entrance.

Holmes must have at last felt my legs shaking and confused the reason. He offered me his jacket. I smiled and said, "No, I'm fine. Thanks."

He said softly in my ear, pretending to kiss my neck, "Once more I remind you, Watson: from the moment we walk through that door, we must do whatever we can to make sure we stay very much together. If anything threatens that constant proximity, we'll find an excuse to leave. I pledge that to you."

I stopped cold, despite myself.

He searched my eyes and then kissed me hard. I again quickly surrendered, responding passionately, already a fool for his loving attentions. The guards at the door watched us share that mother of all French kisses.

With that, Holmes declared our names to the guards. A guest list was checked on a smart phone. Photos of myself and Holmes were called up and held up alongside our cheeks.

The guards exchanged glances and simultaneous nods. We looked like ourselves. Great. I assumed my picture was the same one Holmes had on his seating chart. Were there similar staff photos of instructors floating around? Seemingly so.

We were then wanded with some device that looked like an airport's handheld metal detector. Holmes was patted down, then myself.

We were at last pronounced cleared to enter.

The doors opened. A sexy old Bryan Ferry tune blasting from within: *Limbo*.

Holding tightly to one another's hands, Holmes and I stepped across the threshold.

17

The first man who greeted us was wearing a tuxedo. He was slope-shouldered and had an under-slung chin. His dark hair was in deep recession at temples and forehead. "Mr. Holmes," the ferret-faced man said cloyingly, taking Holmes' hand, then mine. His handshake was damp and limp. "So delighted you could finally muster the spark to join us," he said to Sherlock.

The stranger then smiled wetly at me, brazenly sizing up my body—his reptilian gaze focusing mostly on my breasts and legs. "But then you had the perfect tinder to ignite the fire in this beauty," he said again to Holmes. "Very pleased to make your acquaintance, Ms. Sacker. We're all quite thrilled to have you here, too. I very much look forward to getting to know you better, Jona."

The little man licked his lips and said almost regretfully to Holmes, "It's a small town in its way and we're careful, of course. I heard there was some unpleasantness with the local police for you both . . . ?"

Holmes shrugged. "Nothing that couldn't be easily explained away. I'm tutoring Jona in math, albeit extra-curricularly, at the behest of her guardian, which is to say her paternal uncle. All very respectable and there is even a business arrangement in place. And don't worry, we also took care not to be followed here. Jona drives every car like she's stolen it. Quite the thrill-seeker this one. Nobody could possibly follow. And we wouldn't wreck this evening for anything, Mr. Clay."

So this was the man on the motorcycle, the adroit hacker. "I'm so glad to hear it," Clay said. A pale scar—almost something like the acid splash on my hand—was visible on the man's left cheek as he turned from us to lead us deeper into the club and on into a kind of great room.

Clay's arm swept before us, welcoming us to a mahogany and scarlet lounge with bars at three corners and what appeared to be a leather upholstered dance floor—or, no, on closer inspection it was a kind of central and sprawling leather or vinyl couch that could accommodate dozens in the center of the room. A communal bed, I guessed.

For now, it was empty.

I swallowed hard. Holmes squeezed my hand and said, "We both need a solid drink. What's your poison, Jona? I recommend something with a caffeine mix that you can nurse. We mustn't entirely lose our edge, after all."

"Black Russian? No, rather, rum and Coke, yes, that's what I want."

"Cuba Libras," Holmes said. "Yes, perfect. We can switch to cola, straight up, later and nobody will know the difference. Very sound strategy, Watson."

"*Sacker*," I said. "But my lover would stick with Jona, or darling . . . maybe sweetheart."

Holmes took that more smoothly than I expected. "Yes, he would, of course. And so he shall."

I scoped the place some more while Holmes and I waited in line at the bar. I spotted a few cheerleaders, still in their jumpers, though they looked a bit pawed over already.

Then I saw Breeana, very much out of her school uniform. Unselfconscious, already dewy with a light sweat and beaming, Breena, was nearly fully nude—just sheer panties and a transparent bra on. She moved through the hall, shaking hands and giving Mayfair kisses . . . tolerating squeezes of her mostly bare ass and the occasional stroke of a brushed hand across her generous breasts.

God, she might as well have shed what was left at this point.

Holmes saw and said tartly, "Brazilian. Who'd have guessed?"

"You never guess, Holmes," I said.

He gave me this look then laughed. "Jona, you're a treasure."

Even as he said it, another of the cheerleaders, Andrea Page, shrugged off her jumper's straps and unbuttoned and cast off her shirt. She reached behind and unfastened her bra's clasp.

It seemed a signal to the rest of the squad. All but me, of course: I was counting on my first-timer status buying me a pass on that kind of exhibitionism, at least for now.

"I'm told there are private rooms upstairs," Holmes said. "We'll get in some requisite face-time, make some connections and see if we can't pry loose some useful intelligence in conversation. Then we'll *get a room*, so to speak. We'll get out of line of sight and bide time until things begin to break up." He gave me a wry look and said, "For, after all, even Viagra has its limits. They can't all go for all night, surely."

The party had hardly started and it was already a disgusting, disturbing scene: Nearly all of the cheerleaders had now stripped down to just their panties or thongs. Instructors age twenty-something to upwards of fifty or even sixty were brazenly pawing and copping feels from my bare-breasted, presumed peers. Most of the men were not physically appealing, and yet they were shedding their clothes, too.

And here was the other thing that surprised:

There were also some younger guys who were obviously there to play counterpart to the female students—these were definitely high school-age dudes but unknown to me. Possibly they were students from the all-boys Catholic school across town. An older woman or two were already engaged in unselfconscious PDA with the underage guys: So this was also cougars' night out, I deduced.

Holmes watched me watching those couples. I shrugged and said tartly, "At least the Professor is an equal opportunity blackmailer."

"That's one way to put it," Holmes said dryly. He leaned in and kissed my throat, again setting me tingling. Into my ear he whispered, "Many of the adults here, they're not educators, you know."

I didn't as a matter of fact. I said, "How do you know they're not that?"

As I looked around me, I rested a hand familiarly on his hip and then kissed him passionately again, very aware of Breeana watching us.

I told myself I was behaving "appropriately," just as Holmes had coyly pledged to Professor Groves that we would do on this charged and treacherous night. I was simply playing the role assigned me, I assured myself. On a heady impulse, I shrugged off the straps of my jumper and fumbled with the buttons of my blouse. I tugged its tails from my waistband and left it fully open. My bra was black satin. My fingers were absently fumbling with the catch between my breasts: I hadn't quite decided to *twist* . . .

Holmes caught my hand in his and kissed me. He said softly but firmly, "That's quite enough, Jona . . . Don't make my job harder, please."

The look he gave me: I fancied it a mixture of a young man's desire for a pretty companion and a colleague's conscientious protection of his partner. Not for the first time, I hoped none of it was simple acting on his part.

Holmes, looking to change the subject I suspected, said, "To your earlier question—about how I know they're not teachers—you know my methods. We observe. We deduce."

Even as he said it, his fingertips brushed down my throat, then further, trailing excitingly between my breasts and tracing the definition line leading to the dimple of my navel. Holmes lightly thrust his thumb inside my belly button, tickling me and eliciting a giggle.

I was suddenly cognizant of how many were watching us in this moment of playful intimacy. I guessed the throngs were making certain they'd chosen rightly in terms of bringing us into their rarified fold—in ushering us into their outrageous, anything-goes carnal coven.

So far, I thought, we were doing a fine job of making the grade, simultaneously living up and down to tawdry expectations.

And besides—a delicious fringe benefit—playing the part expected me granted me the right to do to Holmes all of the things I desired but that would possibly otherwise remain unrealized fantasies.

Holmes said, "I count six medical professionals. Two surgeons, and four psychiatrists, specifically. Two attorneys, three judges and a bank president. At least four corporate-level human resources professionals, three retired naval officers and one former Chicago police detective—that one emphatically not working undercover, I hasten to add."

A bit frustrated because he had me all worked up, but still smiling into his eyes while really wanting very much just to kiss him again, I said, "Is that all?"

Brandi Carlile's *Thrown It All Away* playing (some unknown DJ seemed to share much of my musical tastes), Holmes said, "It's hardly been ten minutes. The place is crowded. Check back with me in another ten." A little tilt of the head; he said rather apologetically, "Forgive me for this: I forgot to mention the chairs of the county Republican and Democrat parties are also here, leading us to the further deduction that Moriarty is no political partisan, either."

Holmes sighed and cupped my chin in his hand. "And now I suppose you'll be wanting an explication of the afore-mentioned deductions about these people and their respective trades—all that informs this first volley of conclusions?"

"God no," I said, "at least not now. As you said, I know your methods." I added, "Breeana's watching again, and so . . . " Another passionate kiss, this time at my initiation. Holmes cupped his hands around my hips, pulling our lower bodies closely together . . . his leg insinuating itself between mine. I let that leg of his carry some of my weight, moving slowly deliciously against his thigh. Was it my imagination, or did his thigh rise to press harder against me as he searched my eyes?

There came a point when Holmes fleetingly risked leaving me alone for a moment to order us our first non-alcoholic drinks.

Seeing me alone, Breeana zeroed in on me like a buxom and now fully bare heat-seeking missile.

"When are you really going to join the party, Sacker? You know, loose the duds?" She gestured at her own bare, smooth body, glistening with a thin sheen of perspiration.

I looked down at my unbuttoned blouse. It really was getting rather humid and my breasts glistened with a sheen of sweat to match hers. I wondered then if somebody wasn't playing with the thermostat to further encourage disrobing.

"I'm getting there," I said firmly, surprised to hear a bit of slur in my voice. I know my limits—I hadn't drunk *that* much, and it wasn't done on an empty stomach. Soldiering on, I said, "This hasn't been my every Saturday night for who knows how long, after all. Not like it has been for you, I suppose."

It wasn't *quite* a dig. I then decided to try and make a kind of winning joke of it. "Anyway, the idea of Mr. Merz—" that was our mutual math-calculus instructor and a man with the worst halitosis and dandruff—"seeing me like you are now? I just can't get there yet, Bree. I'm sorry, but I can't. These ugly old naked dudes? I mean . . . " I shrugged and said, "Maybe after a few more drinks . . . " I made a face.

Breeana said with what surprisingly seemed to be authentic commiseration, "It will get easier, I promise. And switch to Long Islands. They serve 'em wicked potent, here. Couple of those and you'll get over the hump. And that really needs to happen, and soon, Sacker. You see you need to do certain things and you need to do them *where they can be seen by others* in order to be fully trusted and invited back. This whole place, these wonderful sexy nights? They absolutely depend on all of us sinning alike and together, *in the open*. There's a good reason these get-togethers are secretly called 'The Red-Handed League.' You see, Sacker, if we're all breaking the silly law together, then it ensures nobody narcs, or rats out the others."

"I do see. And I'll get there, I swear, Bree. Just a few more drinks . . . "

"Great. Can't wait. Long Islands are the answer, like I said." One fist on her bare hip, leaning into me just a shade closer, she thought about it and said in an almost flirty way, "Any bi-tendencies, Sacker? The guys, *all* the guys, of course, *like* that in a girl. At least a little bit of it. You're very hot . . . we could put on a little show, just the two of us, now. I'd be happy to, well, to bring you over." Something in the way she said all that briefly put me in mind of a vampire.

Breeana deftly tapped glasses with me and said, "Anyway, I'm mostly with Mr. Thompson these nights. *Mostly.*"

Thompson was the boys tennis coach. "Not bad, you'll admit," she said.

"Oh, he's plenty hot," I said.

"Swapping and couple hook-ups are also pretty much part of the expectation here," she said. She did that with a hint of hopefulness in her voice, watching Holmes at the bar. "Maybe next Saturday, the four of us?"

I saw Holmes watching us. It was clear he felt a certain urgency to rush to my rescue. On the other hand, we were here to investigate and we could hardly do that if we stayed completely glued to one another.

The night's soundtrack was shifting now—going darkly erotic: Chrysta Bell's *This Train* throbbed in the air, a Lynchian song calculated to serve as background music for hard, slow-grinding sex.

Some impulse seized me. To my own surprise, I raised my hand, my fingers stroking Breeana's right nipple to stiffness. It was the first time I'd ever touched another woman like that. I sensed the Squad and Holmes watching. I leaned in and kissed Breena; teased her tongue with mine. The contact mostly excited me.

Breeana took advantage to twist the catch on my bra; my open shirt still mostly obscured my bared breasts. Pulling away, I said, "Yeah, maybe, but next time, ok?" I nodded Sherlock's way and said, "If I can get him on board. He's surprisingly shy in some ways."

Breeana, eyes unfocused and lips still parted—I took dark pride in having reached her—gotten her wicked vixen's blood up in at least some measure—said, "Well there's weeknights for just the two of us, until next weekend. We should spend time together like that, don't you think? Might help you loosen up faster next time. And anyway, we click—right? I know I want it."

Right. Maybe I wanted it a little, too.

"*Maybe,*" I said. "It *might* do that. I might love that."

As Holmes moved rather too quickly back toward us, Breeana drifted off. I could tell she was bothered Holmes didn't spend more time dwelling on the wonders of her fully exposed body.

For his part, Holmes didn't comment upon our observed kiss and my near toplessness. I was older than Breeana, after all: I was of legal age in a way she was two months shy of, *if* public record searches didn't lie on the point.

I accepted my drink—just cola now, he assured me—and tapped glasses with Holmes. "Think the Professor will show his face tonight?"

"Highly doubt it," Holmes said. I noted him stealing glances at my right breast in profile. "I think he's more of a watcher . . . and probably from some safe distance."

Less thirty minutes later, the leather-upholstered pit at the center was a tangle of glistening, writhing couplings. I'd never watched others have sex in person; I was surprised how it fascinated me . . . the feelings it stoked. If felt a little wrong to stand off from it.

And the numbers of simple spectators—those like Holmes and myself at the moment—were swiftly dwindling. I said urgently, unable to keep my hands off Holmes, now stroking his hip through his pants, "*Darling*, I see our options as leaving now and losing face, diving into that awful fray over there, or—"

"Or going upstairs," he finished for me.

He signaled the bartender. He said to him, "A bottle of cabernet sauvignon and two glasses. But before that, there *is* a private room available upstairs?"

The bartender, a pale and lupine man who I believed lived mostly by night, smiled meanly and said, "Pal, there's *always* a room available. Most come here, they like to be seen." He nodded and smiled wolfishly in the direction of the glistening knot of bodies. "But if you actually want *privacy*, sure there's a room." His smile turned still more lascivious as he ogled me and his hand selected a set of keys from a board next to the taps.

Holmes, unflappable, accepted the opened bottle and a couple of deep crystal-cut glasses. He motioned his head at the pile of coupling people and said, "As for *that*, maybe next time." Holmes suddenly leaned toward me with this nearly feral expression. "Tonight," he said, "I'm not sharing this beauty. Tonight I can finally have her and in a proper bed."

Holmes leaned in then, kissing me hard and actually biting my bottom lip. I bit back, harder; actually drew blood from his mouth. Licking Holmes' blood from my lip, I smiled and said for the benefit of the bartender, "That's just for start-ers, *Mr.* Holmes."

As we mounted the stairs, licking another drop of his own blood from his bottom lip, Holmes said, "We'll give it maybe an hour, then get out of here. Have to say, this has all been fairly disappointing. It's nowhere near as illuminating or reve-latory as I'd hoped. We're going to leave here with no new or worthwhile data, I fear. We haven't even had a useful interac-tion unless you got something more from that girl than a sto-len kiss. No, this has all been about them measuring us. And endeavoring to compromise us, of course."

That put me in mind of the nickname Breeana had put to this thing. I said it to Holmes and cited its dish of a source.

"The Red-Handed League," he repeated. "That does about cover it. Well, at least so far, we're okay, I think. Behaving *appropriately*, as promised, wouldn't you agree? But we need to wrap this up and fast. Next week, if we should have to come back here, far more will be expected of both of us. Exclusivity of partners won't be an option."

I was certain of that, too: Breeana had said it was so, after all. And, rather drunkenly, I'd concluded, this night I'd just about painted myself into a corner of Sapphic contact with my fellow cheerleader during the coming school week. How was I going to manage that if Breeana remembered (surely she would) and pressed for it (again, surely that would happen, wouldn't it)?

Holmes bumped shoulders with me in a comradely way as we made a curve and mounted the final flight of richly car-peted wine-red stairs. "Anyway, it's almost over tonight. We'll have some wine, watch the clock and then get out."

Watch the clock? Fuck . . . No! My God, I desperately *wanted* to ravage him once we were alone in that room. I wanted this strange and wonderful man to ravage me. I had a sexual craving of heretofore unknown proportions.

He twisted the knob to our room, then toed open the door with his boot. He stood very still at the threshold and lowered his head in a posture of dejection. Voice thick with apology and perhaps even a hint of fear, he said, "Oh, Jona, I'm *so* sorry. I truly am."

The room was dark and dominated by a big four-poster bed; the sheets were turned down in sinful invitation.

There was a private bathroom off to the right.

There were also cameras. They were subtle enough, but as he nodded at them, I spotted them all too easily. Each and every subtle camera was trained on that big, lush bed. My heart raced as this erotic epiphany seized my imagination. So here it was: We were still being tested—still under close scrutiny even in this "private" space.

There was in me this strange and heady mix of exhilaration at the prospect that now Holmes would surely *have* to make love with me . . . and this kinky subtext of knowing that the act would be observed, probably even recorded for "posterity" or more likely, the purposes of eventual blackmail.

Somehow, the sexually thrilling prospect of the former eclipsed the dark kink and potential disaster embodied by those all-seeing cameras and knowing somebody was on the other side of them, perhaps watching us right now, in real time . . .

Some unknown party—the Professor, Breeana?—who would watch every single thing that happened in this room between us.

Holmes whispered rawly in my ear, "We can leave *right now*, Jona. To hell with all this. We can simply walk away, now. We'll make some excuse."

Standing there with a wine bottle in one hand and two goblets in the other, Holmes awaited my verdict. I thought I knew the answer he wanted from me. But my feelings—my urges—were running in quite the opposite direction, all possible consequences to us be damned.

MR. MORIARTY

*He is the organizer
of half that is evil and nearly
all that is undetected
in this great city.*
—Sir Arthur Conan Doyle

18

A gaunt silhouette illuminated against a flickering wall of television monitors: twenty screens in all, fed by at least three times as many cameras.

There were cameras in ten rooms, the central pit, the men's and lady's rooms, the parking lot, four pointed at the various bars and another camera in the long lonely private hallway leading to this very room in which the one man sat. The last camera was trained on the room's door so nobody could sneak up on the figure basking in the flickering light of pulsing screens.

For now, all attention was focused on monitor number six—the feed from the room currently occupied by the new teacher at the school, the rather mysterious Mr. William Scott Sherlock Holmes, and the newish, fetching student, "Ms. Jona Sacker".

A new teacher and a new student, conveniently coupled—yes, already apparently intimate.

Apparently.

Of course his skepticism was mildly piqued. He was still questioning his decision to let them in this evening, despite the prize the girl's uncle posed as a potential asset—the final, necessary puzzle piece to the far grander scheme resting on the tawdry bedrock of this distasteful pleasure palace he found himself administering with a mixture of revulsion and undeniable fascination.

The Sacker girl's legal guardian—he was an unexpected windfall and a panacea, all-in-one.

If this silly young thing was all she appeared to be.

So far, teacher nor student had done anything sufficiently *compromising*—hence much of his nagging doubt.

Oh, there *was* that passionate kiss Jona Sacker had wetly planted on the lips of his very naked and equally just-underage niece, but that was hardly enough to do anything with: It was of no real practical use at all. No jury would get too worked up about two attractive young women mere months apart getting consensually friendly together *like that.*

No, far greater leverage was required on these two newcomers.

Tenting long fingers under a dimpled dagger of a chin, the man leaned in, watching that particular monitor and the two figures still hovering at the threshold of the room, still looking at that big inviting bed and whispering together.

The man fiddled with knobs, but couldn't make out any of their words. The couple had fallen eerily silent. The result was this tableaux that taunted him like a high-definition silent film: A young man, a younger woman—still a girl by legal statute—a bottle of wine and a bed.

The girl ran the back of her bare and bronzed arm across her damp forehead. Her torso, the exposed upper portions of her full, proud breasts, were dewy with an enticing sheen of perspiration that glowed amber in the low light.

As the night got on, the man watching all those screens usually ordered the air conditioning steadily backed down throughout the facility: heat, sweat and the scent of bodies stirred to passion seemed to further stoke the rabble's baser instincts. The sultry closeness of bodies packed tightly together, perspiring so freely, further teased the pheromones. *Everything*—even debauchery of this sort—had to bow before simple science and not-to-be-denied chemical imperatives, after all.

There was also the fact that all of the party foods and the drinks were secretly chemically enhanced: a cornucopia of carnal aides including Spanish Fly, Ecstasy . . . even Viagra where its need was suspected.

And, if it seemed efficacious toward a desired end, perhaps even the odd dash of Rohypnol.

The man had almost ordered that last served up to Jona Slacker while she was still downstairs, where the room could have had its way with her unconscious, fully yielding and pretty young body.

That had been Breeana's idea, but one he ultimately resisted on this first night and mostly for the very reason of the proposal's source: Breeana too often let emotion and jealousy cloud her logic. But she was young and still learning, of course. Now Holmes and Sacker were alone together with a bottle of wine laced with still more Ecstasy. All that would rest on a foundation of more of the same that had been secretly served them in their mixed drinks earlier in the evening.

The man watched Holmes pour the wine; watched the two figures sip.

More intangible whispers. Something very fiercely being argued between them—fiercely but frustratingly unintelligible; the girl shaking her head yes, the man seemingly resisting, shallowly shaking his head side to side.

This went on for another glass, the girl clearly pressing her case. At last the man, this Holmes, gave a shallow shrug.

Then languidly, the girl shrugged off her already-open blouse, at last fully exposing her upper torso.

The man leaned in closer, blue-gray eyes narrowing. His study of the unfolding scene of budding intimacy was, ultimately, coldly detached.

Jona Sacker tugged down on her jumper rather less deftly than she might have just a few minutes earlier—she was obviously compromised by all the drugs and alcohol now.

She stepped out of her school uniform and then skimmed off her black satin panties.

Taking the man's equally sluggish hand, Jona placed it there on her splendidly ripe bare breast. Holmes seemed to marvel at his hand there, then at the vision of his fit young companion as she stood fully revealed to him. Then, smiling crookedly, Holmes began to undress.

Each room was equipped with cameras *other* than the ones on the walls and ceilings. There were also hidden cameras in the headboards, and secreted in the bedposts, meticulously blended into wood patterns and swirls—tiny, high-definition cameras situated to give almost point-of-view perspectives of the couplings undertaken upon each of the rooms' generous beds.

There could be *no* doubt—these two weren't faking some coupling, not at all, for the Professor had *the angle* now. More importantly, he had them captured on film and fully and utterly compromised. This was true and raw sexual congress that he was seeing and recording for future use against the pair.

Standing behind him, her breath coming rather raggedly with stoked passion, Breeana, clad only in a towel, still faintly reeked of sex despite a just-completed shower: once again, the heady scene both repulsed and beguiled the Professor.

Watching over his sloped shoulders she said to her strange, darkly brilliant uncle, "There, are we happy now?" He could hear the jealousy in her tone. "They're getting it on, *and how.* That's no safe sex there, Unc. I told you these two are for real. He's no cop. And Jesus, she looks like she's receiving God."

Moriarty's niece stared very hard at Jona Sacker, her long, strong legs wrapped so tightly around Holmes' striving, sweat slicked hips.

"And she's no faker—that much is certain," Breeana said. "That much is for sure, Uncle." A beat then, "Just look at her, the little bitch is coming all over the place, and so is he, obviously. Cum city."

That was all put quite indecorously, of course, the Professor thought. Yes, quite crass, but that was Breeana, again—callow and still so much to learn about, well, everything.

Still, facts were facts.

Again, as in all things in this world, free will and decision was an illusion, a romantic's silly conceit. Science ruled supreme. Anatomy was destiny and biology always trumped choice . . . at least that was true in all the inferior others.

Not for the first time, Moriarty felt at once aloof and piercingly alone in the world.

19

Despite the cameras and the lingering unknowing of whom precisely might be at the other end of all those unblinking lenses, I never wanted to leave our wonderfully warm if heavily compromised *private* space of so-delicious passion.

I held Holmes tightly against me as his body continued to convulse inside me, making mine do the same in softly shuddering response.

We were a damp and desperately clinging tangle as I nursed him down there with hidden muscles, milking every last bit of his essence from him. The resulting wet spot was increasingly cool as it spread under my damp bottom. The room was thick with the sweet scent of our bodies' urgent, hungry mingling.

Holmes said softly, thickly in my ear, "I'm sorry again we had to do this."

"My God, I'm not sorry at all," I whispered bluntly back. "This was sublime. I loved every bit of this with you."

Holmes said nothing about what the experience we'd just shared was or wasn't for him. He just said hoarsely, "We should go soon, don't you think?"

"Just ten more minutes," I begged. "Just ten more minutes like this, of being one person. Don't move a muscle or you'll make me crazy again."

He searched my face. I could tell he was deeply conflicted in this moment of stark vulnerability and absolute nakedness in every sense.

The logician and cold magician was clearly at sea—swamped by the delicious rogue wave of our mutual passion, all of his once firmly fixed compass points blown to hell and gone, at least for this moment. I loved seeing him like this—fully human and confused . . . and I especially loved that I had done this to him. I felt very powerful and at last the teacher . . . I taken him to a new place, one beyond his imagining.

"Things have just become very complicated between us," he whispered in my ear, "haven't they?" Despite himself, his fingers raked through the thatch of hair between my legs—I was decidedly not Brazilian this season.

"Oh, yes," I whispered back, my body shuddering a last time around his. "It's all very complicated now, Mr. Holmes."

And I wouldn't have it any other way, I thought.

We showered together and made love once more in the shower—there were more cameras there to perform for, but after what they'd already captured, what was a little more?

So I let myself think Holmes wasn't performing for the cameras this time; that he craved me for, well, *me.*

And anyway, I was hopelessly beguiled by this man, my body and heart fully engaged by him. I'd never given myself over to a man with such abandon as I had with

Holmes—whispering dirty things in his ear and offering him carte blanche to use my body any way he saw fit. *Whatever you want from me,* I'd vowed, *I'm completely game. If you want it, I want it.*

We at last reluctantly dressed, said our groggy goodbyes to some others along the way and made our way uncertainly to the car.

Once we were safely inside, Holmes said, "Now, either way, *he* has something on us, of course. Or he thinks he does. We'll see now how he tries to use it. This next part should be fascinating."

"Think that will take long?" My tone was still mostly dreamy and sleepy. I yearned to be stretched out naked in bed with Holmes in a truly private space now, savoring the afterglow of our coupling. Instead we faced a tedious commute.

"Not so very long at all, I expect," Holmes said. He was getting a cigarette going with an uncertain hand. My own hand, strangely sluggish, drifted to the driver's door console and flicked the power window switch, cracking the window on his side.

Holmes continued, "Question is, if he goes at you first—and I think he will—he'll have to give some sense to your "uncle" of what exactly his leverage against you is." Holmes hesitated, then said, "When that disclosure inevitably gets back to Chief Briggs and to your Mr. Groves . . . ?"

Why did Holmes have to threaten our still yummy buzz with the revelation of that terrible specter?

I didn't want to think about any of that now—I simply couldn't do that.

No, all I could think about was the wonderful way my body felt and the fact I still wanted more of the same with Holmes. I'd never felt so . . . *wanton.* Fully sated in a way I'd never been before, I was still somehow restlessly and faintly hungry for more of the same with Holmes. I thought about pulling over on the side of the road somewhere and urging Holmes into the back seat.

But seeing Holmes was still turning it all over in his mind. I instead said, "Whatever the consequences, it was wonderful being this way with you. You were beyond wonderful. What you made me feel tonight—the places you took me too with your body and hands? There still aren't words, Holmes." I hesitated and said, "But you took a bit of a bigger risk, you know. I mean, coming inside me like that, without asking first and without my agreement or permission . . . . Weren't you afraid of making me pregnant? "

Holmes' startled expression brought me up short. He said with a rare hint of panic, "Are you saying I was *wrong* in my deduction about you and birth control?"

My deduction?

Birth control?

Without waiting for a request that he explain himself, Holmes—more in the style of familiar, imperious Sherlock—said with just a dash of defensiveness, "I told you I studied your social media sites, Jona. You being a swimmer and posting shots from events, I drew the obvious conclusion about your being on the pill."

Half-disbelieving we were talking about this after *that*, I gripped the steering wheel harder and said, "Help me out here, please? You've utterly lost me."

Sensing we were in a potentially precarious place, Holmes placed a calming hand high up on my bare thigh, his fingertips just under the hem of my jumper. That was comfortingly familiar of him, at least, something Holmes surely wouldn't have thought of or presumed of doing just a few hours ago. *He wants me too, now*, I told myself with a kind of giddy triumph. *We've turned a corner.*

"It's just that your breasts are fuller in recent pictures, but they're also clearly not artificially enhanced—certainly not surgically manipulated," he said. "I know that for certain after seeing and, more, caressing them. And your complexion is notably clearer in recent months. I therefore concluded you're 'on the pill' to use the parlance. You simply show all the signs and we had already established that you were in a committed relationship until relatively recently."

Once again, it was *so* cold, so scientific. Yet so devastatingly accurate.

But then I supposed that Holmes might be expected to approach even sex in that way—as something to be coldly analyzed and then used in whatever way necessary to achieve some desired result.

But I also felt some flailing need to best Holmes now—to hurt him just a bit in that moment. I said rather too firmly, "Tonight was your first time, wasn't it? This was your first time making love, wasn't it?" I glanced at him and said, "*I'm* your first, aren't I?"

For so many reasons, I hoped I was right—I was unfeelingly and fully focused on that confirmation in the moment. I desperately wanted to be his first and *only*, *ever*.

He shot me a look back. Holmes was clearly, nakedly stricken by my apparent observation and deduction. Yes, my conclusion clearly struck him as an indictment; even an affront. I instantly felt awful for having done so.

Holmes said thickly, "You could *tell*? You *knew*? Did I really do so terribly badly?"

I found myself reaching across to take his hand. I squeezed it hard. "Oh, Lord no! You didn't fail at all, darling. My God,

I've *never* felt the things you made me feel. I nearly passed out the first time you made me come." I hesitated, then confessed, quite honestly, "That was the best sex of my life." A little wicked smile. "At least so far."

"Thank God," he said too quickly, quite defensively. But I could tell he believed me. "Because I did my due diligence, I promise you that," he said. "I researched, copiously. Oh God, the research: I watched so much so-called 'romantic couple's porn' I thought my eyes would bleed. I—"

I immediately tuned him out.

Yes, it would have been exactly like that for Holmes, just as I'd already begun to inchoately realize before he rather unpalatably confirmed it for me.

Even our first lovemaking had been a kind of science project or intellectual exercise for my strange suitor—a sort of an experiment: that's how Holmes had at least approached our intimacy this evening. He'd undeniably gone into the experience that way—as a scientific exploration with the two of as guinea pigs.

But had it somehow changed for him in the *doing* and the *feeling?* Had it become something more in the actual sharing? I could only pray that was so.

Sighing, I said, "I *guessed* it was your first time, that's all. Your priorities are . . . they're *so* different than those of other men tend to be."

I took solace from that memory of his expression as he climaxed and the certainty I'd felt in that moment that, yes, we'd fully connected, and *deeply* so, however briefly or fleeting it might prove to be for him later in the shadow of that shared ecstasy.

Holmes said softly, "This with us, it's very real for you, isn't it, Jona? Your feelings are twisted up in this new physical side of our relationship now, aren't they?"

How did he possibly think it could be otherwise?

Probably because it *was* otherwise for him, I thought dejectedly. He only had himself to use as a yardstick for the rest of the human race, and he was by no means a reliable unit of measure against anyone else I'd encountered in my still fairly young life. No, Mr. Holmes was a very singular entity.

I said carefully, "After all that, baring our bodies for one another, joining them and being one person with all those sensations between us, after looking into one another's eyes in that moment of intimacy and complete vulnerability as we came together, is it *really* so different for you, Holmes?"

He stroked my cheek, his hand again trailing down my throat. Looking straight ahead, perhaps somewhere far down the road, so to speak, he said, "You simply must comprehend how this is so far outside my experience, Jona.

"I simply have no reference points at all for any of this," he said. "As you correctly surmised or intuited, I have no remote precedent for what we've shared tonight. I'm still processing." He shook his head. "You'd expect that last word from me in this context. The human computer utterly undone by a carnal hour or two. Isn't that how you see it? Don't lie—not just because I'd know, but because there are no secrets between us, no barriers anymore. As you said back there, while we were still, well, joined: We've been one person, so much as that thing is remotely possible."

Thank God. Ignoring his central question, I instead posed one of my own: "Would you change anything tonight now if you could?"

He wet his lips. "No. I don't think so."

"Do you regret anything about this night and what we've shared?"

"Only the inevitable embarrassment you'll experience when Moriarty plays his card and your boss and mentor learn there's a sex tape of us out there in the world. When they know that you *knowingly* had sex on-camera to try and build a case. There's no real defense or justification that will satisfy your bosses for this development. I'm sorry, but I think you've trapped yourself into following my career path—going private, I mean."

Practical implications and consequences were simply too much for me in my present emotionally and sexually aroused state.

I took his hand with my right, slowing down a bit so I could drive more safely with one hand, and said, "Chasing criminals, solving crimes . . . all your nicotine and your crazy amounts of caffeine: You're clearly an addictive personality who chases stimulation in *all* its forms. I wonder how sex could be any different for you now that you've discovered its potency and potential for distraction in your downtime?"

"Oh, make no mistake, I *do* want it again," he said thickly. "I'm very much the addict to stimulation you declare me to be. But what does all this make us in the larger sense, Jona? My physical desire for you is fierce, even now. But the emotions I conclude you'd surely require of me as well in the longer-term are likely elusive, at best. I fear that I'm quite probably simply not wired in that way, as you must see."

That was *quite probably* true I confessed to myself.

I would, of course, continue to hope for far more.

20

Our lovemaking in Holmes' bed was just as piercing as before, but some part of me couldn't help thinking of him watching romantic porn, poring over sex manuals and trolling sleazy websites for pointers on effective intimacy and pushing bedmates to ecstasy.

This time, it was different in another way, too: Not quite so raw and all-consuming in a hungry, almost primal sense: this time, or so it seemed to me at least, there was real sentiment involved, and, blessedly, it seemed to run in both directions.

But of course, ever the exceptional student, Holmes again expertly played my body like—well, like I had to imagine he'd play his violin.

Lolling, spent and damp in his arms, I pointed at his violin and said, "Play something for me, won't you?"

"Now? Really?"

"Just something soft and sweet and very slow, please."

"You have a particular piece in mind?"

"Something by Bach . . . one of the violin solos?"

And so Holmes played for me for the first time on this night of delectable firsts. He did so softly, his eyes closed as he moved slowly and nakedly around the bedroom as he played.

It was exquisite and I told him so.

He at last put aside his violin and stood by the window, a slender bare silhouette.

I pulled back the sheets, exposing my bare body. I shivered a little from the resulting cool air across my skin. I said, "Now come back to bed, darling. Press up tight against me and hold me all night to you, please, Holmes..."

I awakened at four in the morning, the room still quite dark but my mind racing. After laying there a while, listening to Holmes breathe in his sleep, I slid from bed naked and opened my laptop.

I began running names.

Almost eerie in its symmetry to Sherlock Holmes's stingy online footprint was that of Mr. Moriarty: there was precious little on any Professor Moriarty—his first name and even its simple initial remained a seemingly deliberate secret—nothing to be found beyond an Amazon.com author's page populated with abstruse and arcane works on mathematics I doubted I could have waded through with a gun to my head.

And Breeana: of course I Googled her, too, and for the first time.

She'd been almost like the grand hostess at tonight's event. Or, to be more indelicate, albeit possibly more coarsely accurate, she'd been like the Boss Whore in a ritzy bordello.

Yes, it had seemed very much to me as if she had the run of the place. The staff seemed to defer to her in every way. The bartenders catered to her drink needs and the DJ had rushed to fill each of her song requests.

Once I got past the usual social media sites Breeana frequented or partook of, I was left with those other sites that promised you information on anyone in exchange for a credit card charge: arrest records, phone numbers and the like.

I had no interest in those, of course.

But there were one or two such sites that also listed known or suspected relatives to entice you into that usually fruitless credit card use.

A single name among them bounced for me, and how. Sharing a sliver of computer screen acreage were these two names:

Breeana Brònach Rourke and Professor Moriarty.

It seemed she was actually the Professor's niece.

Of course: How could it be otherwise? He must be the uncle math tutor she'd alluded to at the Round Table days before.

Yes, my partner's bête noire was a blood relative of *my* bête noire.

Too perfect: Too terrible in its sinister symmetry.

I rose and shook Holmes awake. "Watson? What's wrong? Don't you have any sense of the hour? I really don't think I'm quite up to another round of—"

"It's the game, Holmes," I said, cutting him off. "The game's afoot! Come now and see!"

I took his hand and tugged. He frowned and said, "Yes, of course she is. I already—" He cut himself short and said, "Dear God, you've been Googling, haven't you?"

So much for my blossoming deductive powers.

21

Sunday morning: Chinatown, shimmered in the steady, needle-spray rain.

Breeana was at her laptop, working in iMovie to edit all the footage of Holmes and Jona loving one another that had been captured from various vantage points.

Vindictively, Breeana found herself consistently choosing the most clinically explicit of the available footage—lingering penetration shots, unflinchingly and up-close captured climaxes and so on.

Breeana had this vision for her day: She would edit the film and burn a DVD to be gotten off to the bitch's uncle with an ultimatum that Uncle Moriarty had yet to shape.

As she assessed the latest snippet of explicit footage, Breeana impulsively decided that next Saturday—when Jona knew that Breeana undeniably held the upper hand—*then* she'd put Jona through a properly improper *initiation*.

Yes, she'd make Jona endure some multi-partner action. A gang-bang! Yes, *that* was surely the ticket! Let the roomful of all those horny, mostly out of shape faculty members have their way with the hot-blooded bitch.

After her spate of dirty movie-making, Breeana planned to venture out of her uncle's loft and down to Wo-Hop for lunch.

Then she'd wander the neighborhood in the rain; a nice Sunday stroll and time with herself before the return to dreary, uptight Portsmouth and the depressing private school so lousy with all of its dumb, slutty girls and their pervy older teachers.

And there was the sad fact of the other thing she dreaded, come Monday: the torture of Mr. Holmes close by but so utterly untouchable now that she knew what he was capable of giving a girl in bed.

This time her uncle leaned in over the girl's proud, straight shoulders. He closely studied the snippet of footage currently running there in the editing preview panel.

He *tsk'd-tsk'd*. "You simply must show more full frame footage capturing faces for the purposes of our blackmail, my dear. These are simply too gynecological to serve those ends. Still, quite spritely, isn't she? And how randy they are, together!"

The tone of his voice suddenly shifted, grew sad. "But I fear now this particular bit of film is time wasted on your part, my dear."

She said uncertainly, "Uncle?"

"As I said, you spent too much time dwelling on that girls private parts," the Professor said. "My examination of her young body was not only far more dispassionate, but also far more comprehensive, luv."

Frowning, Breeana asked, "How? Exactly how was it *more comprehensive?*"

"Mine was head to toe—decidedly not dwelling, as you clearly did, upon those certain sordid bits common to all of your vexed sex, my dear."

Her uncle gestured at the close-up view currently occupying the screen. "If one looks at the bigger picture, so to speak," he said, "then one notes that this girl's physique, particularly her shoulders and thighs, suggest much swimming. Those mature muscles suggest not casual dips, but rather, intense and competitive sport, sustained over time."

"She swims, too?" Breeana advanced her film to a wider shot of Jona's tanned and toned body. "Granted, it's a great back. Very nice ass, too," she said grudgingly. "Her legs are long and shapely, but not too muscular. Maybe I should consider swimming? Are you saying I need to be in better shape, uncle?"

He granted his young female kin a frosty smile. "It's good exercise, if one likes that sort of thing."

"I've Googled the bitch every way I can think of and I got back *squat*," she said. "Couldn't find any social media accounts or really *anything* for a Jona Sacker."

The old man smiled and said, "Isn't that lack of information online about her suggestive in itself, goading one to look in different ways? It's an alias, my darling one. Her real name is Jona *Ormond Watson*. She's several years older than you, though she actually looks a shade younger." He leaned in, kissed his niece's cheek. "Probably all that swimming. Kept her young and fit."

"I'll give it some thought," Breeana said defensively, taking her uncle's assertions as a not-so veiled hint.

"You should also eschew the coffin nails, my dearest blood," he said. "It absolutely eats the collagen out of one. That lamentable vice ages you faster than anything and your looks are, after all, an asset to me that are, on their own, alas, all too *fleeting*, I fear."

And *shit* but the wicked old man could be *so* very *cruel.*

But since she and her uncle had partnered these past two years, her private bank account had swelled to dizzying proportions. She'd never have to really apply herself in college, would need no career or actual straight-arrow trade in the end.

She was already well on course to retire a rich white-collar criminal, and well before the age of thirty. All thanks to good old Uncle Moriarty . . . clever (if occasionally cruel) Uncle Moriarty.

He said, "Ms. Watson is a college student majoring in criminology with a minor in forensics. She's working undercover for the Portsmouth police, I've learned. That sporty Mustang she drives is a loaner. It actually belongs to her college instructor, who I take as untowardly smitten with the minx, by the by."

"Some undercover cop," she scoffed. "She's all over social media under her own name, you're right," Breeana said wonderingly, staring at her computer screen. "Jona *Watson*. So not careful. Pros wouldn't let her have any of this stuff out there unless it was specifically for show—you know, like all the special accounts you shaped for me."

He waved a long-fingered hand as it swatting aside invisible gnats. "Not so terribly surprising: they're small-town police who, from their callow and shallow perspective, dropped a comely amateur into a high school to chase libidinous instructors and silly young girls yearning to explore their budding sexuality. In their hubris, these police probably never expected Ms. Watson to need to spend more than a week or two moving among all of you—if even that—just briefly snooping about and attracting potential suspects, then reporting back and pulling out fast."

"And her guardian," Breeana said, "he's a set-up, too?"

"By logical inference, of course he must, be," her uncle said bitterly. "And more is the pity, alas. So much for his usefulness to us—which would not have been inconsiderable, I assure you. It's a terrible loss and one I must find a way not to let stand."

Breeana sighed and said, "I see now about the film and its worthlessness." She toggled back to iMovie and pulled down the menu, staring to zero in on "delete."

"Wait my dear," her uncle said, his cold, moist hand closing over her mouse hand. "It never does to be hasty in destruction. It strikes me now that some version of that film may yet have utility for us."

Breeana turned around in her chair. "Explain that."

"Even if Jona Watson is police after a fashion, it doesn't necessarily follow that Mr. Holmes is that same sorry thing. Absent more information, for now, he remains an enigma. *For now*, I stress. So we'll use the film to try and blackmail Mr. Holmes. If he's a teacher and only a teacher, he'll be beside himself once confronted by our threat. If he's truly an official investigator of some kind, this sex tape could still be leverage of no small import, I should think."

"But she's of age," Breeana said. "Jona Watson's in her early twenties."

"A sex tape is a sex tape, my dear. Reputation matters, particularly for credentialed and sanctioned investigators. Ethics are paramount for such types. Sleeping with that girl, whether she is of age or not, means Mr. Holmes has ceded the moral high ground if he is perhaps also official in some capacity."

"Okay, so you can maybe use the film against him," she said. "Trash his reputation with it, sure, I get that. But right now, what about Jona? She's supposed to start training tomorrow with the squad. If she's a spy, I don't want her around me or the other girls. Too risky."

Moriarty took up a chair next to his niece and tented his fingers under his chin. His head was moving in that eerie, side-to-side motion that came with her uncle's darkest decisions. It always reminded her of a snake, preparing to strike.

Breeana awaited her uncle's certain-to-be terrible verdict.

"I'm contemplating a kidnapping of Ms. Watson," he said. "Perhaps a few hours in the company of Mr. Enoch Drebber would pry answers from her. Upon further reflection—sifting through the data about her I now possess—I'm revising certain deductions about this young woman. To that point, and even with unwitting chemical enhancements exerting their influence, unless she's a complete *hedonist*, Ms. Watson's uninhibited and eager willingness to be intimate with Holmes knowingly on camera is also highly suggestive. It speaks to a disdain or unconcern for consequences that is suggestive in itself in other, and in far more grave respects, I fear. Yes, I think Ms. Watson is keeping important secrets about herself and her own welfare, even from Mr. Holmes."

"What are you saying?"

"Not yet fully sure myself," Moriarty said. "I need just a bit more data to be certain."

"Don't tease about this, Uncle. Not this time. Please . . . "

Moriarty grudgingly relented. "Very well. In advance of more concrete information, it remains closer to pure speculation than discerned fact. With that caution, I confess that I am fairly certain Jona Watson is in some way ill, or, at very least, she is threatened by an underlying condition. I lean strongly toward the latter for the moment. Yes, she quite strikes me as a sensual fatalist, living life to the absolute top because she knows her end is always potentially near. It's implied in her reckless abandon last night, and in the way she pushes sports cars to the very edge that elude even my best spies ability to match. In the way she throws herself into sports past the point of injury. It seems in nearly all respects she is drawn to heady stimulation like some nail to a magnet. Her choice of a lover in this Holmes is certainly proof of that impulsive extremism. Something quietly but desperately at once threatens and drives her, I'm sure of that. Something medicine can't fix or stave off, I suspect. She lives her young, hectic life like one having been handed a death sentence of unknown but possibly close-term execution date."

That set Breeana back on her heels, and more than a bit. The old man rarely called such things wrong, but he also usually gave voice to such predictions with more hard facts at his back. But then, she had pressed him hard for this particular hypothesis.

A bit rattled, she said, "Uncle, if we do kidnap this girl— this *woman*—and if we put her in the hands of Drebber . . . ?"

A wan smile. "Yes, child, in doing so, we set in motion a predictable and bloody chain of events that will certainly and inevitably climax in Ms. Watson's execution after some degree of suffering."

He smiled sadly and comfortingly patted the back of her artificially tanned hand. "But if I'm right in my just-shared other surmises, then we can console ourselves with the fact we may actually be doing Ms. Watson a sort of favor in curtailing her protracted emotional and mental suffering she is already currently enduring. You must confess that it is surely a terrible burden to walk through all of one's life with one's demise clinging like a deadly shadow to one's heels."

Sunday morning: Holmes had gone out for Starbucks and a stack of Sunday papers. Dressed only in one of his white shirts, I lingered over coffee and the daily rags—the sections *not* containing daily police blotters and the more prominently played crime reports that were the only parts of the newspapers seemingly of remote interest to Holmes.

It had been a while since I'd actually handled a physical newspaper, having become accustomed mostly to following occasional headline links via Twitter. It was kind of a nice novelty to browse over the pages.

As we sat by the nonworking fireplace in our chairs that faced one another at angles, even as I read, I irresistibly in my mind moved us to Baker Street, with its *working* fireplace, high ceilings and rambling layout.

I could easily imagine an infinity of Sunday mornings with this strange, but exciting man I increasingly was coming to love.

For a moment, all was quite perfect.

Then, irresistibly, my stomach began to churn as I thought of the fact that tomorrow I'd almost certainly have to face tough questions from my creepily smitten professor and Chief Briggs about what happened between myself and Holmes Saturday night.

Was it better simply to tear off that terrible bandage and get myself summarily fired by admitting up front what the two of us had done and that there almost certainly existed a visual recording of that cardinal sin we'd heedlessly, perhaps even selfishly chosen to commit?

After all, we could simply have feigned an argument or something like one and, as Holmes had suggested—departed the scene, our virtue and respective covers uncompromised.

Yes, it was probably better to endure all that ignominy now than being found out later, or—the ultimate nightmare—to have it come out during some eventual court proceeding, the strategically divulged revelations almost certainly derailing the prospect of a successful prosecution of Moriarty and company.

Still, I could live in this moment and duck reality for just a bit longer, couldn't I?

Smiling at him over my coffee cup's travel lid, I said, "By the way, how's my math homework coming, Holmes?"

"Done," he said, not looking up. Then he suddenly checked his iPhone again. He'd been doing that obsessively, about once every five minutes over the course of the past hour.

"What are you expecting, Holmes?"

"Word on a location," he said. "It's concerned with your cheerleader friend who has that so interesting connection to Moriarty. Anyway, our digital footprints are more akin to a toxic spill than to an actual footprint or animal track, of course. You can hire services, employ 'cyber cleaners' to try and expunge your online life and myriad web explorations that might look unsavory to another, but it's very hard if not outright impossible to leave virtually *no* digital trace at all of yourself, not as things sadly stand these days."

I smiled and said, "Yet you have somehow done that very thing. You're virtually invisible online, Holmes. How in hell do you manage that? Beyond your eBooks on the various sites, there's no trace of you on the Web at all, or at least none I can find."

He folded the last of his sections of newspaper and tossed it across to me. I caught it on the fly.

Holmes briefly, swiftly raised himself, pressing down on the arms of his chair and crossing his legs under himself. He said staring at the empty fireplace, "I have friends—or rather, family—in high places, as I've remarked in your presence. No idle boast, that. Consequently, I get the kind of treatment usually reserved for MI-6 operatives or accorded to under-cover FBI agents. It's colloquially called 'the man without a profile treatment'. This family of mine, or rather his agency, more exactly, sees to it I remain a cipher on the Web. I'd be positively crippled in my activities otherwise, I fear. In a world in which everyone seems to be a narcissist who shares every little thing going on in their sordid and drab little lives—sharing all that drivel in real time for a non-existent audience in nearly all cases—even simple anonymity can be its own incalculable asset."

God.

I said impulsively, "I don't suppose this mysterious and powerful relative of yours could expunge or redact my online life, too?"

Holmes searched my face for a moment, weighed my words. He said judiciously, "For my *permanent* investigative colleague, I'm sure such a service could be performed. Yes, I think—assuming our association is to be a *long-term one*—that investment of effort on his part could be managed, particularly if we're to be partnered for any duration beyond this particular case. In that context, it's almost a necessity."

He seemed to already envision us as come kind of independent detectives in a formal and continuing partnership.

Given what I was envisioning having to admit to my "controllers" in a few hours, I certainly didn't rule out that prospect.

"Then by all means, please go for it," I said.

Sleet lashed the windows, but it was cozy in this warm room with Holmes.

"I hate the thought of this weekend ending," I said. "I dread those damned girls and having to be with them in practice tomorrow. To be with them naked, if only in locker rooms. I dread the notion of having to trust Breeana and her closest friends not to drop me during practice.

"You know, I can think of six, maybe seven pyramid formations in which failure to execute a catch correctly could leave me paralyzed or dead," I said. "I know a lot of people kind of sneeringly don't regard cheerleading as a sport, but it's actually far riskier than baseball or even football. There's at least as much athleticism involved as in gymnastics. Maybe even more, because it's coordinated with the efforts of others, not done solo, like parallel bars or vaults."

Holmes considered that. He said, "I could forge a note in the guise of your so-called guardian asking you be excused for medical reasons." He looked around and said, "I believe I might even have some plaster and an aluminum crutch from an old case squirreled away around here, somewhere. Scenario: you finally really snapped your ankle tendon, and so . . . "

No. I said, "Not crazy about gimping around in a cast and all that unnecessary itching." Holmes tapped his fingertips on his chair arms. "On further reflection, it occurs to me—let's hope not too belatedly—that you don't even need to be John Clay with access to your iPhone to find a wealth of online information about Ms. Jona *Watson.* I am going to see you *are* wiped from existence in that sense. Is there anything you really simply feel you must keep?"

"A Tumblr account. It's protected and so private. It's kind of my, well, it's like my diary."

"Then I hope for your sake—and maybe my own, soon enough—that it's very well protected indeed," he said. "Anything else?"

"Everything else can go. Please. Wipe it all out."

22

S unday afternoon found shadows growing longer in every sense. I kept getting flashes of Professor Grove's disgusted face. When we'd gotten home from the "orgy" I'd found a flurry of texts asking how I was and what had happened at "The Party."

I had answered back shortly about being safe, explaining further about having had to leave my phone behind and why that was. And, sadly, I revealed "The Party" produced no actionable revelations beyond my awkwardly eye-witnessing several teacher-student couplings.

I was in a position to give them names of perpetrators and victims to focus on going forward, although the concept of their being "victims" was admittedly a hard one for me to get my mind around in context: To the last one, each of the young girls and young boys had seemingly been intent and eager to give their all. They were enjoying themselves . . .

Professor Groves and Chief Briggs: If—no, *when*, for I'd all but unilaterally settled on face-to-face confession—they learned I'd slept with Holmes, and *on camera*, they'd think *me* same as a whore. They might even be right about that: I'd chased sensation and I'd let my heart rule my head. Childish. Selfish.

Destructive.

I was looking for a distraction again as this Sunday wound down. I said, "Maybe see a movie?"

Holmes looked appalled. "I don't do movies, Jona."

Another look around his rooms. "No television around either, I see."

"Lord no," he said.

"You apparently don't own a single novel." I jacked a thumb at a row of books lined along the floor against one wall. Nonfiction, to a volume.

"Fiction? Of what practical use is that to me?"

I checked *The Times* entertainment calendar again. I said, "There's a concert. Classical violin. My treat if you're up for it. Save you from playing more of the violin for me." I held up my debit card. By this time tomorrow, I expected it would likely have been confiscated, so why not stack a little more on while it still spent?

It had been a nice, if fleeting, career path that I'd been on prior to Saturday night.

Yes, I told myself, awaiting Holmes' verdict, *Jona, you're the perfect idiot. But at least you've moved on and found the best—if strangest—love of your life. You've got that at least, if you can just hold onto it. If you can just hold onto* him.

He nodded. "The concert sounds wonderful, Watson. Let's do that. Dinner after is on me."

In the gloaming, Breeana said, "Have you decided, Uncle?"

Moriarty smiled unrestrainedly. It was a terrible thing to see since it came so rarely. His head was doing its strange sideways oscillation again. "Yes," he said. "My dear, ring Mr. Drebber for me, won't you please?"

23

This is another memory I will always cherish: Holmes, his eyes shut, a beatific expression on his face and fingers moving up and down the neck of some imaginary violin as we sat together in the concert hall.

Later, huddled under our umbrella, Holmes said, "There are three running surveillance on us now. One's obviously for hire, perhaps by *your* professor."

Nodding, I said, "And the other two?"

"They are my Professor's, I should think."

"So we let them keep following us?"

"Not this time. Something is different about these minions of Moriarty's."

I frowned. "Different how?"

"Moriarty's present shadows are decidedly ex-military," he said. "The woman is clearly defrocked Mossad and the man is former RAF. With the prowess and skills for mayhem they surely possess, it's best we lose them. Why employ mercenaries when simple shadows would do? No, this positively reeks of some deeper ill intent."

"Then just losing them won't do much good, not long-term," I said. "They followed us from your place and so will just go back there to wait for us."

Holmes smiled. "We've already made the down-payment. I say we break into 221B and put up there. I'm sure if Mrs. Hudson found out she'd simply regard it as a romantic impulse on our part."

"Right, but to the larger issue of those two behind us right now?"

"We lose them, Watson, just as I said."

So how *do* you shake a tail being executed by a former Royale Air Force commando and an ex-agent of the Mossad?

I began rattling off potential strategies: Jamming a set of revolving doors was my first offering.

Holmes on that prospect: "Hard to trap two in one of those swiveling doors without trapping yourself, and anyway, they likely carrying assault batons more than capable of breaking even the tempered panes of glass in such doors, Watson."

My next thought was the subway—a last minute leap through closing doors, either on or off a train. Holmes: "Clichéd and fruitless. Trains run in straight lines to fixed destinations after all, Jona. Mr. Moriarty has an *army* of these types I expect. They'd simply pick us up again at some subsequent station."

"Then police," I said. "Briggs could call some city cops and—"

Holmes just shook his head. "City cops against highly trained commandoes gone rogue? Even *I* wouldn't put the poor police through that inevitable slaughter."

"What then?"

Holmes checked his watch. "A different matter for the moment. Have you Googled yourself, lately? Why don't you do that right now, Jona?"

I did as he asked, though it seemed a crazy time for it.

But, rather dizzyingly, nothing showed up. Absolutely *nada*. It was like I never existed, at least digitally.

"You see, that's not the only sort of thing my relative can make disappear, Watson. Birth records are an option, too. But to other concerns of the moment, we just need to keep walking a bit further." He slipped his arm through mine. "By the way, are you familiar with the term *rendition*?"

I nodded. "I am. So in what Middle Eastern or Balkan hell hole do you think these two might end up, ultimately?"

"Knowing my family member's proclivities for absolute closure as I do," Holmes said darkly, "somewhere that is much the same as nowhere."

Breeana said, "When does this kidnapping happen exactly?"

"Tomorrow, mid-afternoon," the professor said.

"Where? At school?"

"No dear, we can hardly give the police more excuse to poke around *there*. So I think we make it happen in the city. Perhaps lure Ms. Watson back to campus. After all, very bad things frequently happen to comely coeds in such places."

She wrinkled her nose and said, "Why 'mid-afternoon'? When this happens, if Holmes is maybe more than a teacher, he might come after me directly, you know. So might whoever is controlling Jona . . . I think this might make me the easiest target for the cops."

"Acceptable risks because I know you are more than capable of playing these older men as you so deftly play all older men. Failing working that angle, I also know you're capable of brassing it out, so to say, for the mere hour or two needed for me to get you a top-flight lawyer who will leave them positively shattered with litigation, my dear. You're never far from me or my paladins in any sense, you can take comfort in that. I'll let nothing happen to you at their hands, Breanna. You *know* that. At the same time, I very badly want for Mr. Holmes to feel profound panic and loss, the sooner the better. And, ideally, I need you to observe that state of his in its happening, my dear. It will give us further and priceless insight into Mr. Holmes—to what and who he truly is."

Midnight. Bare-skinned and spent, finding it a bit harder to regain my breath or to quiet my pulse in the afterglow this time for some reason, I spooned up against Sherlock on the floor of our new shared apartment.

A bit uneasy for some reason—feeling unusually vulnerable and craving some kind of tacit reassurance—I tried to keep a sleepy Holmes awake and distracting me, even if it meant pointless small talk. I inquired, "Who gets the first shower come morning?"

"Me of course," Holmes said drowsily. "I'm the one who has to take much slower public transportation back into the city, after all. Now please hush and go to sleep, Jona. If I don't get some rest now, you might be the death of me."

Those words were hardly any comfort.

I lay on my back and began to take deep, steady breaths, trying to calm my still-racing heart.

24

M r. Enoch Drebber finished sharpening his knives, then left his daughter to finish balancing the register and to close down their restaurant for the night.

Preparing gourmet delicacies and inflicting agony: these were his two, God-given skills.

He'd heard it said somewhere that if you could make your passion your vocation, then you could be truly whole as a person . . . be truly complete.

Despite a missing eye, Enoch Drebber felt *very* complete, and therefore very blessed.

He stepped out under the scant shelter of a rusting fire escape's first landing, the rain falling hard all around him as he lit a cigarette in his little dark oasis of dryness. The rain pattered hard on the corrugated steel above his head and soaked the rutted pavement of the alley. With each suck at his cigarette, the glowing ash intermittently made his rather jaundiced skin look orange and his scraped-back black hair to appear auburn.

His phone vibrated. His eyes narrowed as he saw the name in the caller I.D. panel. *Always at such odd hours.*

And, as usual, no salutation or chit-chat; not even a hello, just that strange and rather cloying voice:

"There's a job's come up." It was the usual opening, more or less.

Drebber said, "The subject?"

The familiar voice with its soft British accent said, "Female. Early twenties. She's police of some kind in training. She's quite athletic and may even have some self-defense training given her career interests, so we'll bring her to you."

Drebber grunted his affirmation. "Any sense of her tolerance for pain?"

"Well, there is at least one tattoo, a complicated one, and on the wrist, right at the pulse point. So let's say at least a better than moderate tolerance for pain can be reasonably deduced."

Yes, the accent was definitely British he reckoned for the umpteenth time toward no good or useful end . . . probably a middle-aged man—again, these were old and familiar patterns of thinking. Drebber had never met this very peculiar but steady employer and had decided several jobs ago that he likely never would.

He said to the voice, "And hoped-for outcome this round? What are my rules for engagement?"

The question was somewhat academic, as this client rarely elected for nuance or appreciable degrees of *engagement*.

"Open-ended in terms of the latter," the professor said. "But to your central point, ultimately, I expect her time with you to prove terminal. Let there be no ambiguity on that point. I can't ever have her being found, let alone talking."

Drebber smiled thinly. "Then anything goes reaching that destination?" He could barely conceal the elation he felt—it had been many frustrating months since a client had granted him lease to take his foot fully off the brakes.

"*Anything*. Please do indulge yourself this once, dear fellow. I want the girl's disappearance to provoke a response in a particular man. Having said that, the body will never be found once you're finished, so we're not going for effect in that sense. No need to leave a face or other identifiable traits as I've asked for from time to time in the past."

Drebber smiled. "Then please tell me what you want to learn from her first, before I *indulge* myself, sir."

Breeana stood with her hand on the door, preparing to head downstairs to catch her ride back to Portsmouth for another school week. She said uncertainly to her uncle, not sure she truly wanted to know, yet somehow driven to inquire, "And when Drebber's done? What will become of whatever's left of the little bitch?"

The old man rubbed the back of his neck. "Didn't I tell you? One of your recent initiates into the Red-Handed League is the owner-operator of a rather vast private landfill. Tomorrow night, your fellow student will bed down with discarded tires and similar rubbish, for all the time there is, my dear. Tell me—any prospect of getting some of Mr. Holmes' DNA that we can deposit there with her just in case she *should* somehow be found down life's sometimes uncertain road?"

She wished. But, no. Breeana said, "Wouldn't a certain DVD suffice?"

Another frosty smile. "Perhaps, but instinct tells me that would be a bit too pat—would evoke undermining suspicion even from such as the Portsmouth police. But once you finish your editing of this film—which appears to be becoming your opus given the unprecedented amount of time you've devoted to the enterprise—might it not be easier to merely have Clay upload the film to YouTube for all to see? As we've discussed many times, simply destroying a reputation can be even more devastating than destroying a life, after all. And anyway, males, particularly, tend to literally destroy themselves when all face has been lost. Suicide under such circumstances is practically a statistical guarantee, particularly among men aged twenty to fifty-five."

Math again, she thought. Science. The old bastard reduced everything, it sometimes seemed, to numbers and formulas—to infernal laws of probability.

Too often, he was also right.

A long drive back into the city: I was also back in my stupid uniform that I'd never see the same way again in the wake of that crazy, lurid Saturday night party.

And God, the Sunday laundering that must be required by the other girls to clean their uniforms up for another school week? All those jumpers must be like plaid Petri dishes.

Later in this school day, it would be gym clothes for cheerleading practice after school.

Then, there would be the showers and seeing the squad all doe-naked again—another unwelcome call back to that sleazy Saturday night and memories of them striving, bucking and rising under faculty who I couldn't quite bring myself to make eye-contact with anymore.

I dreaded it all.

As I turned the corner, I saw Holmes was standing at the door to his room as usual, vetting email, I supposed. Or maybe he was checking out dirty new Snapchat photos now that he was at last securely "in" the dirty secrets circle and so now explicitly a *player*, at least in the cheerleaders' eyes.

Speaking of girls: The other cheerleaders were gathered tight-in around Breeana's locker, giggling and sniping.

I heard Breeana say, "No, there was no faking, I'm tellin' you. I've got documentary proof. And, what a *whore*: I'm talking cream pie city, bitches, over and over! . . . Nah, there was no safe sex there. I've *seen!*"

I kept moving, blushing furiously.

Lunch—no room at the inn this time. The other cheerleaders' chairs were spread out to pointedly leave me no seat at the Round Table. It seemed for some reason I'd already been dismissed; locked out on what was supposed to be my first day of practice with the girls on my first day back to school after finally making my Saturday night debut at the sex palace.

How odd.

And Holmes was not at *his* usual table for lunch, I noticed. That was a first, too.

Yes, everything seemed more than a bit off now.

Troubled more by Holmes' absence than the cheer squad's collective snub, I ended up at the misfits' table. Even the geeky girls looked liked they knew something terribly tawdry about me.

Brilliant: It was going to be a very long day and a very long and terrible week, I sensed.

Two more periods until chemistry class with Holmes and I still hadn't gotten a glimpse of him since before first period when he was standing in his doorway.

My phone vibrated—a VIP list alarm that had a solitary VIP in its directory—that was Mr. Holmes, of course.

It was an email: "Rendezvous at Ducks Hall—I'm with Professor Groves and Chief Briggs in the former's office. There's been a major development. Make some excuse and come here at once if convenient. If not convenient, come anyway.—SH"

On the spot, I made up my mind and headed to the office. I made up some story about a stomach virus and sprung myself. Then I burned down the road for the city and campus.

At least, I consoled myself, the three key men in my life at the moment seemed to be on cordial, if not even *cooperative* terms this harrowing and unhappy Monday.

That wasn't nothing, I kidded myself.

Wind chased freshly fallen leaves across my path. I checked the rearview mirror frequently. All clear so far. I checked the dash clock: I should be in Holmes' class now.

Both of us missing from class would set tongues wagging in all kinds of directions, I thought. Not that it mattered anymore: I truly left Cattulus believing I'd never go back. More intuition, I supposed, though I had no real sense why I should think my undercover stint was closing down beyond the probable reality of my being fired when I inevitably confessed in a bit what I had done with Holmes.

Yes, the more I'd thought on it, the more I'd concluded any secret-keeping on that front would threaten a successful prosecution of the Professor and all his minions.

Another dashboard clock check: Yes, I decided, I'd made up enough ground to buy myself the time to stop at my dorm and change out of this old man's fantasy school girl outfit for my summary dismissal.

At least I could look like an adult for certain "dressing down" and subsequent termination.

I palmed into a parking slot in a soft skid.

An incoming text arrived from Holmes just as I shifted into park: "Where r u?"

I pecked back: "On way 2 meet u. Just stopped at dorm 2 change clothes. Won't take minute."

As I turned off the engine I saw there was a vagrant huddled on a bench in front of my dorm. Odd—you didn't see many of those around campus; the university police were pretty diligent about chasing the homeless off. But it did happen, now and again. In mild precaution, I pulled my gun from under my seat and slid it in my coat pocket just in case.

Another text arrived as I slid out and used the fob button to lock the doors.

Holmes: "Dorm? The city? Change clothes? Why? What meeting??"

I typed back: "The meeting you summoned me for with Chief. Not going in dressed like slutty school girl."

Holmes: "??? Did not summon you. I'm still at Cattulus! Come back at once. Could be trap!"

This chill.

Then more shadows on the ground next to mine: two silhouettes on the ground, male and female.

Reaching for my gun, I looked up just in time to hear the trigger pull.

I felt the sting in my chest and then there was the white burst behind my eyes as the stun gun lit me up.

Electrical charge! I thought, immediately terrified.

My doctor would be mortified—electrical shock to my faulty heart was a potential death sentence. A charge like that, I'd been warned, could be lethal for me—trigger that long-dreaded arrhythmia that would put me down forever.

Like I said: white light, then all was *dark*.

EXCERPT: INTERCEPTED EMAIL FROM BREEANA BRÒNACH ROURKE

L ast period and that empty chair, sitting there front and center, and practically screaming for attention, Unc.

Holmes is wholly focused upon it, of course.

His hard gray eyes locked with mine. Accusing, and all wrath.

Raising his eyebrows, Holmes stabs at his iPhone. As he does that, he says, "Family emergency has come up. Mrs. Banks will sit with you until the bell."

Another look my way: Yes, pure hatred, uncle. Pure and bottled rage, desperately seeking expression.

We need to prepare for this man's vengeance. It will be terrible and spastic, I think. I'm really scared for myself right now.

Holmes is walking over and leaning down . . .

Yes, this is me again, although this is sort of like dictation, Uncle. Whispering in my ear, Holmes is saying to me, "You write your relative this war is between *him and I*. If he crosses the line and hurts Jona, I'll visit corresponding consequences on you, my dear. You tell Moriarty that. Write him right now, just as fast as your fingers can type."

So I'm doing that. Uncle, I believe every threat this man is making. I know a bluffer. This dude is not bluffing! And he knows your name! He knows we're related!

I'm going to at least hurt him back, or try to . . .

I'm going to tell him the secret that the bitch is keeping from him.

It's ten minutes later, and I'm alone for the moment . . . away from Holmes anyway, but under guard. I'm *scared*, uncle.

I definitely need that attorney. I need him an hour ago!

Holmes is like a mad man.

25

Surprised to still be alive, I came to, naked and lashed to a table that sat in the center of a chilly concrete room.

Somehow, I felt strangely calm in the first moments— reassured just to be alive, despite my doctor's long-ago warnings about the risk of electrical stimulation to someone with my variety of congenital heart condition. In theory, that stun gun's blast should have caused a cascade of mounting arrhythmia that could have killed me.

But then my new reality began to sink in.

Stripped and tied to a table in what looked like makeshift butcher shop. There was a hose connected to a spigot on the wall—drainage facilitation.

Maybe better to have died from electrocution. Almost certainly that would have been better.

My fucked-up heart and my resultant statistically foreshortened existence—I'd been told time and time again not to expect to see forty, probably not even thirty—had consigned me to years of preparation for a very different kind of death than the one I was facing now.

This promised to be bloody.

And yet?

Even though he seemed to be back in Portsmouth, based on our last texts exchanged, I still firmly believed that now that Holmes knew I was in trouble, he'd find some way to rescue me.

It was a childish and possibly deluded cocktail of superstition and faith that was fleetingly giving me hope, I couldn't deny any of that, but it was what I truly felt in the terrible moment.

A swarthy, gaunt man with an eye patch smiled at me. His skin was a sallow yellow and hair black and slicked back.

He said, "Ah, awake at last. And now we can begin." He wrung his hands and cracked his knuckles.

I said firmly, as authoritatively as I could. "You need to know I'm a plain clothes police officer. You need to untie me, let me get dressed then you can drop me just anywhere. But you need to do that *now*, before I'm harmed. Do it, and I'll give you at least a three-hour head start before I call in the dogs to chase after you. Seems generous to me, under the circumstances."

My calm at having survived my possible electrocution and my trust in Holmes to find and save me were already beginning to ebb in equal measures.

Tough as I was trying to sound, I could hear fear in my voice. Professional as this misfit was, he and his "friends" probably detected it, too.

A man and a woman shared the room with us. They were armed. They were decidedly not the two that followed us earlier, of course: Holmes' still-mysterious relative had made that other male-female team vanish, just as Sherlock had promised would happen.

The one-eyed stranger just smiled sadly and shook his head. "Sorry, but no. You see, you are *already* a corpse Ms. Jona

Watson. Your death is an inevitable outcome. Having said that, and to prove the truth of my assertion, let me say now that my name is Mr. Enoch Drebber. That is not an alias. I of course would not reveal my real name if I thought there was any possibility at all of you divulging it at some point. You are going to die here. But that isn't to say I'm not willing to bargain with you. I am prepared to commit to a diminishment of your suffering if you cooperate with me, cheerfully and fully. I need some critical information from you, for a certain man, you see."

A feral smile: "Believe that I'll stop at absolutely nothing to obtain it. I will zealously embrace any form of debasement of myself or to you to get what I want. I love to make others suffer, it's really that simple."

My body was shaking so hard now; my jaws hurt from straining to keep my teeth from chattering.

Still, I tried to be as hardboiled about it as I could be with my terror-choked voice. "You are in *so* over your head, mister. Let me tell you precisely how I see things."

A curt shake of the head. He held up a hand to silence me. "Stop, just please please, *please* stop. Let me show you how things truly are, Ms. Watson."

He held up two knives. One was long and sharp. The other glowed blue-red from having sat in an open fire somewhere just below my sight lines—I could smell if not see the blaze; caught glimpses of trailing wisps of smoke curling up toward the naked light bulbs dangling overhead.

Drebber said, "As I've said, Ms. Watson, I've been granted carte blanche to do to you all that I wish until certain information is in hand. Do that, and I promise you a quick death But, before you answer, just so you know I truly mean business, there is the matter of getting at least some little bit or two off you. We'll do that right now."

The blade hovered near my left breast. The man, this Mr. Drebber, said to the armed woman, "Put the gag back in her mouth, please. While I savor much of what I do, I'm just no fan of the noise. I prefer to concentrate squarely on my work."

The woman moved to do that.

As the rag was stuffed in my mouth and the blade's-edge hovered at my nipple, I finally lost some control of myself: My heart raced crazily—another threat to my life in that sense. My knees knocked, furiously. I felt this tingling in my lower back and then between my legs and realized I was about to lose control of my kidneys.

Despite my nakedness and the coldness of the basement, I was suddenly bathed in sweat and my heart was pounding even harder. I would have begged and offered up anything then, if only I could have spoken.

Mr. Drebber smiled a last time and said, "This pain is going to be terrible, but it is merely the start of something even worse if you do not learn from this brief spasm of agony."

The blade—his cutting knife—hovered above my breast. The other knife, its heat radiating against my skin, was at the ready, presumably for the purposes of scalding cauterization.

Drebber said, almost paternally, "Now take a deep breath, dear. Try to experience this pain in full—it may give you the vital impetus to surrender to me early what I would like to know and so spare yourself even worse agony."

There was a loud noise and blood spray—blood in my eyes, across my lips.

Drebber's smiling face simply seemed to evaporate in a spray of pink and white.

The other two were just turning, raising their guns, when they were also shot in the head. There was more warm, bloody backsplash across my bare belly and thighs.

Four men in black body armor burst into the little underground bunker. In a muffled British accent, one called out, "Clear, sir. You can come in now. The parcel is safe and secure."

A large, portly man in an immaculately tailored three-piece gray suit entered. He was leaning heavily on a cane.

He made a pained face at me. "Oh dear, God," he said in a soft British accent. "Do quickly clean and cover her up. And get those ropes off her, right now. After, *immediately* signal my brother she's fine and that he should proceed with his end of this bloody mess."

The big man waited until I was decent, then smiled pityingly at me and said, "It's fine now, Ms. Watson. You're perfectly safe." He held out a pudgy hand. "My name is Mycroft Holmes, by the way."

This other, older and decidedly portly Holmes sat alongside me in a black SUV as we made a brief detour back to my dorm so I could shower and once again try to change clothes.

As we drove across town, I gave Mycroft Holmes a closer inspection, trying to use some of my Holmes' methods.

In profile, there was something of Sherlock Holmes in the hawkish nose and decisive chin. This one had familiar, hard gray eyes, too, but that was about all they shared in terms of physical traits.

Mycroft Holmes weighed perhaps two-hundred and seventy-five pounds. His hairline had deeply receded at the temples and his remaining hair was graying. His British accent was still very present in a way that my Holmes' was not, and the cut of the man's big suit was decidedly European.

I said, "Thank you for everything, Mr. Holmes. I have to ask, who are you exactly? I mean in the sense of—"

"In the sense of my affiliations," he finished for me. "My employment situation, so to speak. That's what you want to know more about, isn't it? Sorry, but that's simply not up for discussion. I'm afraid I can't talk about *any* of that to you, Ms. Watson."

"Please, call me Jona. And yes, I understand. I won't press."

That slight smile he gave me—I thought he must think it to be solicitous. If so, he was wrong. Like my Holmes, I sensed this version, too, sometimes "modeled" what he took to be expected social behavior. He said, "Anyway, you've been through a terrible ordeal. If you require someone professional to speak with, I can see it arranged."

"No, really—I'm quite fine, thanks to you."

Mycroft suddenly frowned and produced a handkerchief made of powder blue silk he handed to me. He pointed at his left cheekbone.

I nodded and dabbed at my corresponding check with his handkerchief. It came away bloody—not my blood of course.

"Keep the handkerchief," he said with tart distaste. He flicked some lint from his pant's leg. He said, "You have Sherlock to thank for your rescue, really. You see my brother maintains a kind of network of operatives—all unfortunates, young and old—to do his bidding from time to time. Yet these wretches are, at times, surprisingly effective in executing my brother's rarified errands. Take this present episode for evidence of that fact."

The homeless woman sleeping on the bench outside my apartment: she must have been one of these *irregular* agents of Sherlock's. I wondered at that aloud.

"Quite so," Mycroft said, curling his lip. "A Miss June Stone, I believe. One of two dozen of her sort who've been playing threadbare guardian angels to you these past few days. They have no appreciable reach into Portsmouth, of course, but here in the city, they're virtually all around you, a rag-tag army of guardians. Miss Stone witnessed your abduction. Fortunately your kidnappers simply pitched your dropped belongings— including your purse, keys and mobile phone—back into your car. Miss Stone then followed them in your Mustang and used your phone to call my younger brother. Sherlock then alerted me as I was *in situ* here in the city." A slight clearing of his throat, and an added, "And, since I'm not without certain resources."

Mycroft Holmes shook his head, more distaste pulling down the corners of his mouth. "This sort of cavalry thing is really not my line of work, Jona, but what *can* one do under the circumstances when it's one's brother asking?"

He smiled, obviously remembering the expected *bon mot* from a British gentleman who'd just saved a woman's life: "And, of course, an attractive damsel in jeopardy? How *can't* one come to her proverbial rescue?"

He patted my arm then and said with palpable relief, "And here we are. I'll wait down here while you freshen up. Don't worry—others of mine have already checked and cleared your room. It's quite safe. Brother asks you be brisk about all your cleaning up and changing. You see they've taken a Miss Breeana Rourke into official custody. He'd very much like you to be there for as much of her interrogation as possible."

As we pulled into the Portsmouth Police Department's parking lot, I said, "Once again, Mr. Holmes, of course I can't thank you enough. You literally saved my life of course. Will you be coming up with me?" I hoped so. Despite his quirky frostiness, I liked this man, even trusted him.

Mycroft quickly raised a thick-fingered hand. "For myriad reasons, no, my dear. Primarily because my role in this affair would be *impossibly* difficult and awkward to explain to such as these. Far above these police and their pay-grades, to coin a phrase. If I'm reluctant to tell even you what my exact position is—fond as I already am of you—please believe I positively balk at the notion I might have to divulge my employment's true nature to small-town *cops.*"

He smiled then and added, "But there is something you *could* do for me—a thing that ensures my presence there in the most useful sense. If you'd just permit me . . . ?"

Mycroft opened a black leather case resting on the seat between us. It was about the size of a shoebox. He eyed my clothes—I'd opted for black flats, blue jeans and a blue blouse topped out with a black velvet blazer.

He handed me a silver pin—a jeweled, running wolf—and said, "It's also a listening device of course."

How could I object after he had saved my life?

He pinned it on my lapel above my left breast, then he took my hand and raised it to his lips for a brushing kiss. "Ms. Watson, please believe it's been my rare privilege to serve. I confide to you my brother thinks the world of you and that simple fact, I'll also confess, is a phenomenon unto itself, entirely without a precedent. I can't tell you how that astonishing fact recommends you as a young woman of extraordinary character and quality of spirit in my eyes."

After squeezing my hand a last time, Mycroft gave me another pitying smile. "I just sincerely hope for both your sakes you can endure our Sherlock over time. He's often an infernal devil to live with, I fear." His mouth turned down. "I speak from long and painful experience, of course."

26

Venomously, Breeana said to Holmes, "What exactly did you do to my computer, you bastard? That probably wasn't even legal, you know! What did that thumb drive do?"

Holmes shrugged and said, "I'm not the police. As to this business of having done something to your computer, I have no idea what you're talking about. Maybe your attorney will find some way to convince himself of the reality of this fantasy you're spinning, but I'm not going to waste time as you try to muddy the waters with your flimsy and transparent lies, Ms. Rourke."

Holmes tapped the end of an unlit cigarette on the table-top impatiently, watching her, searching for useful cracks in her veneer.

Breeana seethed. She turned sharply to Chief Briggs and said, "I asked for my lawyer at least an hour ago. I'm not saying anything more until he arrives *and* I want this not-a-policeman out of here right now." She nodded at Holmes. "Believe, me, my lawyer will use that too, you know—you cops letting some amateur criminologist and a university professor participate in arresting me, and in screwing with my personal computer. You're going to lose your badge, old man, I promise you that.

My family is going to sue your ass and this rich little city all the way into the ground. You *better* believe it."

I didn't see Groves in there now so I figured he must have moved on—the other professor she'd alluded to. Maybe Groves was looking for me. If so, I hoped he wouldn't find me in this cramped little darkened room on the other side of the interrogation room's one-way glass.

Cowed by the legal threat, a red-faced Chief Briggs blustered, but then firmly dismissed Sherlock.

Disgusted, Holmes rose and left the interrogation room.

He joined me in the little room on the other side of the glass. To my surprise and delight, Holmes smiled and then gathered me to his chest on first sight. He said, "You're really quite all right? Really, Jona?"

"Yes. Really. But Mycroft got there just in time. If he'd been even a second later arriving, it would have been very bad."

He let go of me after a few seconds and jacked a thumb at Breeana. "She's a tough one. Not giving a single inch."

I said, "Has she talked about us? About you and me, and you know, sex?"

"No, for whatever reason, she's apparently choosing to hold that card for now," he said.

Standing so close to him, wanting to put an arm around him or to take his hand but knowing it wouldn't be welcomed at this moment, and certainly not in this setting, I restrained my strong impulse for more direct contact with Holmes. I said, "This thumb-drive stuff and her computer—it really happened, I take it?"

"Of course."

"To what end, Holmes?"

"The device—something, again, of Brother Mycroft's—gives at least as much as it takes. It sucked off what I hope to be salient information and then it wipes the hard drive. It also similarly infects and destroys other devices it has had contact with . . . sends out destructive emails and texts and plenty of clever little, innocent looking attachments and myriad Trojan horses that also annihilate any receiving devices. So hopefully, that recording of us, along with much of Mr. Moriarty's digital archives and attendant hardware, is now so much ruin. Digital scorched earth."

"Fingers firmly crossed that's true. Does she know about me? I mean that I'm alive?"

"No, Watson. I thought it better she thinks things are going her way for the moment. And less likely, as I think further on it, for her to bother to raise your name in vain in front of the chief and your instructor if she thinks you're dead. On that note, your police friends have no idea you were a captive for the moment. Groves would probably have suffered an apoplexy if he'd known what was happening."

"Speaking of names being raised, has Moriarty's come up yet?"

"Only because I at last did so," Holmes said. "Blank stares from your mentor and the chief upon first hearing. I wish I could say I was surprised. They'll Google him of course and find an obscure and self-published author, then think me still more daft. Morons."

"No need to twist the knife, Holmes. What about Breeana?"

"She has stonewalled, steadfastly, just as I've said."

"But what's going to happen to her?"

"She's poised to *lawyer-up* as you heard her say and I'm now dismissed because of her further legal threats. Relieved that you're safe and my cover now blown, I propose we return to Baker Street and prepare counter-strategies to thwart Moriarty's inevitable wrath."

"I'm all for that," I said, suddenly yawning deeply. Crashing blood-pressure, I supposed. With Holmes at my side, I at last felt truly delivered . . . *really* safe.

As we were leaving, a tall and slender man in a black suit and carrying a matching black leather briefcase approached us. I said, "The attorney, I presume."

A German shepherd curled in a corner perked up, then began a low, guttural growl.

Holmes' eyes flickered the presumed attorney's way—sizing the lawyer up in that characteristic way he and his elder brother had in common: gaze running up and down, then left and right. I wondered what that incredible mind of Holmes' was processing about the attorney.

"That man's a lawyer by appearance only," Holmes hissed urgently, stopping us as the stranger rounded a corner. "But he's not *really* a lawyer, of course." Holmes then looked to the dog that was nearly going berserk, barking and snapping at its leash. Holmes said, "That's a bomb-sniffing dog, Watson! Hurry, there's hardly time before—"

The explosion buried the rest of Holmes' words. The concussion of the blast preceded its sound and heat.

Holmes, a few steps ahead of me, was flung back against me. We sprawled together on the floor as the sprinkler system kicked on, soaking us through.

So many terrible creams—cries of terror and of pain. Holmes struggled to his feet and offered a hand, pulling me up.

Fire was already spreading through the police station, but Holmes moved toward the point of first destruction, forcing his way through to the interrogation room. Half-deafened, I dogged his heels despite his barely heard urges that I flee to safety with everyone else.

We at last made it into what was left of the interrogation room—its interior wall that joined the hallway was nearly obliterated. Inside the scorched room lay strewn and splashed on the walls the remnants of Chief Briggs, Breeana, two police officers and the suicide bomber disguised as an attorney.

I wouldn't have been able to identify any of their bodies but for the recognized remnants of their still-burning clothes.

"They're all lost," Holmes said in frustration. "We need to get out of here quickly—the place is fully engulfed and the roof is compromised. This place is going to be a total loss."

THE FINAL PROBLEM

I think that there are certain crimes
Which the law cannot touch, and which therefore, to some
extent,
justify private revenge.
—Sir Arthur Conan Doyle

27

A shared cab ride back to the city this time.
I desperately wanted another shower. My wet
clothes smelled of smoke and cordite and were chilling me in
the autumn air, despite our insisting the cabbie turn his heater
up to its maximum setting.

As we traveled the empty spaces between Portsmouth and
the city, Holmes briefly spoke on the phone with his brother.
He winced at some feedback on the line, then glanced at my
chest. Holmes pulled my gifted pin loose and slung it out the
window. He said into the phone, "Nice try at keeping tabs on
me, brother mine."

A fleeting smile then he said, "*Yes*, Mycroft, of course I
know you had to try. You're never one to pass up a rare and
promising opportunity to further secure your state of near
omniscience. Given circumstances and services rendered, all
is forgiven, *this time*."

When he hung up I said crossly, "That was gift to me, you
know."

"And you also know it was a device to spy on me, just
as I said. You should understand here and now that my

relationship with Mycroft is complex. He'd simply kill to have a recording device in my proximity twenty four-seven, believe that. You can't imagine the lengths I have to go to in all my living quarters, every day, to maintain privacy from him. It's all tedious but essential ritual."

"Tell me about more about Mycroft," I said.

"Not much I can tell, as you probably have already heard from the horse's mouth. He's seven years my senior. That's about it in terms of what can be disclosed beyond what you already know or perhaps have correctly concluded for yourself."

I supposed it truly was. And there was some definite tension there, at least from Sherlock's end. Maybe one day I'd know why. Maybe.

Silence for a time, then I said softly in the deepening dark, "Moriarty actually killed his own niece. He coldly and deliberately had her blown to pieces. And, my God, he found someone who isn't a Muslim extremist to all appearances to do the deed. What kind of man can order someone to suicide like that?"

"Indeed," Holmes said. "One would conclude the bomber was another blackmail victim—probably one willing to sacrifice himself to save another from Moriarty's attentions. And I wonder if the Professor decided to sacrifice his own blood because he thought he'd be getting you and I in the bargain. But what choice did he have? He was invisible to the authorities until I put his name out there. Breeana was a wild card and a potential path to his door if she cracked. The moment we arrested her, I gather her fate was a forgone conclusion in her uncle's mind."

"And so he sacrificed her, like a pawn. My God, what a monster."

Holmes raised and then slowly lowered his hand as if to say, "Just so."

That same hand next reached out and took mine. He squeezed hard. "I thought I'd lost my Watson," he said. "It was a terrible half-hour or so of not knowing that it was happily otherwise." I thought I heard a slight quaver in his well-bottom voice. I leaned in and kissed his neck. I said, "Thank God for you and your strange and mysterious brother."

Holmes rested his hand on my knee. "Anyway, we both smell like a chimney. Really must scrub up and get into some fresh clothes. You know, I'm afraid things really must only get worse from here, Watson. Moriarty's ego has been damaged in the most profound way. He's been forced by circumstance to murder kin. His response will therefore be fierce."

Holmes had ordered our cab to drop us a block short of Baker Street. "Must keep the new nest safe as long as we can," Holmes said. On the other hand, Brother Mycroft had seen to it the Mustang was already parked safely out front when we reached our new place. The Ford's keys were waiting in our new mailbox. I retrieved my computer from the Mustang's trunk and followed Holmes up the stairs to our apartment.

He said over his shoulder, "Must you really fiddle with that thing tonight?" He shrugged and said, "But then I suppose your dubious professor must surely be beside himself by now after the bombing and no contact with you for several hours. He's probably owed at least a bloody email of assurance you're okay, eager as I feel to let the man stew in his miserable juices."

A low rumble of thunder; more cold rain began tumbling down.

Holmes keyed us in with a portable set of lock-pick tools. He held up a hand as the door opened with a creak. He said softly, "Careful now. Must be very quiet up the steps."

Padding naked and freshly scrubbed through our new flat, I returned to find Holmes fully dressed and sitting crossed legged and hunched before the window, looking down on the street.

He said acidly, "Please turn off the light but stay close by the switch. There's a masked man down there with a flashlight. The professor somehow knows where we live now. I've just been given a few threats now in Morse Code by flashlight. Time to respond."

I slid on my shirt and quickly buttoned it up, then skimmed on panties. I stood by the light switch, as Holmes ordered. "But I don't know Morse Code," I said.

"I'll direct the speed of your switch flips, don't worry," Holmes said. Then he added, "The man down there, he just signaled, 'Cost my dearest blood. Reckoning required.'"

Holmes wasn't having it. He said, "Jona, here we go—it's all about lingering light, and fleeting light. Listen carefully and flip the switch exactly as I say!"

Later, Holmes would tell me with my ordered switches I'd signaled back, "Your crimes killed her. I was just gun, you pulled trigger."

From where I stood, I could just see the faint bursts of light on the glass as the response came. Holmes translated: "He signaled 'Surrender or face annihilation.'"

I said, "Do you think that's the professor himself down there?"

"No, probably just a useful tool. Time for our response, Watson . . . "

I signaled back with bursts of light and dark, "If no surrender?"

"Desolation," the Professor responded through his minion. He flashed on, "Property searched. Network down. Unacceptable."

Holmes read to me that last admission. He couldn't suppress a wicked smile. "I'm simply delighted to hear that it worked," he said to me.

Then came the next threat: "Will see destroyed if persist."

Sherlock shared that threat and searched my face. I shook my head no.

Holmes smiled and gave me more light-flipping instructions. Holmes said that we said, "You've lived as an enigma. Will perish an enigma too."

A last flashed message: "Settle your affairs."

The stranger then dove into a taxi that crawled curbside and slid off with a skid.

Holmes drew the shade, then padded over to my side.

He traced his fingers down my breastbone, tracing its contour through my shirt. "No more distractions this night. He'll need some time to prepare something properly terrible for us once he's assured we're really not standing down. This might be our last good night together, and for quite some while. We should savor it."

28

I emerged from another shower to find a full breakfast set out on the floor. I said, "Holmes, did you prepare this? If so, how on earth . . . ?"

"Cupboards are still decidedly Spartan. While you showered, I snuck out to get the morning papers. When I returned, I found this waiting on the floor, along with two proper door keys on matching fobs and this short, handwritten note. He handed me a slip of paper. I read:

"I see you lovebirds couldn't resist taking up residence early and who could blame you! Welcome, and *Slàinte!*" — Mrs. Hudson.

I hugged Holmes tightly and said, "It's good to be *home.*"

"Anyway, it's a true Scotswoman's breakfast," he said, "but she warned me not to expect it in perpetuity. This is a one-off, she swears."

The food was delicious; the coffee was black and exceptionally strong. Even Holmes found it satisfactory. I found myself incrementally adding more and more skim milk.

I gestured at the messy pile of newspapers already strewn across the floor. "Anything revelatory on the two or three pages of all this that you actually bother with reading?"

"Not really. Though you should know, echoing your aside last night, that *Muslim extremists* in fact seem to be the go-to fall guys for the explosion in Portsmouth last night. Isis comes up in several reports. There's a lot of muttering about some suspected sleeper cell."

"Well, there you have it," I said. "Someone's covering their tracks, and they're doing it with a backhoe."

"Even if the surviving Portsmouth police knew of Moriarty's existence, it's doubtful they could go *there* as an explanation to the press. After all, even in simple description, the Professor comes across as a kind of pulp-lit arch criminal."

"It does sound a little absurd, yes."

"Speaking of absurdities, the high school is calling in grief counselors today of course," Holmes said. "As though any of those girls, even her squad mates, felt anything less than terrorized by our Breeana." He laughed rather darkly and said, "You know I actually received a text late last night asking if I'd continue to play teacher there until a 'suitable replacement' could be found?"

He scoffed and said, "As if that is even possible . . . "

"But I take it your being irreplaceable aside, that you didn't say yes?"

"Of course not," he said. "I must devote all focus to Moriarty now, and to stopping his so-called greater plan."

"Yes, and you need to fill me in on more of that. On the other hand, I need to start thinking of an alternative way to make some money. I can only assume Chief Brigg's death effectively ended my employment. Also, I haven't been paid a penny yet in salary. All I have is my debit card which is probably already frozen."

"Don't worry about money, presently," Holmes said. "You still have classes to complete, of course, but Brother Mycroft already has eyes on you. If you have a resume, you should email it to me. I took the liberty of working on exploring a kind of consulting gig for you with dear brother. Believe, me the work will be stimulating. And potentially lucrative."

"What *is* he, Holmes? Is Mycroft, well, some kind of government agency head? Maybe some British spin on Homeland Security?"

"Close enough," Holmes said, "although I sometimes suspect Brother Mycroft *is* the British government, as I seem to remember remarking in earshot of you. I suppose you might describe him as a kind of clearing house for the government back home and a primary link to your government's most secret echelons. He is the ultimate hidden man, the one who links disparate dots and discerns emerging threats. He then takes whatever steps necessary to extinguish those threats before they can manifest themselves. When he eventually passes, as we surely all must do—but in Mycroft's case, most probably from over-indulgence in one of his favored French restaurants—only *then* do I truly fear for the safety of the realm."

Holmes gave me a dire look and said, "Please never tell him I said any of that. His ego already makes him well nigh insufferable."

"Are *you* on his payroll, Holmes?"

He frowned; I'd struck a nerve. "There's a kind of retainer," Sherlock said grudgingly. "And then we negotiate other consulting fees, but on a case-by-case basis. Take this matter of Moriarty: I told you, his real objective was not compromising these girls. It's always been about controlling their parents. The Professor was very selective in making his blackmail choices. Working with Mycroft, *I've* helped to connect dots that even my brother, working largely alone, had not. This is, in the end, about control of literally all the knowledge in the world, Jona—the overt and the covert."

Holmes lit a cigarette. He pulled his empty wine goblet closer to serve as an improvised ashtray. "Have you ever heard of Project Carnivore?"

I nodded. "Yeah, I actually *have*. In the wake of 9-11, it was the FBI's attempt to scarf up basically every cell phone transmission, email and even text messages back in the days when people mostly still had pagers with a kind of early version of that function."

"What you might not know is that it was an evolutionary spinoff from an earlier project called 'Omnivore,'" Holmes said. "That first one didn't quite work. But long after Carnivore, and more recently after Julian Assange and Edward Snowden and various other surveillance and intelligence hemorrhages, Omnivore got freshly dusted off and executed all-too effectively in its latest incarnation. Then it aggressively morphed *further*. It presently exists and continues to evolve, sucking up data on a scale that defies imagination.

"It essentially captures anything and everything stored in digital format," Holmes continued. "Everything, everywhere. It then records and sorts all of that data by user and stores it in a searchable database that also defies imagination with its bold intrusiveness. Imagine it, Watson—every one of your emails, texts and smart phone photos, all of your web searches . . . even MS word documents sent to the cloud or to your Kindle for back up—intercepted and then archived, under your name and fully searchable. Imagine every element of your online or digital life captured and every sliver of it then cataloged. Just the notion of their web searches recorded, stored and discoverable would justly send most people into a blind panic."

It *was* terrifying. I said, "And I take it Omnivore is what this Partington installation in Portsmouth is tied up in?"

"That's it exactly," Holmes said. "Omnivore is run out of that base. And it's the mother lode of everyone on earth's individual closets and all of their attendant, closely guarded skeletons, captured and consolidated in one place. And if control of that unthinkable repository were to fall into the hands of a master blackmailer like Moriarty?" Holmes arched his dark eyebrows. "Think on that . . . "

"So this is the Professor's end game," I said. "He intends, essentially, to try and blackmail the world?"

Holmes laid a finger to his nose. "Conceivably, that's really it, Jona. That's just what's at stake here. Moriarty means to blackmail the entire sorry goddamn world."

After a quick trip out for more wine and a wedge of sharp cheddar, sitting together on the wide windowsill, naked and entwined in another delicious afterglow of lovemaking, Holmes said, "You must have been terrified being alone with that killer, at his mercy. He's in my files, of course. He was a sadist of near epic proportions, Jona."

I said softly, "Strangely, only at the very end, when he was about to begin cutting into me, was I truly beside myself. Then, for just a fleeting, terrible moment, I *was* scared in a way I've never been before. Before that, I truly believed you'd somehow save me. And you did just that. That man was just about to go to work on me, and then he was quite dead. Who was he, exactly—beyond being a sadistic monster, I mean?"

"A cipher, mostly. Apart from being a stone-cold torturer and killer, he also had exceptional culinary skills. He once actually appeared on television on something called *The Iron Chef*, whatever that is, a few years ago. The professor subsequently set him up with a family restaurant for cover. They say his offerings were quite excellent. His Zagat reviews were stratospheric, for what that's worth."

Holmes was quiet a moment, then he said, rather portentously, "Jona, this is very difficult to ask, but I simply have to do it. Please forgive me these next few minutes, I beg of you."

Oh God . . .

Now my heart began racing almost as it had even in my final moments at the mercy of that crazy cook-killer.

My mind also raced, grasping for possibilities about what might be looming.

Had I in some way pushed too hard pursuing our romance?

Did Holmes fear our growing intimacy and was he now planning to break it off or to stamp on the brakes in some way?

As I began to think of things to fill the awkward silence, Holmes pressed on:

"Funny or odd as this may seem to you, Jona, apart from myself, the two minds I most respect in this world in regard to their deductive prowess are those of my brother and, I must grudgingly confess, Professor Moriarty. When both of those men have arrived at the same deduction, one I so clearly and mystifyingly myself was blind to—*inexcusably* blind to, Jona—then I have to cede hallowed ground and consider the possibility these two cold and amazing brains are right in their independently arrived at deductions."

Holmes' right palm was pressed warmly to my belly. His left rested on my shoulder. Outside, the rain still fell, hard and steady. The streetlights and signage glowed in the growing, rippling puddles.

"Holmes, you've lost me completely," I said carefully, staring down at the glowing, rain slicked street.

"Have I really lost you?" His hand gripped my shoulder more tightly. "You see, darling, Breeana confided to me one of her uncle's deductions while I detained her in the classroom, while we were awaiting your police friends. It was probably her uncle's idea to do that."

"Why," I said breathlessly. "Why did she do that?"

"To hurt me I suppose," Holmes said. "Then, quite chillingly, Mycroft soon after confided the same deduction to me."

"And why did your brother do that?"

"I suppose, in his way, he actually meant to spare me possible hurt."

"That's doesn't make sense . . . It seems a contradiction."

"Only these two singular men's motives in divulging what they deduced are at odds. The revelation is the same."

"This deduction, Holmes," I said carefully, "what is it about?"

"It's about you of course." He kissed the back of my neck in what I knew he intended to be reassurance, then wrapped his arms close around my torso, hugging me more tightly to him. "This has to be done," he said as much to himself as to me. "Please forgive me, Watson but I really need to know. Are you *ill?* Perhaps . . . " His voice cracked and he said, "Perhaps *terminally* ill?"

I began to shake. I knew Holmes felt my trembling, of course. It was an answer in itself.

"Terminal isn't really the right word," I said finally, my voice ragged and thin. "It's not an illness per se," I continued. "It's more of a condition. Congenital. Here."

I took his hand and placed it between my bare breasts. "My heart is a kind of time bomb. There's a sort of arrhythmia, untreatable, that *could* one day kill me. It's been dormant, there, since my first day alive. It's inoperable, even today. So I'm on an anticoagulant. Consequently, I can bleed like crazy if cut. If that mad man made some kind of cut or amputation, I'd have likely bled out, despite his plan to use a hot knife to staunch my bleeding."

Holmes took a deep breath and held me tighter to him. I sensed he was confronting something he realized even he couldn't overcome. I also sensed this was another kind of first for him, one that, just like the loss of his virginity, he'd always associate with me.

I said softly, "Holmes, it could happen to me five minutes from now, or *never*. These two men—your brother and your enemy—how'd they each figure it out?"

He said, "They arrived at it in the same way I might have if I wasn't . . . you know, *smitten* with you. If I'd been fully and *dispassionately* observing you as I do observe the others. The clues were there in so many ways. They were manifest in your sustained and various risk-takings: driving sports cars fast, solitary vacations and exotic beaches. In impulsively embracing an undercover assignment without proper training and in the way you recklessly, heedlessly pursued our intimacy and moving in together just as quickly as I proposed it."

I said, "And you're not *also* an extremist in pursuit of sensation? What we did took your impulsive cooperation, too, you know. And you're not just as much a fatalist with your insane espressos and all that deadly nicotine you pump into your lungs? What's your excuse for risk-taking, Holmes? Any secrets you want to share with me?"

"Jona, I'm being serious; You live like someone for whom there's no tomorrow because you clearly and all too really feel that way yourself. But it took Mycroft and Moriarty to make me see it, hard and clear. I've been badly off my game where you're concerned." He nuzzled the down at the back of my neck, and said rather hoarsely, "I suppose you could take it as a backhanded compliment."

I kissed the back of his arm and said, "I'm so sorry, Holmes, but I *am* determined to take that as a compliment. I should have told you, of course. Starting this love affair and keeping something so important as my condition from you was horribly selfish. But I—"

His fingers were at my lips. He said, "Hush. No apologies, and no regrets, Jona. As you said, we could have only tonight, or we could have many more nights like this, perhaps stretching out into years. Anyway, involvement with me is hardly a promise of safety and tranquility, either. And, anyway, none of us in this life is promised tomorrow, right?"

Tentatively, I said, "So are we okay for now? I'm going to confess this now, regardless how it may terrify you, darling. These past couple of days—even with all its bloodshed and bedlam—have truly been the happiest I've ever spent."

Holmes urged me to turn around. I did that, wrapping my legs around his waist as he kissed my mouth; his body stirred against mine.

He said, "I'm just relieved you're capable of tolerating me, whatever comes. Very few are capable of hanging in there with me. Not even fellow professionals or elder brothers, most times."

"So whatever becomes of us, no regrets, *really?*"

"Really, no regrets," he said. "I never regret anything I do, Jona. What earthly thing could it change if I did give into regret? What would be the bloody point?"

29

Shortly after lunch, Professor Groves at last surfaced again. There came a volley of texts begging to lay eyes on me, to please allow my professor to see for himself that I was truly okay.

So we agreed to meet at this Starbucks . . .

My instructor was still clearly shaken as he greeted us, still eyeing Holmes with a mixture of fear and loathing. Yet he didn't let his aggressive antipathy of Holmes get in the way of his own hand-wringing at suffering "a too-close call."

Groves said, "Do you know if I'd been fifteen minutes later leaving the police headquarters I'd have been in that room when the bomb went off? My God, *I'd* be dead now, just like Briggs, wouldn't I?"

Did he say that to try and elicit pity?

I resisted the urge to tell my instructor Holmes had actually been running *toward* the impending explosion he knew was coming. Sherlock didn't resist going there: "Could as easily have been Jona and I, if only we'd tarried a moment. We were actually *in* the building when it exploded, you know. How many miles away were you, exactly?"

Gripping his cup harder, Groves shook his head, ignoring the question and said, "So what do we do next?"

Holmes shrugged and said, looking rather tired and bored, "What's *left* to do, really? Please do tell me if you have some useful notion about what a next move might look like, *Professor*. The local police, such as they were—and that was precious little from my admittedly tainted perspective—are decidedly in tatters. Moriarty's niece was atomized and the bawdy house they used to compromise all these rich dullards has been raided and shut down. The bigger game has gone to ground."

Holmes sipped more of his jumbo espresso, then flicked lint from his black coat sleeve. "At any rate, my secret client is satisfied that any threat to his daughter is now safely negated. I have to concur. The Professor will move on to some other enterprise, to some other place. So, following Mr. Moriarty's admittedly dubious example, I, too, shall cast eye toward potentially greener pastures."

Surrendering to Holmes' studied belligerence, my instructor gave me a pitying look and said, "Whatever else he is, this expatriate Brit is *not* an idealist, is he?"

Holmes stood and moved to the register to have his favorite barista mix him another twenty-dollar coffee drink.

I tossed him the keys to his Mustang. "Thanks for the loan of the wheels, Professor. You'll find your LoJack in the glove compartment. That was really a crass move, I'm sad to say."

He nodded, taking that. He forced an uncertain smile and pocketed his keys. "You'll be back in classes tomorrow, then?"

"What choice do I have," I said. "Figure my job—and attendant work credits— disappeared with so much else wiped out by that bomb. It's all over."

The professor rubbed his jaw, watching Holmes waiting at the counter for his refill.

"Not necessarily," he said. "I don't for a second believe your friend will surrender the chase. This other Professor—this

Moriarty—has pricked your colleague's ego and interest. No, I think Mr. Holmes will stay on the trail for a while longer, at least. Tell you what—finish out the week working with him. I'll work it out from the university's end. I think there is still work for you to do, albeit clearly not undercover work, anymore. Despite his boorish behavior, I *do* have an appreciation for Holmes' deductive and investigative skills. Only a fool would deny those qualities in him."

More than a bit skeptical, I accepted my instructor's offer and said a cool goodbye.

When Groves was gone, Holmes straddled his chair, armed with a fresh and heaping cup of steaming death. "Cynical as this may sound, you probably could have exploited certain urges and held onto that sports car for a while longer, you know, Watson. I rather enjoyed having on-demand wheels with that sort of horsepower."

I reached across the table and closed a hand over his. "No worries. I have a car of my own. It's at campus, so we'll have to cab it one more time. It's an Audi. Not sporty like the other, not close to a muscle car, but it's perfectly fine."

That was all silly bravado—my own car was two steps, *just maybe*, above a beater.

Holmes nodded and suddenly held his fingers to his lips. He checked the door, presumably to ensure Professor Groves had indeed left, then reached over and tugged my coat from the back of the empty chair where I'd carelessly slung it.

He reached under the collar of my coat, at its back and showed me a silver disk that had been secured there with a thin strip of two-sided tape.

Holmes dropped the metal disc on the floor, then ground it under the heel of his Doc Marten. It crunched softly.

I said, "Some kind of a listening device?"

"Yes, another bug of some kind."

"And you're going to tell me Groves put it there?"

"Who else?"

He frowned and reached into his overcoat's pocket. He showed me his vibrating smart phone. "It's Mycroft," he said. "He's requesting—that's pretty much the same as *demanding*—an immediate audience with the two of us." He smiled and said, "An invitation by name for you. Astounding. It seems you've pierced the inner circle with my big brother."

"So we go to him?"

"Of course. Mycroft's coming to you yesterday was something unprecedented. He's a man of limited stamina and fixed horizons. As you can probably deduce from his girth, my brother's not remotely given to motion for its own sake."

"Where are we going, exactly? He's so secretive about his job that I can't imagine we're being invited to an office or official installation." I smiled uncertainly. "Or am I maybe somehow wrong about all of that?"

"On the contrary—it was a perfectly sound deduction based on what you know of Brother Mycroft," Holmes said. "No, we'll not be going to his office, wherever that may be. Rather, we'll be going to his private club. But rest assured that it's a suitably unusual place all on its own, and one entirely befitting my queer elder brother."

30

The Diogenes Club occupied a four-story, austerely gray, old tomb-like building near Wall Street.

"I won't spoil this for you," Sherlock said. "You really must take it in as it comes. Having said that, from this moment on, you must not say a word until Mycroft or I allows it. Really, Jona, not a single word, not even a soft cough, if you can manage it. This club actually demands total silence. *Total silence*. If you want a drink or some other refreshment, you'll gesture to a waiter and then write a note for it. You'll see no members interacting beyond an utterly silent game of chess. Any noise from even a guest can result in a strike against the longest-standing host club member. Three strikes, and a member can face banishment."

I gave a short little laugh. "Then how in God's name are we going to talk to your brother?"

Holmes brushed my wind-blown hair behind my ear and said, "They have what's called the Stranger's Room. It's the only place in the stodgy dump were anyone is permitted to speak. Consequently, it's quite soundproof."

God. "Leave it to your brother to join such an absurd club," I said.

Holmes smiled, his hand poised at the doorbell. "Joined? Hardly. Mycroft is no joiner. He practically founded the place."

A slightly meaner smile: Holmes adjusted the collar of his coat and said, "Really, no other club would have the bastard."

With that, Holmes stabbed the doorbell with a thumb. Frowning I said softly, "Maybe broken? I didn't hear a thing."

"It's all done with lights," he said. "Now, hush, really!" A pale, slender finger held to his lips.

Smiling but silent, I leaned in and kissed his fingertip.

Holmes was in the process of giving me a mock-cross look and then a kiss but he terminated that move for contact as the door opened on eerily silent hinges.

An elderly, very thin and birdlike man in a tuxedo glared at us. He focused most of his attention on Holmes and then crooked a finger, gliding silently back inside to hold the door for us. He shut it behind us without sound, then again crooked his finger to bid *Follow*.

On tiptoe, I followed the two black-clad men up a spiral staircase to a paneled, second-floor room with a scattering of wing chairs, an old leather couch and a bay window overlooking Wall Street.

The little man in the tuxedo held up five fingers, then he vanished.

"So, we have a few minutes," I whispered.

"So it would seem," Holmes confirmed. "And there's no need to lower your voice now. This place is quite soundproof, as I said."

"Then you've been here before? That odd little penguin evidently knows you and to whom you're connected."

Holmes nodded. He shook out a cigarette and lit it. "I told you, Mycroft is a sedentary man who moves only in a decidedly cramped and exceptionally undemanding orbit. His brownstone is just across the street, in fact. If he has an office, I correspondingly expect it must be within a block or so of here, as well. But yes, as you asserted, I tend to find myself mostly called here for the odd audience, from time to time."

I crossed to the big, rain-streaked window to get some distance from Sherlock's cigarette. A motorcycle cop sat astride his bike below, shivering in a waterproof poncho and looking up hatefully at the cold rain dampening the late lunch hour bustle. He spotted me staring at him and nodded.

A heavy tread on the groaning steps of the spiral staircase; there was still just time to impulsively ask: "Holmes, are your parents still alive?" Brothers—the thought put me in obvious mind of family.

Yet the question seemed to startle Holmes. I sensed I was being given unearned credit for an astoundingly astute deduction: there wasn't an intact family. I could see it in his eyes.

He hesitated for a moment, eying the doorknob as the heavy footfalls reached the landing.

"Just one of them is still around," Holmes said. "My father—but only a shade of the man he once was. A kind of specter."

Perfect and probably deliberate timing on Holmes part: he fell as silent as the rest of the building as the knob twisted this door's too-seldom used hinges gave out a tiny but tortured squeak.

Short of breath from climbing all those stairs—the building was grandfathered in and so could legally forego elevators—Mycroft stumped in on his cane. Florid-faced from his climb, he still managed to beam at me. He closed the door and patted my shoulder. "So pleasing to see you again, Ms. Jona Watson, and so soon? Although once again, I find myself wishing the circumstances decidedly different."

I patted his beefy arm and said, "Something tells me circumstances will never be otherwise, Mr. Holmes."

"*Mycroft*, my dear, please." He said it with a sad smile that could only be taken as agreement with my observation about the probable conditions of any future meetings. Mycroft said, "On a far happier note, I've taken the liberty of ordering drinks sent up. They'll arrive through the dumbwaiter over there. A fine and exceptionally dry red wine. Cigars for you and I, Sherlock."

Holmes said, "Very kind of you, Brother Mycroft."

A scattershot of wind-driven rain struck the window. Drawn to the sudden commotion, Mycroft moved to the bow window and gazed down at the street. He waved an arm, gesturing that Sherlock and I should join him there.

"It's a splendid view," the elder Holmes said. "I constantly forget that. From here, one can see it all—the sweep and variety of the city and those who choose to call it home."

He gestured with a meaty hand and said, "Take those two, right there," Mycroft said.

Taking up a seat on a ledge by his bulkier brother, Sherlock peered down and said, "The two women taking cover from the sleet under that canopy across the street? The beautician and her client, the left-handed lesbian lawyer?"

"That's right," Mycroft said. He gave his younger brother a challenging, cunning smile. "What else do you make of them, Brother Mine?"

A monogrammed and now damply clinging smock made it clear enough to me the cosmetics profession of the one woman—she was also taller, a bit overly made up. Yes, clearly she was some kind of hairdresser. I voiced my observation as my Holmes sized the two up with his characteristic, sweeping-here and darting-there glances.

The younger of the Holmes brothers smiled at me and said, "The smock is a too-easy pathway to the right answer, of course. But subtract the smock and one still can arrive at no other occupation for the taller of the two women," Sherlock said. "Beauticians and cosmetologists might be very adept at making others look what the rest of society regards as won-derful, but they rarely look so smashing themselves. They tend to use themselves and their co-workers as guinea pigs, of course—pushing the styling envelope and serving as early adopters of the edgier and more avant-garde aspects of their ghastly trade. Take that very electric fuchsia fingernail varnish for one thing—much too gaudy, particularly in the fall. Very against, or, to be more charitable, very *ahead*, of current fash-ion. The hair—that tint is also quite outside nature or vogue. So, a beautician."

I nodded and said, "But the *left-handed lesbian lawyer?*"

Sherlock nodded and said, "It's early in the afternoon, but she's obviously headed home, given the grocery bag she's car-rying—bread and a bottle of wine are visible at its top. Her blazer is workday appropriate of course, but rather severely structured in the shoulders and she's wearing it over that V-neck T-shirt in a kind of defiant statement. She is therefore her own boss and sets her own hours. The leather attaché case hanging from her right arm—which makes her left-handed, by the way, because she's using her dominant arm to support the grocery bag—is monogrammed. It's common enough to see the same bag on the shoulder of innumerable lawyers in this city, male *and* female. It's the bag of the moment for those in the trade."

"Our attorney has also recently gone through a break up of course," Mycroft said. "Or, perhaps she was widowed, although I favor the former hypothesis for obvious reasons."

I was at sea again. I said, "Explain this break up stuff, please."

Sherlock ground out the stub of his cigarette and got another going. "She's in a kind of recovery mode," he said thoughtfully scrutinizing her. "Wine bought at this hour of the day almost always portends alcoholism or solace in a bottle. I favor the latter because she so no signs otherwise attendant with an early afternoon drinker.

"As to the seriousness of the relationship that has ended," he continued, "it's signaled by that *other* bag she's carrying in her left had, the one from Toys R Us. Clearly there is a child in the mix and—"

"*Children*," Mycroft cut in, gently correcting his younger brother. "*Children*, Sherlock. You see, she's purchased a Disney Princess doll *and* a Lego Batman set. We can therefore assure ourselves of there being a boy *and* a girl child at home."

"I concur," Sherlock said, "and I stand corrected on the issue of the progeny. Given the body language and closeness with which they are standing together, this beautician is our lawyer's frequent confidante and has some of her own romantic interest in her client. Look at the way she's playfully peeking into the bag to see what the fixings for dinner will be. There is at once an intimation of flirtation and a simultaneous hint of jealousy we now observe in our hairdresser's realization that there is a bottle of wine in the mix—a particularly fruity and rather sweet varietal, which few men indeed would be likely to tolerate, let alone favor. So, again, there is a *woman* who will be dining with our lady attorney this evening."

"Yes," Mycroft said, "As I reflect upon it, I suspect this is a kind of family first date and a pivotal introduction to the children . . . The toys, viewed in this new light, now become rather more like peace offerings than comforting consolation prizes."

"Or strategic distractions," I offered.

"Quite so," Mycroft said smiling. "Couples do enjoy their play time alone, of course. But enough of this chinning one's self. One could lose hours in this window, just observing along these lines. It's the perfect spot for people-watching and for the mild exercising of the deductive muscles."

"You're right," I said. "And I could easily spend the rest of the day watching you two do just this sort of thing," I said. "It's really pretty wonderful to behold."

Mycroft gestured at the couch and said, "Please do sit down, Jona. I'll ask Sherlock to see to our wine when it arrives in our little elevator over there."

I sat down on the couch, again at some distance from my Holmes and his poison cigarette while Mycroft settled his bulk into a big distressed leather chair I took to be his kind of unofficial throne in this room: The contours in the old leather cushion hinting of the particular bottom accustomed to resting there that I glimpsed before he sat down put the thought in my head that this room was indeed Mycroft's office—if he indeed had such a place—and that this chair in which he now sat was his exclusive and de-facto office chair.

There was a soft buzz across the room and Holmes balanced his cigarette on an ashtray stand at his end of the couch. He rose to fetch the wine and cigars.

As he did that, Mycroft smiled and said to me, "By the way, my dear, one has used what little influence one possesses this side of the Atlantic to exert gentle force on certain parties to ensure you're paid for services already rendered. And, from now on, you're on special retainer at the same salary by Her Majesty's government as my personal operative. I've also spoken with the university officials, and your prior arrangement for credits is firmly in place and now fully executed. You need only show up once more there to clear out your dorm room and to accept your diploma."

He glowered and said, "And let's be clear on this point and with no argument: your compromised instructor is very much out of the picture. I should be very surprised if he still enjoys tenure this time next week. In a few months, I doubt he even retains his liberty."

As he fiddled with the corkscrew, Sherlock said, "So who's to join us?" He nodded at the fourth goblet that had come up in the dumbwaiter.

"The head of our fair young friend's supposed family here in town with whom she's supposedly quartered, is whom we await," Mycroft said. "It was pure happenstance that Jona's former handlers selected the Professor's primary and to-then elusive but so necessary *quarry* in order to accelerate the consummation of his planned high-jacking of Omnivore.

"Once the Professor—via Jona while still in disguise— had the taunting taste of our soon-to-arrive guest, he simply couldn't let it go.

"Now that Moriarty's conniving niece and his house of ill-repute are no longer viable assets for his crimes, the Professor is seemingly doubling down—scrambling to find some *other* means to gain sway over one Mr. Jared Phelps."

Sherlock handed us both glasses of wine and then sat down again on the opposite end of the couch from me. As his brother fiddled with his cigar, Holmes eyed his cheroot, then placed it on a side-table, presumably for later enjoyment.

Thank God for that. The cigarette smoke was bad enough—but dueling cigars? *My God.* I was already craving the shower I'd be taking upon my return to Baker Street. And there was no denying the cigar smoke challenged my lungs.

"I do hope you're keeping Mr. Phelps under guard, Mycroft," Sherlock said. The obvious notion, if the man is completely impervious to blackmail, would be to assassinate him, then shift focus to his inevitable successor."

"There simply is no successor of that kind in place," Mycroft said. "I place sufficient trust in Moriarty's near-omniscience to presume the Professor knows that, too. And Mr. Phelps seems of very good character indeed. No, Sherlock, I fear the Professor is instead focusing on Mr. Phelps' wife, Annie. She is rather much more compromised, and in ways her husband does not begin to grasp."

Mycroft made a sour face and said, "Let's not beat around the bush. It's this way: this woman comes from extremely humble roots. She put herself through school with funds gleaned from certain dance establishments, and, yes, some very low film work of a sort. DVDs of the latter still exist, though they are quite outside the knowledge of her devoted, powerfully placed husband."

I sipped my wine—felt this wonderful numbing on my tongue's tip: it was smoky, dense and sublime. I said, "The goal being, I suppose, to protect this man from any revelations about his wife's past while somehow shielding this man from the Professor's clutches?"

Mycroft nodded and sipped his own wine. "Yes, that would be the hoped-for outcome, at least to a starry-eyed idealist. I'm afraid I'm no such a creature. I'd love to keep the wife's secret and will endeavor to do so until such time it threatens the greater good. My simple hope for now is to take this man willingly off the playing field. Engendering confidence in my brother and your own skills as investigators and agents of real effectiveness are key to that strategy. If we succeed in making this man agree to take his wife and go abroad for some measure of time— under competent guard of course—it will then be incumbent upon you and brother Sherlock to neutralize Moriarty or at very least succeed in nullifying the threat he presently poses to her and, by extension, the infinitely more valuable husband."

I wet my lips and said carefully, "Forgive me please for thinking wrongly if I am, but it seems to me neutralizing Mr. Moriarty would be the easier, surer path. But having said that, *really* neutralizing him would almost certainly take some kind of assassination, wouldn't it?" I looked into my glass and ventured, "The Professor just doesn't strike me as the quitting kind . . . "

"One has to acquire a target in order to direct fire of that rarified sort, Jona," Mycroft said dryly. "And rest assured, I'm not asking you or even my dear brother to serve as state-sanctioned assassins. It's not Sherlock's line of trade or even really mine."

Mycroft sampled more of his wine and said, "Happily, we're perfectly fine simply achieving a holding action for a few days. Certain heroic efforts are underway to redirect key components of Omnivore, even now—essentially undermining if not even reversing gains already made by the Professor through his Portsmouth blackmail operations. With some luck and perseverance, in two days, three at most, all of the professor's current assets will be rendered moot and any pressure he might further endeavor to exert over Mr. Phelps or his wife will be ensured to be gratuitous."

I thought about that then said, "Unless he's simply the vengeful sort. Which I think he is."

Mycroft was dismissive of that prospect. "That's quite out-side my reading of our nemesis' personality. He's too logical and coldly analytical an animal to wield destructiveness sim-ply for its own sake or for petty revenge. No, I think when the Professor finds a door closed, he simply seeks a new avenue, rather like coursing water seeking its own level and path of least resistance."

Pea-sized hail now struck the window glass, propelled by the gusting wind. A tornado siren howled from somewhere, its banshee cry oscillating as it twisted in circles to raise the alarm.

The wind leaned its bully weight against the glass again, the frames groaning.

The brothers exchanged a look and shrugged. Mycroft said simply, "This building has no basement, and it's positively riddled with windows."

Sherlock refilled my glass—I'd nervously shot-gunned the first in a kind of pulsing burst—a mix of nervousness and exhilaration being privileged to witness the Holmes brothers going toe-to-toe deductively.

A light over the door flashed. Mycroft took a puff of his cigar and said, "Jona's former *guardian* elect has arrived. If nobody objects, I'll handle first discussions."

But this one time the elder Holmes was wrong in his deduction; it was not through any fault of his own.

He couldn't see who was coming up and so had no data to impel him to a different conclusion regarding the identity of the person on the other side of the door.

But the man who entered the room with the three of us was clearly a cop—city police—a plain-clothes detective, to be precise. He was a not so tall, yet not so bulky a man. He was ferret-faced, with gray streaked hair and too-small, very dark eyes. Confirming my conclusion about his profession he said to me, "Detective Gregory Lestrade, ma'am." Turning to the men he said, "Mr. Holmes?"

The brothers simultaneously said between puffs. "Yes?"

Looking mildly confused, the police detective focused squarely on Sherlock and nodded as if they were already acquainted. Half-smiling, I put down my wine glass and pointed from one Holmes to the other. "I said, "Sherlock and this is *Mycroft* Holmes. They're brothers."

The cop turned to Sherlock. "I'm here because I found this address on a slip of paper in the pocket of a man's jacket about twenty-minutes ago, Mr. Holmes." The cop's dark eyes looked at the three of us searchingly, then said, "The man was quite dead, I should add."

Damn. I wanted to say, "Jared Phelps?" But I held my tongue, waiting to see how the Holmes brothers would field this twist.

The cop—this Lestrade—lamented, "Two whole weeks without crossing paths with the city's only consulting detective. It's one day short of a record."

So there was some history between Lestrade and Sherlock Holmes.

Sherlock waved a hand as if brushing aside a fly and said, "There *are* the infuriating lulls when the criminal class deeply and profoundly disappoints, Lestrade. I fear we've been dwelling in that sad gully, together. But I take it we now have a case as you allude to a body?"

"There's that." The detective said to Sherlock, "So this man here is *really* your brother? There are actually two of you?" He jacked a thumb at Mycroft. "Can't say as I see it."

"I am his elder brother," Mycroft said. "We're to take it that Mr. Jared Phelps is dead?"

"That's right. How do you know that?"

"We were expecting him." Mycroft drew again on his cigar, then expelled a stream of pungent, blue-gray smoke and said, "I was facilitating a contact between the dead man and my brother, the consulting detective. I'm simply a connector, so to speak, detective."

The cop's dark, too-small eyes sharpened. "Yes," he said sibilantly. "I see."

Sherlock balanced his cigar on his ashtray's edge. He rose and steered Lestrade to a corner by the rain-streaked window, still being pelted with hail. "How did Mr. Phelps die?"

"A single gunshot to the head. He was found in his car. We believe it was self-inflicted."

I thought to myself, *So he's moving beyond the sullied wife* . . .

Lestrade said, "There's another body in the mix. You see, this looks like murder-suicide. It appears Mr. Phelps shot his wife, then left the house, drove to a parking lot about three blocks from here where he placed the barrel of his automatic against the roof of his mouth, and there he pulled the trigger."

"And there's more," Lestrade said. "Across town, a Mr. Matthew Burnett and his family—a wife and an 11-year-old daughter—were found shot to death in *their* home. We've been told Mr. Burnett would have constituted Mr. Phelps' probable successor at his workplace."

Well, my thesis was blown to smithereens . . . and drenched in more innocent blood.

Moriarty wasn't emerging as some "Napoleon" of crime, as Holmes had once described him, but rather as a mad-dog killer.

His voice now pure and pained gravel, Holmes said to Mycroft, "Scorched earth."

Lestrade said, "Sherlock Holmes, I need to know what is going on and what you know about all these people. I demand a suspects list, right now, for knowing you, you certainly already have one."

At this point I began to tune out, to keep my own counsel.

I'll confess that until the precise moment of Lestrad's revelations about the murders, I'd secretly tended to think of Professor Moriarty as a kind of dark-side-of-the-moon version of Sherlock Holmes:

Hyper-intellectual, coldly logical.

Very Mr. Spock, so to speak, but maybe the evil, mirror-mirror edition, a goateed and coldly homicidal Mr. Spock— the one from the other side of the looking glass.

Looking disgusted as Sherlock and Lestrade verbally jousted, Mycroft stubbed out his less-than-half smoked cigar. "Damnation," he said so only I could hear. "Moriarty's obviously written off Omnivore. Scorched earth, indeed, as Sherlock said."

I whispered back, "Why don't I feel like that should come as better news than it seems right now?"

"Because you're canny—well-attuned to human weakness and guile," Mycroft whispered back. "As you all too well grasp, this is no victory. It's a tantrum and a closing out of the Professor's interest in Partington. It's simply a bloody intimation Moriarty must have something still bigger, possibly even darker, that he is shifting his sights to now."

31

In my far more sedate Audi, the driving rain sloshing over the overtaxed wipers and the visibility just this side of white-knuckle lousy, I was half-listening to the Handsome Family again.

Squinting to try and stay in our lane and a safe distance from whatever might be in front of us in the whiteout rain, I said, "Your brother thinks Moriarty has moved onto something even bigger than Omnivore, whatever that could possibly be. Your thoughts?"

"Mycroft's just guessing," Sherlock said bitterly.

He tapped a cone of cigarette ash into the wet wind through his briefly cracked window. "But I'd only be guessing too, at this point." He glanced at me and said, "You know how much I abhor such foundationless flights of fancy."

Sighing, Holmes tipped his head back against the seat's headrest and closed his eyes. "My God, but how I dread the days ahead and all the tedious waiting for some sign of Moriarty's next enterprise. My God, the interminable and terrible waiting."

Holmes turned his head and gave me the most pitying look. "I selfishly confess I'll desperately need you to try and distract me while we endure this unknowable interval together. I'll be more than a handful, Jona—bank on that. Deprived the stimulation of a definable problem to solve, I'm really quite a beast to suffer in my own right, I'm afraid. This wait for Moriarty's next surfacing is going to be particularly hard on you, I fear."

There was a long moment of hesitation from Holmes.

I said, "Knowing it could be that way, can't you just try very hard to have it be otherwise?"

He shook his head. "We are who we are. And Watson, I'm simply abysmal, even dangerous to myself and to others faced with inactivity. I inevitably look for . . . let's call them artificial stimulations. Chemical distraction is my pass-time of choice, too often."

I saw that my knuckles were even whiter now than they'd already been from gripping the wheel in fear of the weather conditions. I consciously relaxed my grip. Holmes saw me do that, of course. His restless, sharp eyes never missed anything that might provide him psychological or emotional insight into another.

Forcing a smile, I said, "So, what—in your down periods you somehow manage to consume even *more* coffee and cigarettes than you already blow through? Is that what you're saying?"

I really hoped that was all that he was saying.

Holmes gave me a long look. "We both know that's hardly possible. No, it's usually cocaine, if I'm flush. Sometimes opiates—maybe prescription medications. Until the case drought blessedly subsides."

"Is it the same for Mycroft?" I wondered.

"Once, sometime ago, it might possibly have been like that," Holmes said. "But my brother's embraced asceticism.

Not sure that same capacity is in me. Mycroft strives for a kind of stillness. I desperately crave action, motion, even if it must be undirected or artificially provided."

For a solid week, I spent an intense period of sharing rough but heady sex, early morning newspaper scavenging and incredible coffee binges with my increasingly difficult to live-with lover.

In theory, a woman has infinitely more capacity for sexual activity than a man can ever match.

In reality—my particular reality, of course—I couldn't begin to keep up with Holmes as his "engine" slowly but steadily turned in on itself as not only Moriarty, but the whole of the city's criminal class seemingly went dormant—all the murder and mayhem slipping into an unrelenting interval of unknowable duration that ran Holmes to the ragged edges of manic collapse.

It was a fearsome thing to behold—let alone to try and hold back with one's body and increasingly tested affection.

Yes, Holmes simply and truly couldn't cope with stillness and placidity, just as he'd warned. He was drowning in the calm seas of inactivity.

Watching that hyperactive, great brain begin to spin against its own drive was a harrowing thing to behold—the more so because I'd fallen so hopelessly in love with the man.

Irresistibly, I increasingly imagined how many terrible similar periods of this particular brand of torture might lay in wait when Holmes would again be confronted with similar, inevitable fallow periods.

I wasn't sure I could endure another few days like the ones I was struggling through with Holmes now—trying to bind him to the world and to anchor him with my sex and 24-7 companionship, so desperately trying to keep my lover from imploding.

A Sherlock Holmes deprived the stimulation of a crime to solve was indeed the forbidding challenge that Holmes had fairly warned me about those many days ago. Trying to stare down the abyss with Holmes was a sublime and exhausting experience.

Of course I had lived with an expanding black hole at my periphery every day for the same as all of my life. I had successfully done that for all my years and would for all of my remaining years as I walked with the threat of my own death every step along my path.

But this thing of Holmes' was something well apart from my sort of personal, perpetual hell. I ran from the constant threat of my death every day of my life, while Mr. Sherlock Holmes ran from the constant threat of the normal and mundane life most would welcome.

But Holmes was in no way content to simply exist, just to *be*.

Somehow, someway, my burden seemed to me to be so much easier to shoulder than this thing pressing down upon Holmes that I'd sworn to stand witness to . . . and sentinel against.

After drumming the tabletop hard for more than an hour, little rivulets of blood were actually starting to leak around his fingernails' edges as he desperately sought some new distraction—some problem to set his fantastic mind to.

32

For two more indescribably terrible weeks, I endured this awful limbo with Holmes in Baker Street.

As he steadfastly, stubbornly deployed his irregulars, trying to catch any hints of Moriarty's probable next plot, restlessly trolling crime blogs and wading through newspapers, I moved in more furniture—his, mine and some stuff we picked out together in thrift shops when I could at last drag him away for some fleeting distraction elsewhere in the city.

It was the comfort and reassurance of nest building . . . at least it was so for me. Arranging furniture, hanging pictures and touching up paint was my therapy for dealing with the stress of striving to hold together a disintegrating Sherlock Holmes.

Standing in our sitting room that was slowly taking shape, I glanced over at Holmes and saw he was sitting cross-legged on the floor, engulfed by discarded newspapers, pecking away at his iPad, still trying to connect dots that refused cohesion, a driven, desperate man, wholly possessed but ultimately, perhaps tragically undirected.

It was like watching a stubborn old dog re-trace the same fading scent, over and over, hoping the next chase after an ebbing spoor trail would somehow miraculously produce a different result.

Of course it did no such thing in this case: Every potential thread Holmes grasped and tried to follow led nowhere.

At some point he looked at the carpet, streaked with vacuum cleaner swaths and said rather meanly, "You sweep eccentrically, Watson—side to side across the room, moving backward to the door. It's like the sweeping pattern of someone with obsessive compulsive disorder or a tyro trying too hard to expunge a crime scene."

Hurt, I stared at him. "I suppose I'd take either as a sideways compliment from you as things stand now," I eventually said back. "You're fucking impossible, you know."

Quietly satisfied after a full day of decorating, sitting with legs tucked under me in a comfy old chair and a knit afghan bundled 'round, nursing a glass of strong but cheap Chianti, I read a true crime paperback and listened to Handsome Family's creepy *Far from Any Road*.

Occasionally, I looked up to watch Holmes pacing like a dervish, chain smoking and making a shambles of my carpet sweeper patterns with his endless trekking back and forth.

I maintained my usual watchful eye to make certain he didn't resort to worse poisons than simple nicotine and caffeine, though I was nearly wrung out from my weeks-long vigil at this point.

Just as I thought I was about to lose this battle that increasingly seemed like some fresh but undeclared Hundred Years' War, Holmes froze mid-pace.

He was reaching for something soft to throw at me when he saw that I already saw something was up.

Tugging the ear buds lose by their cord, I said, "What is it, Holmes?"

He showed me his iPad and said hoarsely, "It's a Skype invitation from The Professor!"

This latest digital conversation with Moriarty was truly chilling.

The evil bastard sounded like he was at ragged ends, too, just like Holmes.

But there was thickness and sluggishness to the Professor's tongue—liquor or pills, or possibly both.

Something had the man positively *slurring*. Moriarty's true face was also nearly visible on the screen—he'd backlit himself so his head was a kind of blob with a false halo.

Where the Professor was almost dreamy sounding, Holmes, jacked up on liters of black coffee and God only knew how many coffin nails, was positively *manic*: Holmes' voice raced to the point of being nearly unintelligible at points.

These two badly fucked-up extremists struck me as the drugged-up yin and yang of crime and punishment.

Holmes practically sneered at the professor's ranting, demanding of him, "Are you calling to surrender yourself or are you simply calling to taunt?"

"I'm calling to freshly state terms, dear, dear boy," Moriarty slurred in response. "Calling to school you in how things must be from this moment forward since it's obvious you really were serious when you swore you'd not stand down."

Scowling, Holmes said, "Please, *Professor*, if this is to a scolding, or worse still, some kind of a lecture, I'm going to end this exchange right now."

A guffaw that degenerated into a coughing jag. The Professor said, "Oh, dear Mister Holmes! What exactly did you expect this to be? Did you envision some battle of wits, perhaps? Did you anticipate some chess game, with real people filling in as pawns and bishops? No, Mr. Holmes, you quite damaged me, I'm loathe to confess. You tore family from me and you cost me hundreds of thousands of dollars. The money you cost me derailing my Omnivore gambit is quite simply incalculable."

Holmes, said, "Mr. Moriarty, you're making my night with such confessions."

"You bloody fool! This is *not* fated to be some battle of intellects that you obviously crave. I'm a *businessman*, an entre-preneur. You're simply a stupid impediment to my aims. If you continue to be so, it will result in your inevitable destruc-tion. It's really that stark and simple. So, tonight, already, I have erased a mark or two from your victory column, Holmes. So go, run off now and check your doorstep, consulting detec-tive. What you will find there is simply the first of many such *erasures* that will continue until you fold your hand against me, forever!"

Holmes voice was its own terrible indictment: "*Mr.* Moriarty, who have you *killed*?"

The Professor's voice was equally awful now: "I don't mur-der anyone. I don't lower myself to those foul places."

A hiss back from Holmes: "No, you merely *order* it done, which is even more despicable. Still, it's all the same in the eyes of the law. Any blood spilled upon your orders is still very much on your hands, and you'll be punished accordingly when I bring you in. Now, again, *Mr.* Moriarty, who have you killed?"

"*Mr.* Moriarty," the Professor said in a credible imitation of Holmes voice. "You insist on that phrasing and I know why, now. It's because you cost me my position at university. You ripped my tenure from me. That was all your doing, Holmes, wasn't it?

"I've lately and freshly seized threads of my own, you see, Holmes. I've traced old, half-forgotten tracks. You've been my anonymous Hound of Heaven for years, stalking and harrying me. You've been waiting to tear out my throat, like a crazed cur. You've spun your web with your network of the down-trodden and with your stupid police friends. You certainly know something yourself about using people.

"You sit there in your infernal web, a malignant spider, feeling every quiver of the web you've spun, knowing every twitch. There are seven of my enterprises I now know that you cost me, Holmes. Maybe more. Well, it stops *now*. In tribute to her and in contrition for my beloved Breeana's loss, I draw this line in the sand: You stop this now, surrender this vendetta against me, or I'll kill everything and everyone you love and then, at last, when all is desolation for you—when it will come as a perverse favor—only then will I kill *you*."

Holmes snarled again, "Moriarty, who have you murdered?"

A chuckle: It was like someone dragging the tines of a fork down a chalkboard.

"Ironically, just as you were unknown to me, I was unknown to you, *Mr.* Holmes, at least in the early going. Yet fate, or God, or whatever name you want to assign the perceived-to-be supernatural agency that taints and engages us through this dreadful existence with flirtatious bouts of déjà vu, supposed irony and all these similarly phrased phantoms of circumstance and coincidence we grasp after to give meaning to the meaninglessness we insist demands meaning has somehow bound us together. It began long ago, I see now.

"You truly want to know who is freshly dead tonight? Then simply open your front door, *detective*."

How to describe the terrible change that came over Holmes face as it at last sank in—the identity of this person Moriarty was claiming to have killed?

Despite himself, Holmes said rather dully, apparently accepting the truth of Moriarty's murderous claims, "The Colson kidnapping. You've killed Sabrina Colson?"

The Professor called out, "Hah! Eureka! Now *run*, wretched Holmes! Go run down and check your step! See what's left of darling Sabrina!"

Moriarty's voice was positively manic at this point.

His ensuing cackle was more like a banshee's howl of delighted despair than a laugh. Soon, he was screaming.

I realized then that I was, too.

33

The sirens were long shut off and the crazy cop cars' party lights had at last stilled, the last cruiser sliding off from the curb and heading the other direction up Baker Street from where it had come some hours ago.

Holmes's voice, that silky baritone made raw by so many cigarettes while waiting out the crime scene—his voice that usually thrilled me—was now tortured as it told me the story of Sabrina Colson.

As he talked, I remembered.

This image I will carry with me always: Sabrina's body: to put it in clinical and straightforward terms, it had been *disarticulated*.

Holmes was a hawkish silhouette against the rain streaked window. He said thickly, "I fear I'm going to have to kill Moriarty. I think that's the only way to stop him, Watson. I simply must put him down like the rabid dog he's become."

I handed Holmes another coffee. I stood close to him, staring down at Baker Street, watching the streetlights and the headlights glint on the rainwater-filled potholes pocking the glistening pavement.

"It was the old trap we all face at the beginning of our careers," Holmes confided, nursing his java. "Particularly we who are truly entrepreneurs to use a phrase that Moriarty so twisted. You know: you can't get a job without experience, yet you can't get experience absent a first job.

"So, I inserted myself quite deliberately and firmly into an active police case in order to begin to make my name. It was a kidnapping, and quite infamous in its time—a true cable news sensation.

"The ransom being sought was enormous because the victim's father was suitably rich. The daring and execution of the snatching of the girl, our poor and luckless Sabrina—not to mention the audacity of the ransom asked—these should have signaled to me then something beyond a mere kidnapper was at work. I should have seen then all signs pointed to someone bigger and more malignantly majestic in scale—a true *éminence grise*. A goddamn Leviathan.

"You see, Jona, the mother defied the kidnapper's orders and ran straight to the police," Holmes said ruefully. "The FBI was involved before the father—a software and game design czar of incalculable wealth—even knew what was going on. The child was one of three, but clearly the rich man's favorite of his off-spring—and yes, don't look at me like that. All parents have their favorites, and don't let anyone else convince you otherwise, because I've experienced being second-best, dammit."

Holmes winced a little and said, "Anyway, the case was foundering in the hands of the mere official authorities. The FBI and the local police had reached a dead-end when their involvement became known and the kidnapper then immediately broke off all contact with the victim's family."

A long thin stream of smoke trailed curling across the rain-kissed glass. "The cops and the Feds pressed the notion on the rich father that it was a lost cause then. His daughter had surely been killed as the kidnappers had promised she would be once police or other authorities were known to be involved."

The next, of course, didn't require Holmes' saying, but I did it anyway, in his stead: "So you offered the desperate rich man your services. Probably dazzled him with some deductive insights about himself and he was at his wit's end, anyway—it was his *favorite* child, after all—he desperately sought a miracle and there you were. He leapt at the offer of this desperate, Hail Mary opportunity you embodied, just as any loving and clutching parent would. You saved the rich man paying the ransom, saved the girl and somehow screwed over Moriarty in the process, yes?"

I curled my hand around Holmes' neck and kissed his mouth, slow and hard. He kissed me back, softer, then hung his head. "Yes . . . " Holmes pressed his forehead against the chilly glass of the window's pane. "Yes," he said again. "The rich man and his beloved daughter were reunited and had three short years together because of my actions. My career was launched, even assured in all the right rich circles."

Holmes voice then began to give, sundering me: "And now? And now that *thing* on the porch . . . " His composure completely gave way. I held him close as he was racked with sobs.

I said softly, "Holmes, why didn't you tell Lestrade the truth? You never mentioned the name Moriarty to him."

He took my hand, wiping at his tears with his other forearm. "They'd never find him, and, if they did, do you really think they'd stand a chance taking that man alive and without terrible casualties to their ranks in the trying? I *do* have some conscience, Jona. I'm not prepared to send even Lestrade and company racing into that sort of bloody propeller blade."

I rubbed the back of his hand with my thumb. "So you really intend to go after Moriarty privately, to actually do it alone? You really mean to execute him?"

A dim smile—one that didn't include his eyes. "Well, I do have a partner," he said softly. "And a brother who has friends in high places. But the last of it—his actual killing . . . Yes, that will all be on me."

Head down, unable to look him in the eye, I said, "Holmes, your Professor is a full-on psychopath. I think we can both agree upon that much at least, now. His mind's completely given way. What was done to that poor girl's body—that was the work of a lunatic. Her slaughter makes it clear to me what kind of monster we're dealing with now. And you know I was in line for the same treatment not so long ago. This man is Jack the Ripper with a Mensa-level I.Q. But he needs to be *arrested* and tried. Convicted and then left to rot in prison forever.

"He needs to be made an example of, Holmes. You simply can't play vigilante and murder this man in cold blood. You can't! I can't help but think that would be your undoing in the most profound and terrible way. You're not above the law, as much as you might like to kid yourself. You're an honorable and just man. You're heroic in your way."

"I told you, there are no heroes in this travesty of a world."

"I couldn't disagree more with you."

"Then we'll just have to agree to disagree this one time," he said crisply.

Well, that wasn't reassuring.

I decided to change the focus, just a click or two, at least for the moment: "Well, before you can do *anything* to him, you first have to find Moriarty. You really think you can do that absent any fresh evidence?"

"I've all but settled on the notion it's not really a matter of finding him," Holmes said firmly. "He's far too clever to leave himself exposed. No, I think it's a matter of anticipating his next move."

I let Holmes' strategy sink in. I said, "He started at your shared beginning with Sabrina Colson. Are you presuming he'll proceed chronologically to the next of your then-unknown bouts with one another?"

"He is a mathematician after all," Holmes confirmed. "A self-styled astrophysicist. A man who thinks always in straight lines, in terms of cause and effect."

I grasped Holmes' chin between my thumb and forefinger. I searched his pale eyes and said, "Won't it be a further challenge to cast back and figure out what those cases might have been?"

"That *is* another vexing complication," Holmes admitted.

"Exactly," I said. "Even if he does try to *erase* these people in chronological order of some kind, you're still at the terrible disadvantage of first having to comb through all of your greatest hits, so to speak. You're left to try and figure out who's to be his next victim."

Sherlock Holmes had desperately craved an intellectual challenge and now he had one.

Holmes slammed a fist on the wall. "You're bloody right! It's a gift, not a curse!"

His elation wasn't remotely what I'd been going for, and terrified me in new ways.

34

Back in the Audi and with no rain pelting the windshield for once.

In a way, I missed all the recent rain, actually felt a real and inchoate sense of loss that deeply troubled me. But there'd surely be other rains after all, right?

Now, rather sadly to my mind, it was very much Indian Summer—clammy heat and the trees on fire with crazed bursts of vivid color.

We were presently headed far out of the city, even a good distance past Portsmouth, bound for the scene of Holmes' second, retrospectively arrived at "joust" with Moriarty, or at least so by Sherlock's reckoning.

"Who is this one, Holmes?"

Leaves whipping across our path; the Season of the Witch looming despite the current fleeting bout of heat and sunshine.

It was in October, many years ago this very month, almost to the day, that I'd been given what my maternal grandparents had unfortunately called within earshot of six-year-old me my "same as a death sentence."

Irony. The word came up a lot in my life. Too much, really.

Oh yes, whatever a Professor Moriarty or Sherlock Holmes might or might not think, irony very much existed in this tortured world, and it seemed to be my near-constant companion.

I was born on October 31—All Hallows' Eve. My parents learned on the same date of my congenital condition, this time bomb festering in my chest which medical science had no way to fix.

Yes, irony existed, and God? *She's* a comedian for certain, but not a funny one.

I turned up the volume on Springsteen's "Devils and Dust," trying to smother my train of thought. The lyrics didn't help much: "But I've got God on my side/And I'm just trying to survive."

We were hammering out the long dreary miles alongside some rain-swollen angry river.

Holmes, eyes closed and still riding shotgun, once again indulged a bit of time-traveling in another uneasy, monotone monologue:

"Arni Mosley was his name. He was a kind of mentor to me. Sort of like your Professor Groves, but minus the profound, later disappointment. My mentor consulted with the police from time to time and made powerful enemies in the community. Arni was, in a sense, more or less me, but long before I was really me, if you know what I mean. He was a kind of undeclared consulting detective, that's to say. The problem was, Arni didn't have the sense to do his consulting subtly, as I very much was bent upon doing. So Arni's number of potent and powerful enemies steadily accrued. Eventually, a few of them cohered—yes, they really joined forces. It was a potentially lethal case of dead weight finding its own level, you might say.

"These vengeful but not particularly clever criminals cast around for a kind of planner, and they found a man who could build an exquisite frame for a price. They set about having that man—it was Moriarty of course, *now* I know that, or I think that I do. Anyway, this mystery man dismantled Arni's life and reputation with one orchestrated scandal after another. I'll confess to you that at the time I was at best a sometimes uncertain counterweight to these destructive efforts against my friend, Jona. I was just barely equal to the task. Moriarty was truly formidable."

Sherlock Holmes' *mentor*. Surely he would be made to suffer even more than Sabrina had, if Holmes was right.

I pushed my foot down harder on the accelerator, more fallen leaves spewing and whipping in our wake.

Holmes was proven right: His mentor was a Moriarty target—one already successfully acquired.

And impossible as it had seemed just minutes before to imagine, yes, somehow, this murder succeeded in eclipsing the bloody deposit left on our Baker Street stoop. Maybe it was the fact that a CD purporting to depict the torture-murder of this good man had been left with the terrible remains that gave this killing extra edge.

This coroner also shared a rough time of death estimate with me after several variations on the theme of, "This is totally informal at this point, so don't hold me to this, my dear . . . "

Holmes heard the same data I did, but I sensed the terrible significance of the man's revelation was lost on a reeling, self-recriminatory Holmes.

When I realized Holmes had drifted away, I set off in search of him. I found Holmes in the common courtyard of his murdered mentor's Graystone building.

Holmes was smoking, staring up at the autumn stars that were barely visible through the downtown's light pollution.

He looked at me and said, "What have I done, Jona?"

I gripped his shoulders, stepping into him, getting up in his face. "Darling, you've done nothing *wrong*. This was *all Moriarty*."

He wasn't having that:

"Bullshit," Holmes snarled. "I kicked a goddamn rattlesnake in hubris. I stupidly incited all of this. Moriarty's killing these people only because of me."

He was right, of course, but I tried to stonewall it:

"That's not the way to look at this, darling, not at all." I wrapped my arms tightly around him. "But there *is* something to confront here. The coroner said—"

"I hardly heard the idiot," Holmes muttered. "What could the moron say that could matter a damn to me? Dead is dead."

He checked his watch. "Case number three by my reckoning centered upon one Stacia Lloyd. I'm the perfect fool, stupidly standing out here and moping when there's wild work to be done. We need to move like lightning, Watson. We'll head him off at the next intended victim's and then we'll at last have—"

"No," I said firmly, cutting him off. "No, I'm sorry, my darling, but the two coroners' time of death estimates *are* important. The girl, Sabrina, and your friend, Arni? Holmes, they share *identical* time-of-death estimates. I think the first two, and, sad to say, probably this Stacia Lloyd, and maybe some others you haven't even thought of yet, are already dead, and that they were all killed at once, more or less. Moriarty is simply too careful to make this into some kind of footrace between you, Holmes. And he explicitly told you that wasn't his game, after all—'no battle of wits' as he put it. We are not going to find this man by trying to head off presumed next killings. I don't think we're even going to save a life. Everyone he intended to erase from your victory column has already been dealt with. I know in my heart I'm right."

Holmes was clearly and freshly stricken. The terrible passion of my argument—buttressed by the coroners' identical time of death estimates—had landed with devastating force.

But I continued on: "Holmes, we're not going to beat this monster playing by any rules that he understands or can anticipate. We have to play a game this man has never played before."

"And how on earth do you propose that we do that," he asked disgustedly.

"Well, we need to think more on that," I said.

I did that quite lamely, I knew.

35

It developed in short course there were already indeed seven corpses in all, each one representing a previous and never formally declared Homes vs. Moriarty duel.

The Eastern seaboard was simply too small, or so it seemed to me as the body count mounted, for two such as Holmes and the Professor to ply their strange, and legally opposed crafts and not cross swords, time and again.

Four coroners, plus seven unimaginably mutilated corpses equaled a monolithic time of death estimate: Just as I'd feared, all seven had been killed more or less simultaneously, then the bloody detritus dropped here and there, again, pretty much simultaneously, but with an eye toward subsequent *incremental* discovery.

If this *was* some duel of wits, it was clear to me that the Professor was several moves ahead of us.

Now Sherlock was talking in fast, ragged tones to Mycroft on his mobile: "Like an assembly line of murder and mutilation," I heard him say. "Yes, clearly his mind's completely given way, Mycroft. Quite. Yes, totally insane now, on that point there is no longer any argument."

From there, the two began conspiring.

With nobody but the Holmes brothers or myself seemingly left to kill, they were desperately casting around for fresh ways to "draw the fiend out."

My Holmes grew silent for a while, listening to his brother go on for a time. Then Sherlock said, "I simply have to kill him, of course. Execution on behalf of the community. What other way is there? He'll *never* be successfully adjudicated—not with the probable reach and scope of his blackmail files. No, it has to be this way, and we both know that is so. Moriarty *has* to be stricken from the earth before he can do more harm."

There it was again—Holmes egging himself on to commit a *just murder*.

Sherlock said, "No, still no solid clue—at least for the moment—about where to even *begin* to look. But here's a thought about something we *might* do to provoke a response—to try and goad him to surface, though I confess it's not without considerable risk . . . "

No. Enough of this: My Holmes simply couldn't be permitted to murder *anyone*—not even someone as unremittingly evil as Moriarty.

I was no murderer either, and I had no attention of becoming one.

But I *could* find this man, I thought, and then I could place trust in the legal system if the evidence I could hand the state was irrefutable. Yes, I could gamble and turn this awful man over to the authorities—he'd blown up a police station and killed cops after all—so I trusted those same police to crave vengeance for their own, regardless of the rockiness of the ride possibly getting there.

And anyway, even Sherlock Holmes simply couldn't be right about the supposedly unfathomable scope of this man's blackmail material.

Sherlock was still engrossed in conversation with his big brother: These two towering brains showing off for one another in various and now malevolent ways, the one trying to dazzle the other with some terrible scenario for luring out Moriarty, capturing and then killing him.

Yet the undisputed geniuses were missing an obvious enough angle of attack, or so it seemed to me.

But given Sherlock's dark intentions, I wasn't about to offer my technical insight into what I saw as a sure-fire and relatively simple way of finding Moriarty.

While Holmes remained distracted in his feverish conversation with Mycroft, I pocketed my gun, quietly scooped up my car keys and eased out the door of 221B. On tiptoe, I made my way fast down the stairs and into the night.

Bats chased bugs in the cones cast by the streetlights.

There were more of those perpetual sirens in the middle-distance—again the sound of emergency squads, not police.

I slid behind the wheel of the Audi and set out for Portsmouth, driving fast.

The interim chief of police—very aware of my role as established by his murdered predecessor—was at least willing to hear me out.

It's not like I wanted so terribly much from the man: I simply made an impassioned plea to see Breeana's seized iPhone.

The police headquarters were still in a charred shambles and awaiting demolition, so we met in a double-wide trailer that had been hauled onto an off-lot as a temporary base of operations.

"We've been all over it, Jona," Chief Daniel Lynd said. He was fortyish, held himself straight, but wore a moustache that aged him. He also had intimations of a drinker's gut pouching above his gun belt and a slight tremor in his left hand.

He said, "Emails were routinely and completely deleted from the thing. The girl kept no contact list and never backed the phone up according to the message my tech guy received upon putting in a charger. No incriminating photos were found beyond some semi-dirty selfies. A dead-end."

I reiterated my contention—without putting a name to the person—that there might yet be a relative of some kind culpable in Breeana's crime—the actual murderous architect of the HQ's bombing.

My notions along such lines obviously amused the man.

I was playing Nancy Drew or Veronica Mars in his eyes, I figured.

The interim chief shook his head. "I'm fully prepared to believe there is someone other than this dead cheerleader behind all this—after all, she couldn't and wouldn't have arranged her own slaughter here. No, I agree with you that there is someone else still out there, but her phone isn't going to get us there, ma'am."

Smiling I said, "If you think you've gotten everything from it, then what could it hurt to give me ten or so minutes with the phone? I'm pretty tech savvy in my way. Please let me give it a try?"

He chewed his lip, then swiveled his chair around. He leaned over, opened a cabinet and drew out a sealed plastic evidence bag containing an iPhone. "Ten minutes. You can look at it right here. I've got some phone calls to return. Hope they won't distract you."

He meant to watch me search the phone.

Well, *okay*.

I smiled and broke the Ziplock seal on the bag with a tug at either side. "That's fine. And thank you, sir."

iPhones have a certain feature buried deep in their preference catalogues that even most technically adept sorts often don't know exists.

I wouldn't have known about the feature if not for catching a presentation on Fox and Friends on one of the several big television screens hung on the wall facing the treadmills one morning while working out at the gym.

It was just the kind of thing the Fox News Channel would embrace in a libertarian/paranoid frenzied sort of way, after all.

This particular built-in function essentially catalogues and tracks movements of each individual phone, creating a kind of mini-database of frequently visited places. This is all done to supposedly assist mapping facility and faster future direction requests.

Sitting in the parking lot next to the trailer, I'd first practiced navigating the preference list on my own phone, eventually finding this kind of greatest hits list of *my* most visited recent places: It came up the school in Portsmouth, Holmes' dingy apartment, our new Baker Street digs and this particular Starbucks, in that order.

Here's the *other* insidious thing about this particular tracking feature—even if you disable it, the thing quietly reboots itself with each and every system update.

So chances were that Breeana's phone would serve up a menu of visited places similar to my own phone's list.

This castoff admission of Breeana's about how she was receiving math instruction from her uncle continued to resonate for me . . . that likely had happened at some reoccurring, fixed point, I reckoned.

Even as the interim chief rattled on to some distant subordinate at the other end of the line, his eyes were still very watchful toward me. I held the phone's face where he couldn't see it and raced through the menus, drilling down to that particular, deeply nested function.

Yes!

It *was* still enabled.

Breeana's list of favored places included the Portsmouth School, that sex palace in the sticks and a Mott Street Address. After that, it was a couple of clothing stores and some Chinese Restaurant, also in Chinatown.

It was the Mott Street residential address I committed to memory, of course.

I backed my way out to the phone's main screen after clearing and disabling the feature so none could follow my path, then I continued to somewhat idly fiddle with the phone a bit, running through its Twitter feed to see if any relevant direct messages lingered, checking a few other social media services which, as this chief said, served up a fat lot of nothing.

As he wrapped up his second call, I passed the phone back to the man and whispered, "You're right. Nothing there. Thank you again for letting me try."

Before he could excuse himself from his call to press me further, I smiled, drew myself up and bolted.

Parked next to a Panera and, sucking up its Wi-Fi signal, I ran property searches on county auditor's websites for the Mott Street address.

Nothing illuminating there, either, at least not on face: The building was owned by something called Granger Properties, Inc. The particular address was probably for an apartment or loft—quite likely a rental.

Of course the Professor wouldn't be the kind to leave such an easily identifiable footprint. On a hunch, I looked up the property record again for the bordello he'd run in partnership with his slutty niece, and there it was again—Granger Properties, Inc.

I got out, rooted around my trunk, and prepped a rag, a can of starter fluid and checked my gun again.

As a light but steady drizzle began to fall, I set off for Chinatown to effect a kidnapping of my own.

Taking a note from Holmes, I found myself a young homeless woman and handed her a stack of newspapers. I asked she knock on doors, offering free samples of *The Post* in a supposed bid to hook new readers and generate subscription sales.

I gave the woman the particular apartment number I was truly interested in and made it clear I needed her to memorize the face of the person who answered so she could later provide me with a very solid and exact description of the individual.

Twenty minutes later, she returned, arms emptied of newspapers and hand extended for a promised twenty-dollar bill.

The person she described was male, about thirty, but prematurely graying and balding. She described a beetle brow, dark and deep-set eyes and thin slash of a mouth—"A kind of young version of Mr. Burns, ya know? I mean, from on *The Simpsons,* ya know what I mean . . . ? He even had a kind of yellow color to his skin."

I thought, *Liver disease? Some kind of jaundice from chemical or alcohol abuse?*

But satisfied she'd indeed met the Professor, I paid her, then I went to a Starbucks and used the restroom—wasn't sure when I'd get the chance again. I bought a stainless steel thermos that might also work as a cudgel in a pinch and had it filled with black coffee. I sprang for a bag of scones, then found the parking lot that served the professor's building and began my stakeout.

Ten minutes in, I received a text message: *Watson, where are you? You ok?*

I pecked back: *Fine, just remembered a doctor's appointment. Routine. Back as soon as I can be. Please don't worry.*

Then I typed our kind of special, recently and playfully arrived-at "safe-word", calculated to ensure one another no digital communication between was being coerced or faked: *My-Croft.*

I got back a terse, *OK.*

After, I powered off my phone, just in case Holmes decided to track me. It would be like him to do that, of course.

An hour later, motion on the deck of an upper floor's fire escape caught my eye.

A man, slightly bent, shoulders somewhat hunched, made his way down a back fire escape from the correct floor. He wore a black suit and black overcoat and was carrying an umbrella in one hand and a computer bag in the other. The description fit the one given me by my improvised "Irregular."

I didn't hesitate: As he continued to gingerly make his way down the damp metal stairs, I slipped on leather gloves, slid my Colt in my pocket, sprayed a generous dose of ether into the rag from the starter fluid can and cracked my car door so there was no chance of the man hearing it open as he drew closer.

Some very good luck for me: He meant to put his computer bag in the trunk of a black, new model Impala, its tail facing the front end of my Audi. As the Professor fiddled with his trunk lid, trying to stay dry and manipulate the keys in the lock, I slid out and padded up behind. I took a last deep breath, before springing—I'd already visualized each move in my mind several times before making my approach.

As the trunk lid rose, I straightened the cutting edge of my left hand and chopped sharply at the man's neck, just below the base of the skull. There was a soft, "Uh" and I knew the Professor's vision was for the moment a field of blackness dappled with fireworks.

While he was still dazed and his nervous system going haywire, I drove my left fist into his kidney to further stun him. Then with my right hand, I covered his nose and mouth with the ether soaked rag, holding tight until he went limp and crashed face first into his trunk. I shoved the rag back in my pocket, lifted and folded the Professor's legs into the trunk and cast in his umbrella and computer bag after his body.

Giddy at my success so far, I pulled the keys from the trunk's lock and slammed shut the lid. I ran back and secured a small bag from my car and locked up the Audi.

There was simply no knowing how long the ether would keep the wicked bastard under, so I drove the Impala just a very few blocks to a strip of abandoned warehouses and pulled under cover of a derelict, canopied parking lot, well out of sight of street traffic. I readied my gun, then popped the lid on the trunk, prepared to shoot if the man inside was already awake and combative.

No: A drool trail, heavy snoring. Not a pretty picture.

None too gently or easily, I manhandled the Professor from the trunk and let him fall hard onto the floor of the garage.

I'd deliberately pulled the car up close to a rusty, vented manhole cover—one perforated to facilitate the parking lot's water drainage. I handcuffed the Professor to the heavy grate—it hadn't budged when I'd test my strength against it and so figured it would hold him plenty well.

While I waited for the rain and resulting chilly run off to stir him to wakefulness, I went about systematically sweeping the interior of the Impala and its carpeted trunk with a hand vacuum. At last satisfied I'd left no tell-tale strand of hair—I'd kept my gloves on through the whole "abduction" so I had no concerns about fingerprints—I packed up my kit and bit my lip as I saw the man on the ground at last stir.

The Professor shook his head a few times and then frowned at the immobility of his right arm. He tugged sharply at his handcuffed wrist and then gave an animal snarl. Sensing my approach, he turned all attention to me.

I gave him my best smile, almost gushing, and said, "Professor Moriarty, I presume?"

36

B aker Street . . . warm and cozy.
   Flood warnings in the midst of an unrelenting, pounding rainstorm.

I was cozily back in my favorite chair, sipping Chamomile tea—I felt a sore throat coming on and was trying to head it off.

Meanwhile, Holmes was pacing relentlessly back and forth, nearly attacking his violin.

The door buzzer came as a terrible alarm.

Holmes went to the intercom, snarled impatiently, "Yes, dammit?"

"It's Lestrade, Holmes. We've got a report on a body having been found in an abandoned warehouse district not far from Chinatown. Death came from a single shot behind the eyes."

Well, here it at last came, I told myself. *Here we go . . .*

Holmes pressed a button and said, "Sounds rather like gangland stuff. Probably some Mafia nonsense. Why should I care?

Because there was an iPhone on the body that we were able to access using the body's thumbprint."

Clever Greg Lestrade, I thought, hanging on every word. *I should have thought of that.*

The detective continued though some mild static, "The phone contained enough to convince me this man—a man named Moriarty, by the way—may be linked to that case you were working with Ms. Watson in Portsmouth. The deceased appears to have been the uncle of the young woman killed in the police station bombing there. We think this uncle, this Moriarty, may even have been the prime-mover behind all of that. The missing mastermind, so to speak."

Some static, then, "Thought you might like to come and look over the scene. You know, just in case there's . . . " *something we're somehow missing* went unsaid.

Holmes, eyes flashing, said, "Of course. Down in just a minute." He turned to me and said excitedly, "You're coming of course, Watson?"

37

The body was quite soaked by now—it was still chained to a drainage gate, and it was still pouring rain.

Holmes got in close with his iPhone and started shooting his own crime scene photos. He got a close up of Moriarty's face with that small hole between the bushy eyebrows. The blue-gray eyes, still open, had become eerily opaque in death.

Holmes said, "Still strong indications of powder blast. The shot was then delivered at very close range, from a revolver of some kind I should think, based on the powder burns on the forehead."

"Yes," Lestrade said. "The slug was recovered—or a partial of the slug, at least. A forty-five caliber bullet. Won't be easy to check against anything, even if we should get access to the weapon, I'm afraid. Upon exit, the bullet struck at least two concrete surfaces. It's a mess."

So there was that . . .

"There would be power residue on the killer's sleeve and hands, gloves if she wore them," Holmes said.

Yes . . . For that very reason I'd discarded the gloves down a sewer catch basin, a few blocks from here. The coat I'd dropped in a Salvation Army bin several blocks further east from there.

Wait a minute: My God, did Holmes actually say *She?*

Lestrade said, *"She?* So you think the killer is a woman?"

"A strong woman or a not particularly strong man," Holmes said. "But most likely a woman."

Lestrade said, "How do you get there?"

"The car was deliberately parked close to the grate which was to be used as a restraining mechanism," Holmes said. "Parking close to the grate is a simple matter of convenience, of course. Anyone would reasonably wish to ration effort and exertion. But this killer couldn't lift the man's body from the trunk or shoulder it the brief distance to this spot, not based on the evidence before us. The body was instead dragged over the edge of the trunk—there are black, rubber-induced friction stains on the man's white shirt that would have come from the trunk lining's rubber seal. He was tipped out onto the pavement and then dragged to this spot, the killer's hands hooked under the armpits, as indicated by those black streaks on the pavement left by our Moriarty's shoes' rubber heels as they trailed along."

Holmes leaned in close to the body, almost as if to bestow a kiss upon the lips of the corpse. Instead, like some kind of bloodhound, he drew in a deep breath. He declared firmly, "Ether—the scent is unmistakable," Holmes said. "Probably car starter fluid in actuality, but used in this case to induce unconsciousness. Can you turn the body over, please?"

Lestrade nodded and two techs rolled Moriarty over so his face was pressed to the grate. I winced but made myself look along with the rest at the horrible wound the bullet's exit had made as it passed through the back of the man's skull . . . at all that mess left on the damp and bloodstained pavement.

"There's bruising at the back of the neck just here, you see," Holmes said. "The lividity from the blood settling for the past couple of hours *almost* obscures it, but it's unmistakably there. It's from a karate chop to the neck, delivered by the edge of the culprit's left hand, I'd suspect."

Right again; I had the very hand in my pocket presently to obscure its swelling and bruising.

The ether, the bruised neck: I suspected from the loitering expert's own expression and that of Lestrade that the now quite silent but observing coroner had missed both these points.

Just my luck Holmes would be called in for this one, but that had been a calculated risk, after all: It was a pretty assured fact if police identified the body and if Moriarty was linked to all that mess in Portsmouth that Holmes was going to get a call.

Oh, I'd thought about making that identification hard for them—taking the Professor's wallet and phone . . . any identifiable belongings.

But then I'd thought of Holmes, burning himself out in frustration awaiting some new sign of a Moriarty plot that could never come with the man secretly dead.

I simply couldn't endure that terrible prospect, not being its catalyst, and so this trail of breadcrumbs even a Lestrade could follow had been left in place.

Holmes next asked the Impala's trunk be opened and then, borrowing one of the crime scene techs as a Moriarty stand-in, he demonstrated—with terrible and precise accuracy—every move I'd made in rendering Moriarty unconscious and getting him in and out of that trunk:

"Blow with a left-hand, and then, with the professor dazed, the more complicated move of administering the ether was administered with the right hand," Holmes pantomimed. "So we deduce she's right-handed and fairly strong, for the professor was not a small man after all. I estimate him at six-one and two-hundred ten pounds. She's younger, because I'm prepared to believe she might have been a blackmail victim of the Professor's and we know how aggressively he was using young and even underage girls to his dark ends. It's a reasonable deduction in that sense."

"Sure," Lestrade said. "So we're looking for a fit, right-handed girl from Portsmouth who's been compromised in some way by this man, by his niece or quite likely by both the late niece and the uncle. Well, that certainly narrows the field . . . "

Sarcasm born of fresh frustration.

Sherlock smiled thinly and leaned into the trunk. He said, "She's very meticulous, this one as you can well see. Probably even has some sense of crime scene investigation process, and far beyond those fostered in the general public by simply devouring episodes of *CSI* or *Bones*. Note the fact she took the trouble to bring a hand vacuum along, which is no longer present here at the crime scene."

He pointed at the carpeting in the trunk. "See here the sweeping, side-to-side patterns she made from edge of the seat partition, working backward toward the trunk's edge . . . it's really very distinctive. It's actually strangely famil—"

Holmes stopped cold, broke off in mid-word.

I shivered: The final tumblers had just clicked in his great brain. *I knew it.*

So now *he knew*. He'd caught me, same as red-handed.

Holmes pretended to survey a bit more of the crime scene. He made some further, out-loud deductions I knew to be quite wide of the mark—observations that would send Lestrade and company running into cul-de-sacs and on into maddening dead-ends for days and perhaps even weeks to come.

My beloved Sherlock was covering for me, now.

As he did all that, we never shared eye-contact.

For my part, I tried very hard to look nonchalant, to tamp down the guilty blush I could feel threatening my cheeks.

My head was starting to throb with my elevated blood pressure. The swooning effect it had me scared me a little, for it had set my heart beating fast and uneven in some previously unknown, strange tattoo.

My doctor's overheard voice in my head, a child's life defining memory: " . . . never see forty . . . a miracle if she endures to thirty . . . " A child then, the age of thirty seemed so old—like something a lifetime distant.

I half-listened as even Lestrade began to rather too successfully embroider upon Holmes' scenario, venturing the notion the fit young female killer had walked from the crime scene a few blocks in the rain, then caught a cab back to the kidnap scene.

On the off chance the killer hadn't also walked or cabbed it to Moriarty's lot—had possibly driven there and left a car there for some period during the commission of the crime— Lestrade said that surveillance cameras had been sought in the area but, frustratingly, none had been pointed at the Professor's lot.

So I'd caught another break there: I hadn't even *considered* the possibility of my Audi being captured on some other building's security camera.

Lucky, lucky Jona Ormond Watson.

Angel of Death . . . sporty little self-appointed judge, jury and executioner.

Lestrade and Holmes at last said their goodbyes, the latter quite distractedly.

Sherlock and I walked in silence back to my Audi, the rain blowing in under our shared umbrella that was next to useless in this particular, near-sideways rainstorm.

Soaked to the skin, we drove back to Baker Street. Still no words exchanged.

Once inside, Holmes turned on me suddenly.

I was startled—my heart, already very overtaxed by the past few hours' physical and emotional strains—pounded quite crazily now, freshly scaring me with its crazy beat.

But then Holmes began to undress me; his mouth found mine.

After stripping one another bare we rolled to the floor.

We made love, hard and fierce, and then I melted into him. Although physically and emotionally wrung out, my heart was still going like crazy . . . my mind racing close behind.

38

I was again reveling in the afterglow: We were tangled around one another, the logs crackling in the fireplace whose light cast crazy, dancing shadows. Julee Cruise softly singing "Space for Love."

It was all fleetingly soothing, my pulse and dangerously racing heart were finally settling down. *Thank God.*

But The Professor's sneering face filled my vision and his crazed voice ranted on in my mind now and again—that brilliantly deductive mind of his hurling insults and barbs my way—nasty hurtful things he'd deduce about me and then attempted to use as skewers.

They'd hit home, every devastatingly accurate one of his cruel digs.

But then he had driven it all sideways. The master blackmailer had said coldly, "Everyone has skeletons, Miss Watson, and yours are comparatively tame against those of your lover, the consulting detective. I've spent the past two weeks digging deeply into the history of the Holmes family, my dear. In the course of the past fourteen days of wading through the swap that is Sherlock Holmes' quite miserable childhood history,

I've learned things about him that I will share with the world if I'm indeed brought into a courtroom and put on trial. Every bit as much as he means to destroy me, I will wreak equal or greater ruin upon Mr. Sherlock Holmes and his brother, this mysterious man named Mycroft."

As he squatted there in the white hush of the falling rain, my Colt pointed at the face of this terrible Caliban chained to the ground, I demanded that Moriarty explain explicitly what he meant by those new threats.

Smiling—a terrible, feral grin—the maw of a shark it seemed to me then, Moriarty repeated delightedly, "*Everyone* has secrets, Jona. You and especially your Mr. Sherlock Holmes. Your Mr. Holmes is a murderer, too, you see. He committed the most heinous crime of all. I speak of the crime termed *matricide*."

Moriarty gave me a look of mock-pity and said, "No, don't scowl that way, Jona. Don't scoff. There can be no doubt. Your Mister Holmes killed his mother, and his brilliant and protective elder brother helped to cover up the crime. The great consulting detective liquidated his own mother. *That's* the story I'll tell the world if you don't let me walk away from here, right now, my dear."

I'd pressed for more, of course. There was too much at stake not to get a full account of this terrible supposed crime of Holmes' that I still could hardly get my mind around.

I needed to be convinced of Holmes' guilt in order to relent and unleash a monster of Moriarty's scale back upon the world.

I said as much.

Moriarty smiled and said, "Just so. That's very much to be expected. Very well, then. It's *precisely* like this, my dear Watson . . . "

Verifiable facts about Holmes' childhood and family life were decidedly scant, but there were some bits and pieces to be found, it seemed, if one knew the right newspapers to look for—the news accounts written just long enough ago to have escaped web archiving.

So Moriarty sought out scattered libraries' microfilm stores of forgotten, long-ago news editions. He combed through reels of the stuff.

And he eventually found his answers.

Sherlock Holmes' mother had indeed been killed—a "death by misadventure," the newspapers termed it. There was a strong sense she'd been killed in the process of attempting to kill another—had been taken out by something lethal that she had actually prepared for another to imbibe.

Mother Holmes was Wilhelmina Vernet. She came from a long line of bohemians and artists, all gifted with inherited wealth, and a lucky thing that was as nearly all of them lacked any ambition or drive, to hear Moriarty tell it.

Father was Andrew Scott Holmes, a cleric . . . taciturn, patrician and fiercely just. He was a man of cold reason, soaring intellect and a believer in absolute justice, as distinguished from what others might regard as "the law."

His profession also precluded divorce once a union had been forged.

Clearly, as Moriarty described this Holmes, he was a calamitous match for the arty and flighty Ms. Vernet. But that unbreakable marital union was nonetheless forged.

The uneasy, friction-laden marriage produced two sons— first Mycroft, then, in an early January night seven years later, Sherlock.

My Holmes was only an otherworldly eleven years old when he correctly deduced his mother—devious, and self-centered Wilhelmina, sociopathic and, yes, *murderous* "Mummie"—was systematically poisoning his increasingly frail and ailing father.

Andrew, despite all his terrible self-righteousness and harsh discipline, was the parent to whom both boys were most closely drawn.

It was terribly clear to young Sherlock, or so Moriarty maintained with his wicked grin, that mother meant to clandestinely murder father Holmes to escape their loveless marriage.

Of course, she had already taken a lover . . . another wild one more in keeping with her own beatnik's spirit.

Having discovered the terrible truth, my Holmes emailed his elder brother, then eighteen and just starting college.

There ensued a flurry of emails between the precocious boy geniuses, the elder Holmes questioning this or that leap in logic or bit of deductive reasoning until, at last, in dire exasperation, Mycroft reluctantly concluded that young Sherlock's deductions regarding their mother's intentions were watertight in their correctness.

Based on Sherlock's researches into poison he had concluded was being used against their father, he projected a single dose—two at most— would surely push Papa past the prospect of recovery and set him on the path to agonizing death.

Yes, father had twenty-four, perhaps forty-eight hours remaining, Sherlock had convinced himself. Since he'd been proven right in all his previous deductions, as his elder brother had grudgingly conceded, why should he doubt Sherlock in this further bit of dire logic?

Taking all this in, Mycroft had dithered, begged for twenty-four hours to contemplate matters further.

Exasperated and enraged, Sherlock had further seethed and considered angles, "doing so with an increasing iciness, we can both presume," Moriarty had said to me in his almost novelistic telling.

That very night, Sherlock spied on his mother's dinner preparations. The brilliant boy detective had concluded a week before his mother was dosing father in supper portions.

Young Sherlock saw the measures of poison she had prepared and determined this one to be the lethal dose. Yes, this was the night, for certain.

Little Sherlock waited until the plates were prepared and placed at their settings, then he snuck out the back and shoved a previously prepared and carefully measured stick between the family car's driver's side seat and its steering wheel's horn.

As his mother ran out ahead of his limping, panting father to see what the hell all that commotion was out front, why the car's horn had gone off in such a perpetual din, young Sherlock snuck in through the back door, grabbed a napkin and swapped mother's and father's dinner plates.

At this point, telling this story that had far more detail than he should logically have had access to, Professor Moriarty had given me a sad look. "Ah, child . . . poor Sherlock. I think we can safely assume the boy, brilliant though he was, hadn't fully thought through this action he took that night. The poison that had been administered to his father had been done so over some interval of time, with proportions and so resulting potency ratcheting up as it had to, because sustained poisoning often engenders—rather paradoxically and in this case somewhat tragically—an increasing resistance or even tolerance to the stuff. The poisoner must therefore use increasing doses not just to maintain the damage being done, but to gain ground against the increasing resistance or tolerance to the stuff.

"Let's give young Sherlock the benefit of the doubt in this case," Moriarty had continued. "He probably only imagined his mother would be made terribly but fleetingly ill by the poison he was serving back to her. That precocious and sharp little brain failed to see in the feverish moment of desperation to protect his father the terrible truth of his impulsive action. His father's resistance to the drug, ironically, had been raised to a *terrific* degree by his slow poisoning. The *coup de grace*, then, the final, fatal installment, if you will, therefore required a truly massive dose of the poison to finally reach father Holmes and to put him under for keeps. However, Mother Holmes . . . "

I didn't hear the rest, just thought it: *Mother Holmes had no such resistance built up against the stuff.* Her drug-laced meal served straight-up was instantly lethal to its *virgin* victim.

Moriarty beaming said, "The convulsions would have been a terrible thing to witness, the retching and the swollen eyes all but escaping their sockets as they grew scarlet from the overtaxed and bursting little blood vessels. The tightening of the chest and throat muscles and the resulting internal suffocation . . . Imagine our young Sherlock, seeing it, knowing he'd made that happen, however deserved."

I didn't doubt a word of any of the Professor's story.

That said, I couldn't grasp how Moriarty could somehow have deduced it all in such close and vivid detail simply from old news clippings and the like.

So I put that question to him, expressed my false doubt any of it could be true because of its uncertain provenance: I had only his word for it that any of this was true and who would take the word of a criminal of his scope and scale?

A deep shrug. "Blackmail is a kind of family enterprise," the Professor had said. "A forbearer of mine, one Jonas Santayana Moriarty, learned of the illicit love affair between Mrs. Holmes and that other man. He'd then made an arrangement with a housekeeper in the Holmes' home, also with an officer of the village police.

"Remember the setting, Ms. Watson: A small town, an influential cleric threatened . . . and a precociously brilliant eighteen-year-old student in philosophy and logic named Mycroft Holmes. There was a rallying around young Sherlock, as you might expect. Oh yes—our young detective was indeed found out in his crime by several, in and out of the Holmes family. For you see, though our little Sherlock had the presence of mind to keep his hands covered when he'd swapped the lethal plates of poisoned pasta, he'd not been anywhere so careful in grasping that dowel rod he'd used to create the critically-needed distraction with his father's car's horn that allowed him to make the lethal swap. The distraction he tried to fob off as some other neighborhoods child's prank."

"Confronted with his terrible crime, our young Mr. Holmes' collapsed and confessed the tale in its entirety. He did so in earshot of my ancestor's domestic spy."

Moriarty shook his head and said, "If only I'd read my father's journals earlier—learned much sooner the strange, fated and tangled string of catgut that seems to bind my family's fortunes to that of the wretched Holmes clan. If only . . . "

Looking at the Professor sitting there in the growing puddle of rain water gathering around him, his clothes soaked through and thunder's rumble in the distance, I said, "And so what?"

"And so I know all of this and will share it with the world if only to destroy Sherlock Holmes' reputation," Moriarty had vowed. "I've also tapped into your private Tumbler account, Jona. It's very spritely, my dear. Very spritely indeed. I'll put that out to the world, as well."

"So that's your threat—you'll out Holmes as a lover and killer?"

"Don't you think that's *more* than sufficient? He sleeps with his partners and killed his mother. Reputation is everything. These two revelations will destroy Mr. Holmes' reputation, quite completely."

A little smile. He tugged at his handcuffed wrist. "So let's stop this foolishness now, child. Clearly I hold all the cards. You let me go now. Do that and I'll even deign to drop you back at Baker Street—drive you myself and save you cab fare. It would be pleasing to chat further but under nicer conditions. I confess that you impress me, in your way."

I said, "For all your presumed genius, you're really not all that smart, are you, Professor? You're hardly the chess player I'd anticipated or that you seem to fancy yourself. Maybe it's the drugs or the booze or whatever you're flying on—oh, I can see it's something like that. It's in yours cloudy eyes and slurred speech, even now, after all. Absent your addictions, you might have been a force to be reckoned with, you know. As it is, I was able to find you, to make you my prisoner, and I did it all alone. Nobody knows what's happened between us. Nobody knows we're here." I shrugged. "Nobody needs to know whatever became of you."

The Professor's pointed, spottily-shaven chin trembled. "What do you mean, *might have been*?" He jerked more savagely at his cuffed wrist, sloughing off a layer of skin and drawing some blood in his frenzy. "What are you saying?"

Watching him closely, sizing up the effect of my words, I said, "You've threatened me with supposed intentions but there's been not a whisper, not a hint or a convincing intimation of any preparation to implement your intent. You see, you've failed to make all the expected and clichéd threats, Professor, and that speaks volumes to me."

Frowning, glowering, he said, "You've lost me, child . . . "

"So sorry; I figured you for being quicker on the uptake. Here's the thing, then: This was where you were supposed to tell me there are all these clever fail safes in place. You know, minions who'll let fly with your discovery of Sherlock's secret if certain protocols aren't fulfilled by certain deadlines. Surely you know all the tired old moves. But, clearly, you've actually taken no such steps. It's all in your head—this terrible wisdom you trumpet. All of it dwells behind your eyes and maybe on that new laptop computer in your trunk."

The look in his chemically-fogged eyes was a horrible thing to behold as my own intent dawned upon him. I knew then my deductions about his failure to have yet prepared "failsafes" regarding all his dark knowledge were correct.

So I took a single deep breath, I took aim, and I murdered Professor Moriarty. The shot seemed to echo off all that rain-stained concrete for a very long time.

Strangely calm, I retrieved his computer and I walked blocks to the river. I slung the computer and my hand-me-down revolver far out into the choppy river.

Then I walked another two blocks before I finally succeeded in hailing a cab.

The cabbie was not a talker. That was fine by me.

39

Holmes stroked my cheek and said, "You know I know, of course."

"Of course," I repeated huskily. I stroked his bare chest. "With all your skills, how couldn't you figure it out? Now what are you going to do with your knowledge?"

Holmes smiled sadly. "What *can* I do? I'd certainly not turn you in. You did it to save me—to stop me from crossing that line. I know that. How could I punish you for doing the very thing I'd already prepared in my mind to do? I would have gone through with it if you hadn't beaten me to the finish line."

A deep sigh and he said, "I so wish you hadn't done it though. It was my sin to commit. I can hardly bear the fact of you having to shoulder the guilt and burden of—"

Shaking my head, I pressed my fingers to his lips. "Hush, Holmes. There was no going back, not once the Professor told me a last story. We all have secrets. You have them too, Holmes. I know that, now. Your secret might be the saddest I've ever encountered. My fucked-up heart bleeds for you, my darling Sherlock."

Standing there naked together in the window, our pale bodies dappled with the trailing shadows of the rain running down the glass, Holmes said darkly, "What story did that man tell you?"

I bit my lip, then said softly, "He told me a story about an avenging angel of a little boy and of the boy's wicked and murderous mother."

That was more than enough to let Sherlock know all that I at last knew about him.

Holmes drew me close to him. I hugged him back fiercely. After a time he whispered in my ear, "We've both killed for the purposes of love and loyalty. You did what you did to *save* me." Holmes stroked my back and added, "We'll never speak of either of these episodes in our lives again, agreed?"

Yes. Never. I supposed in that moment that Holmes and I comprised a kind of terrible and very private red-handed league, all our own.

Without waiting for my answer, he kissed me hard—a long kiss that eventually softened and lingered.

Not caring in this moment of utter candor, I said, "You know that I love you, Holmes?"

Holmes swept me up in his arms and carried me to our bed. We made slow, sweet love together, Holmes very much taking his time and making it last.

Despite my exhaustion, about an hour afterward, I awakened, my mind absolutely racing.

There was this strange compulsion to get the last of this tale down while it was all still quite fresh—to close the story of this bloody and dark circle that began what seemed years ago, on that first day when I met Mr. Sherlock Holmes, the wisest, cleverest and most pitiless just man I have ever known.

I'm determined to hold onto this man, to be his partner in every sense for as long as there can be between us.

It's two in the morning now as I type these last words.

I'm so tired. I need a long rest . . . need to let my health recover after these terrible few days. So I'm going to let this blog languish for a while.

For the foreseeable future, I'm going to focus on living in the moment, savoring this unexpected love I've found.

I'm going back to bed now to wrap myself tightly around my man, drawing out his heat on this stormy autumn night as more hail lashes the windows here on Baker Street.

For this moment at least, all is well.

So now I lay me . . .

—Jona Ormond Watson,
Oct. 31, 2015

40

The scream, a nearly inhuman howl of despair, wrenched Mrs. Hudson from her sleep.

Pulling on her robe, she ran dazedly up the stairs and pounded on the door of 221B. When she got no answer, with shaking hands, she used her master key.

She found Sherlock Holmes on the bed with Jona, feverishly administering CPR.

Mrs. Hudson called 911: It would take them fifteen minutes to arrive, the dispatcher said. The elderly Scot called out the ETA.

"Not bloody soon enough," Holmes snarled. He kept at the clearly pointless CPR for several more of those agonizing minutes.

Stopping at last in his attempts to revive her as the too-late paramedics arrived, he placed his hand on Jona's bare shoulder. It was unnaturally cold to his touch—he was noticing just how cold, only now. She'd already been gone a long time.

Yes, as Jona so often had before, she had a mysterious way of short-circuiting all of his logic and powers of observation—even in death.

At seven a.m. on Halloween morning, the paramedics officially called her time of death.

41

"**S**top worrying, Mycroft," he insisted. "The simple fact is, I lack the capacity for suicide. It was terrible luck, that's all. Terrible bad fortune for both of us. She fell asleep and she never woke up. The kindest way for her—for anyone—to go, really. In that, God, if He existed—which of course He doesn't—might at least be regarded as atypically kind."

The Holmes brothers were seated in a room off the main chamber of the funeral home.

Jona Watson had left instructions for a closed casket ceremony. Sherlock Holmes was quietly grateful for that: he'd seen his share of dead bodies.

He wanted to remember Jona in life, laughing, sitting across from him in the morning at Baker Street . . . tangled up bare in his arms and loving with him.

For four days, Sherlock Holmes had been in a kind of barely functioning fugue state following Jona's succumbing to her heart condition.

But his younger brother was returning to the world, a relieved Mycroft thought, though there was still some distance to go.

Working on a rare and yes, a quite unabashed *hunch*, Mycroft hoped the introduction he was about to effect would miraculously firmly bind Holmes again to the wicked old world—to flush out the currently missing icy logician and scourge of crime and abstruse wrongdoing.

As he handed Sherlock another generous glass of whiskey over ice, Mycroft said, "Goddammit, Brother Mine, do stop *lashing* yourself. At least Moriarty is well and truly dead."

Sherlock sipped his whiskey. "I never saw the Professor in life, you know. Never got to stare the man down. That bothers me somehow . . . more than I can describe."

"You may yet get a chance, in a sense," Mycroft said reluctantly. "The body was claimed by an elder brother. That senior sibling would be a Professor *James* Moriarty. Given the malignant antecedents running through that family, this *new* Professor Moriarty may well bear watching too, you know."

Mycroft stared into his glass and said, "The younger Moriarty had promise before he sank into debauchery. He would have been far more formidable if he'd not become driven by his addictions to stimulants and to sex . . . "

"I was as much the perfect fool," Sherlock said to his elder brother. "It could as easily be said that I let my baser instincts and an aberrant streak of sentimentality cloud my mind. I consciously lost the most vital parts of my professional self giving into what perfect fools call *love*. I let my heart short-circuit my brain and *that* proved the capital mistake, didn't it? I was just as much the perfect idiot as Moriarty in the end."

Mycroft shook his leonine head, leaning harder on his cane. "*No*, I don't agree with you, Sherlock. I'll not let you revise the memory of what you shared with that remarkable young woman. Jona Watson was perfect for you in the moments you enjoyed together. She clearly loved you deeply, and I know you cared for her. I never expected to see such a thing happen for you, and I wasn't in any way unhappy to witness it, however dismayed it also left me and however fleeting it proved to be in the end."

Mycroft hesitated and then said, "I confess with some sadness and much regret that I doubt I'll see it happen again in this lifetime. Perhaps you'll take comfort in that, if you truly feel so badly about this now-ended epoch in a sure to be storied life."

"Well, know this, it will never find a sequel," Sherlock said firmly. "I'll never let this clouding of my instrument happen again. And I couldn't endure such loss again. Even now, I sense that it's damaged my faculties. I confess only to you that I look at a stranger and I can deduce nothing. Everyone is opaque to me, currently."

Sherlock drained his drink. He said bitterly, "So I truly don't want and I don't *need* to feel such 'happiness' and its always attendant misery again. It's proven itself anathema to everything that drives me. Wonderful as it seemed in the moment—and I'll confess to an ecstasy I can't begin to describe—in the final analysis, this whole interval with Jona was like flinging handfuls of coarse sand into the works of a finely crafted clock. It paralyzed me at crucial points. You can't deny it, Mycroft. I know that I certainly cannot do that."

"No," his brother said firmly, "I still can't agree. By the same token, I can't believe it was truly a mistake. I view it as something you had to go through and to experience, at least once in this life. Maybe it's true you never will feel love again—maybe you won't do that as a result of this experience, or because opportunity will never present itself again. The Jona Watsons of this rather bland and often disappointing world, I fear, are in very short supply, indeed. But I can't help but think that having known love, and having gone through all this, it will enrich and inform your life and work in the future. Just give it a little more time, brother."

"Maybe," Holmes said. "I can only sit here now and hope that the bloody price will prove worth the results."

Sherlock scowled suddenly. "That man over there, he keeps looking at me, almost with intent. Do you see?"

Mycroft looked over his shoulder and said, "Yes, but it's nothing sinister, Sherlock. That man's actually quite desperate to meet you, brother. I thought you might like to talk to him, as well."

Holmes gave the stranger another look and said, "I don't need a medical doctor, and before you take that as pretense to possibly suggest a doctor of some other kind, you know I have nothing but contempt for psychologists and psychiatrists, so don't even start on that point, Mycroft."

Mycroft gave him a frosty smile. "Yes, Sherlock. I indeed know your feelings on all that, quite fully. Still, I think you might want to meet *this* doctor—whose trade, I'll now point out, you quite deftly deduced, despite your supposedly *damaged instrument*. The important thing for you to know right now, Sherlock, is that you and that man shared a loved one. Come here. I'll introduce you now."

Mycroft reached down with a beefy hand and grasped Sherlock's arm. He urged his brother to his feet. Waving the stranger toward them, Mycroft called out, so the tallish, strongly built and sun-bronzed man could better hear: "Sherlock Holmes, it's my pleasure, my very distinct *privilege*, to introduce you to Jona's brother, Doctor John Hamish Watson."

Well, well. Sherlock sized the man up, then extended a hand to this other Watson.

The stranger gripped it hard. "You knew my sister," he said. "She emailed me about you. If you don't already know it, she thought the world of you, Mr. Holmes."

This Watson's chin then trembled; his eyes glistened. "I can't thank you enough for the happiness you gave my sister during her past few weeks." His composure began to slip further. "And I confess that I can't imagine this world without her in it." He briefly lost control of himself and said, "I became a doctor because of her condition, because . . . "

Dr. Watson simply couldn't finish that sentence, so Holmes supplied the end in his mind:

Because I'd hoped to cure her. I failed her.

Holmes broke eye contact for just a moment. He looked at his feet and said, "I indeed thought the world of Jona, too. I'm so very sorry for your loss, John . . . "

Still gripping this new Watson's hand, Sherlock Holmes gave the man another long and lingering look. He truly liked what he saw. Yes, this was a *good* and a solid man.

Sherlock decided that was a *smart* man and one uniquely capable of providing the desperately needed ballast that Jona's loss had taken from him.

And there was the *other* thing: this familiar, comforting echo of Jona that dwelt in her brother's candid eyes and his open, unguarded quiet smile of gratitude.

In time, he intuited, other similarities that would also comfort him would manifest themselves. Holmes impulsively hugged John Watson close to his chest.

At last breaking their clumsy embrace, Sherlock regained himself.

He smiled quietly back. Clearing his throat to restore timbre to his baritone, Holmes said, "So. Mr. John Watson, I see that you have been in Afghanistan . . . "

THE END

ABOUT THE AUTHOR

Hadley Colt is the pseudonym for an internationally acclaimed author. Hadley Colt's previous novels were published in several languages to excellent reviews and high praise from fellow writers who've declared the author's work, *"subtle, moving and tragic", "non conformist", "bold and extravagant", "reviving", "an explosive mix of humor and action", and who has been described as "an erudite with formidable imagination" and a "master of suspense".*

To learn more about Hadley Colt, please visit *http://hadleydchase.blogspot.com* and *www.betimesbooks.com*
Follow Hadley on Twitter: @HadleyColt